FATALITY IN FLEET STREET

Christopher St John Sprigg

LONDON BOUND

Oleander Press

The Oleander Press
16 Orchard Street
Cambridge
CB1 1JT

oleanderpress.com

First Published 1933

This edition © 2013 Oleander Press

ISBN: 9781909349759

Contents

A Prime Minister Threatens

"THREE HUNDRED YEARS AGO, Lord Carpenter, I'd have had your head on a spike on Tower Hill," said the Prime Minister, the Right Hon. Claude Sanger.

Lord Carpenter made no answer beyond caressing his threatened neck reflectively.

"As it is I can only appeal to your better nature." The Prime Minister's voice faltered with the oratorical trick the wireless had made familiar to millions. Now, however, the trick was submerged in a note of genuine sincerity. "Do you realize what War means?"

Lord Carpenter, Governing Director of Affiliated Publications, the biggest newspaper group in the world, gazed thoughtfully out of the window. He saw London's roofs tossing in a troubled sea below the lemon yellow and gilt heights of the *Mercury's* gaudy building. He saw the sun glitter upon the transparent lattice-work of the Crystal Palace. But he was interested in none of these things. Force of habit made him turn his profile to his visitor, in order to exhibit his famous Napoleonesque profile with the wandering lock of hair on the high brow. Affiliated Publications' 36,563,271 readers had often scanned it admiringly in photographic form. The Right Hon. Claude Sanger now scanned it anxiously for any sign of a chink in the other's armour.

"I realize – better than you, perhaps, Sanger," answered Carpenter.

"You do not realize – you cannot realize!" The Premier's voice rolled thunderingly and his ragged features were a mask of tragedy. "Think of the holocaust of young lives! The incessant jettisoning of our accumulated savings in the bottomless sea of destruction! Remember our widows! Our sucklings instructed in the lore of hate! Our nation's veins drained of their vigour! Whatever hydra Russian Communism may be, it cannot justify this loosing of a ghastly scourge on England and the Empire. Carpenter, at this moment you are answerable to God and the innumerable posterity of our race!"

"Your oratory is as admirable as ever," answered Carpenter coldly. "I think, however, hard facts are all that matter at the moment. In the autumn of 1937, twelve months ago almost to a day, I decided that Russia must be crushed." Lighting a cigar, Carpenter mentioned his decision with the same casual air as if it had been to have his house spring-cleaned. "The deciding factor was, of course, Russia's first genuinely favourable trade balance with an unpegged exchange. That made her, for the first time, a real menace to the established order of things." With the keen enjoyment of an enthusiast explaining his hobby, Carpenter produced a map from his desk. "I determined that this country, striking up through India, should be the executioner. The clash must come sooner or later, but obviously the time for it to come is when we are strong and Russia militarily negligible. I don't propose to justify myself. I am perfectly happy in my own mind about the rightness of my aim. Therefore for the last twelve months the unique power of my papers – I think I can call it unique without boasting – has been devoted to the end I proposed—"

The Premier exploded. "By every device of dishonest propaganda! By the employment of the world's carrion crows as *agents provocateurs*! By methods which are an outrage on the fair name of Journalism!"

Carpenter raised a deprecating hand. "By the very methods which, employed in the services of the Produce More British Goods Campaign, induced you to recommend me for a Viscounty. The methods, in any case, are beside the point. They have resulted in an upheaval of popular opinion which you have as much chance of controlling as of stopping the Flying Scotsman with one hand. The Empire is simmering. It needs only one more puff of flame to make it boil over."

The Premier, arms folded, sagged slowly forward in his chair. He was a poor listener. He had reached his present position largely because he never bothered to grasp what his opponents were saying. The fact that his speeches contained no reference to their arguments gave the public the impression that they were not worth answering. This made him a tower of strength in debate, but it was a handicap in private life.

Carpenter smiled. "That puff of flame has come." He stabbed Russia in Asia with one long forefinger. "Just around here, in an obscure Soviet, an incident has occurred which, handled as it will be handled by my papers, will bring the Empire to the boil. The Foreign Office knows nothing of it. Fleet Street knows nothing of it. But I know, and tomorrow the whole Empire will know, know of it in such a way, that war will be inevitable. The Government that attempts to compromise, even your own Federated Progressive Government, will fall in a night."

Sanger was silent. He rose heavily to his feet.

"Jove, the old boy looks old," thought Jerningham, Carpenter's confidential secretary, as he brought in the Premier's hat and stick. The silence might have seemed profound with the fate of nations, but the words of farewell were formal. Yet at the door the Premier paused.

"I am going back to decide whether to resign or to try to guide the ship through the coming storm," he said wearily. "Probably I shall resign. I'm getting on now, you know. Meanwhile I must warn you that if I can think of any means, lawful or unlawful, to upset your plans, I should take them without a moment's hesitation."

And for a second the elder statesman looked like the red-headed young fighter of his pre-war political apprenticeship.

Carpenter laughed with unruffled good temper. "You see we are none of us pacifists when it comes to the pinch."

— II —

"Take a note, Jerningham," said Carpenter briskly, replacing the map in the desk.

Hands in pocket, the "Chief" of the largest publishing organization in the world strode up and down the room. Suddenly he turned to Jerningham. "What the devil do you mean by wearing that foul tie in my office?" he barked, dragging the offending green object out of the opening of his secretary's impeccable lounge suit. Raised in anger, his voice lost its veneer of refinement and became grating. "You're nothing but a clerk. Remember it and dress like one, not like a Gaiety chorister."

Jerningham flushed. His handsome but weak face twisted with an expression which might have been shame or fury. His hand shook as he replaced the tie. "I beg your pardon, sir," he answered meekly.

Carpenter resumed his pacing. At last he spoke, with the colourless precision of a dictating machine.

"This is to be the main leader page article. It must run to four columns with a streamer headline. The first two paragraphs are to be in bold type. The article should be illustrated by a photo of myself, of Stalin – the most repulsive one in our files – and that photo of crowds lying down flat on their faces in a Moscow street during the Tsarist succession riots – only give it the caption 'Religious procession mowed down by Bolshevist soldiers.' We've used it before, about a year ago. Now begin. 'We must fight or go under! The Brezka Atrocity is the final move in the Bolshevist policy of encirclement stop The object of that policy is the obliteration of the Empire comma the only bulwark between Communism and Civilization stop' That last sentence to be in small caps..."

He halted a moment and spoke down the dictograph. "Hubbard? Bring up all we've got about the Brezka concession at once."

Then in a monotonous voice he continued. The tone was dreary, but the article was one which, like all the Chief's writing, would go straight home to the bosom of the average man, of which Carpenter himself was a glorified enlargement.

"Rotten, Hubbard, rotten," shouted Carpenter, glancing through the meagre file of cuttings brought to him by Hubbard. "Much more than this has appeared! You get more damned inefficient every day."

Hubbard gave a strangled cry of protest. The mildest of men, this was enough to stir him to bitterness. Jerningham felt a fellow feeling for him, smarting in his turn under the Chief's rough tongue. Jerningham knew Hubbard's reputation on Fleet Street. A wizened, parchment-faced old man, he dwelt from year's end to year's end in the dusty library of the *Mercury*. He had never been known to take a holiday or be away ill. Some said he was expiating the terrible day when he gave a reporter, told to write up the obituary of a politician called Armstrong, the *dossier* of a novelist of the same name, whose obituary had accordingly appeared the next morning. Since that morning, it was credibly asserted, he had never been seen to smile again. His perpetual residence in the library was, however, of some value. The filing system he adopted for newspaper cuttings was so elaborate that it was believed no one but himself could grasp it. Imagination quavered at the prospect of his death. But the system was worked by him with astounding speed. He boasted that anything that had appeared about anything could be produced by him in two minutes.

Now, in his agitation, his shaking hand spilled snuff all over his jacket. He brushed his lapels and nervously tapped down the lid.

"Damn it," roared the Chief, "I will not have that disgusting habit here. Jerningham, mop up that stuff from the floor!"

Blinking up at him, the librarian insisted on making his protest. "I am quite certain nothing has appeared which is not in that folder," he asserted.

"Nonsense, nonsense," said the other angrily. "I'll have to get a filing expert in to teach you some lessons, or better still, boot you out altogether."

Even Jerningham was staggered at this outrageous threat, but Hubbard said nothing. His beady eyes regarded the Chief coldly behind his pebble eyeglasses.

"All right," Carpenter said at last, "you can go."

The Chief did not go on with the dictation of his article immediately. Hubbard had gone. He stared ahead reflectively. "Extraordinary that such an unprepossessing fellow should have such a charming daughter," he said reflectively. "When I first saw her in the Advertisement Canvassing Department and asked her name, I could hardly believe it. What a figure!"

Jerningham, kneeling on the floor wielding a duster, thanked his stars that at least he hadn't a daughter working in the office of whom Carpenter spoke in that tone, and knowledge of Carpenter's weakness was by no means confined to his secretary. Very unwise of Hubbard, thought Jerningham, for even he must know by this time how things stood between Carpenter and his daughter.

— III —

The thinkers of England's thoughts sat round in the draughty Board Room at the top of the lemon yellow *Mercury* building which dominated Fleet Street.

In other words, there was a Special General Conference of the *Mercury* called by Lord Carpenter. The "General" in the title accounted for the wide assortment of people who were present, from Editor to the Publisher. The "Special" in the title accounted for the equally notable omissions in the ranks. On the whole, however, the band was sufficiently representative of the hardworking souls who formed the conversation and conscience of democratic England.

At the moment they all looked a little uneasy, except Grovermuller, the Editor. A dapper, silver-haired, bird-like little man immersed in a ponderous-looking review, he sat in the centre of the crescent of chairs. The hierarchy of the paper dwindled in orderly formation to the tips of the crescent, and at the extreme right hand tip was Charles Venables, late society editor, but now crime expert of the *Mercury*. There was a faint air of surprise even on his innocuous face as he toyed with his monocle, and seeing it his neighbour, Perry, the Art Editor, endeavoured to reassure him.

"It's all right. This is a Gathering of the Good Boys."

This mysterious phrase was not lost on Charles. The last gathering had been a Gathering of the Bad Boys – those members of the Advertising Staff whom Carpenter had considered responsible for a dwindling in the *Mercury's* revenue. Carpenter, mottled with rage, had screamed invective for half an hour at his shaken staff. He had wound up by stating that Sergeant Capes, the commissionaire, was a better Advertisement Manager than any of them, and had installed the bewildered worthy in the Manager's office at the Manager's salary until such time as the revenue was restored to its old figure. Meanwhile, the Manager received Sergeant Capes's salary. The Advertising Staff agreed to leave in a body that evening. The next morning calmer counsels prevailed, and the succeeding issue grossed a revenue five percent above the average. That evening Sergeant Capes, gloriously drunk, was thrown out of the Savoy Grill Room, after sweeping Sir David Lowder, the famous advertising magnate, into an alcoholic embrace of kinship. On the second morning all was quiet.

But this was a Gathering of the Good Boys. Charles's neighbour, Perry, for instance, was the only Art Editor in Fleet Street, in fact probably in the world, who made up the picture page in a morning-coat and spats, instead of the waistcoat and dusty trousers more usual to the tribe. Perry's languid accent matched his appearance, both of which were deceptive. In his time, as a stripling press photographer, Perry had been towed by a submarine on an aquaplane in the North Sea, hung by his legs from an aeroplane undercarriage in mid-air, lain on his belly along the smoking-hot bonnet of a Grand Prix racer cornering at 90 m.p.h., all to obtain shots a little more distinctive than those of his competitors. And he had the knack of inspiring his cameramen to go and do likewise.

"What is the Chief's allocution going to be about?" asked Venables, feeling rather like a member of a Fourth Form summoned *en masse* before the Head. Even the nickname the "Chief" was like a schoolboy tradition.

Through the ramifications of Affiliated Publications Limited, whose journals accounted for eighty-five percent of the country's circulations registered at the Audit Bureau, Carpenter now wielded a power in the newspaper world of imperial dimensions. But he still loved to remind Fleet Street in the mellow, paternal tones he had acquired with the passing years, that he was, after all, a "working journalist." Nothing pleased him more than that his staff should visualize his active shirt-sleeved co-operation with them, such as was suggested by that nickname, the "Chief".

"Anything might happen, old boy," admitted Perry. "The Chief may burst into tears and say he has remembered us all in his will. He did that last time. Or he may walk in as he did once, look round in dead silence, mutter, 'Magnificent! Magnificent!' and walk out again. We may all be given a rousing speech and told to look in our pay envelopes next week, and when we look, find the same as usual. That happened once, you know."

This not being helpful, Charles endeavoured to find enlightenment by scanning the thirty-odd men – and women – decorating the office. They did not look at their ease – but it was not an office conducive to ease. Opposite the crescent of chairs was a full-length Orpen of the Chief. Round the walls were hung the remarkable collection of weapons gathered by the Chief in his wanderings. The furniture was massive – blackened oak, burgeoning and heaving with baroque carving. The carpet was inch-deep with pile. The Chief was just going through a period of craving for luxury – a reaction, perhaps, from the year before, when a longing for austerity had stripped his office of all superfluous furniture. The unfortunate results of this craving instantly depressed any visitor on entry to the room, even in the most auspicious circumstances.

In any case, being one of the Chief's Good Boys was, strangely enough, more depressing than to be a Bad one. He that is down need fear no fall. The whole staff of the *Mercury*, from the

Advertisement Manager to the Messenger Boy, Art Perkins No. 25, were, as it were, distributed on two ladders, those on the right ascending in the Chief's favour, those on the left descending. Only the Editor, Eric Grovermuller, by some uncanny gift, was able to remain perpetually at the top, teetering dangerously at times, but always recovering himself by his supreme talent for poise.

Now all of the staff gathered together in that office were near the top of the ladder. Venables had just sensationally solved the Garden Hotel Mystery. Perry had obtained an exclusive photo of the *Macon's* forced descent on the South Pole by a brilliantly improvised organization of speed-boats, dog-sleighs, and aeroplanes. And all being near the top of the ladder, all feared the inevitable approach of the return to the abyss.

"It is the Russian business, of course," boomed out Andrews' voice suddenly from Perry's elbow. Andrews, enormous and shaggy, carried heartiness to an extreme which might have made the judicious suspicious. With reason – Andrews was the shrewdest City Editor in England. More than one famous swindler, expounding his schemes with invincible assurance to this cheery soul, had suddenly felt deflated by a cruel thrust at the weak spot in his scheme, delivered with the utmost *bonhomie*. And the point was subsequently pressed in the City column with a persistence which was attributed to malice. Quite wrongly, because Andrews did not know what malice was.

"You, my lads," he went on, "have the privilege of seeing how patriotism is manufactured, and war made. In twenty years' time your memoirs will be history. Meanwhile, you will probably have been blown to bits, and, anyway, you will not be believed."

"I suppose it's rather a dirty job we're doing," mused Venables. "But a fascinating kind of dirt..."

"Here," interrupted Perry, "is the Chief."

A Reporter Protests

CARPENTER, A BORN RULER of men, knew the value of silences. He waited, with tightly pressed lips, until the last whisper had died away. With a mingled pride he surveyed for a moment the small group of men, the heart of the greatest circulation-getting system in the world. Invisibly ramifying, the arteries of Affiliated Publications carried the world's happenings, transmuted by comment, to every part of the Empire. Down the main artery of the Daily Mercury, with its 2 million readers, pulsing in the Sunday Mercury, through 5 million brains, and trickling at last by diverse routes into the capillaries of hundreds of monthlies and weeklies devoted to subjects dear to heart and home.

Now the engineer of this system, posed before his portrait, seemed lost in thought. Charles Venables looked at him with interest and perplexity. Why had he conjured a demon of War from the vasty deep? Was it, as was whispered, merely for the gainful exercise of certain commercial operations? No – not with that wide forehead and generous mouth.

Was it the sensation of power? Had the peak-faced, pimply little office boy that was the young Carpenter, snubbed by his betters and hating it, stirred again to life, wreaking a revenge for all those humiliations?

Or was he merely mad? Would they lead him presently away to a quiet home drooling gently, while the house he had fired tumbled round England's ears?

But Charles confessed the man inscrutable. Confessing that, he confessed his genius. Few men of the day possessed in greater measure that other attribute of genius, personality. It flooded the room, dominating thirty-odd keen and cynical brains, softening sophisticated temperaments with a queer mixture of respect and affection.

Carpenter came out of his brown study. "Today at Brezka," he began abruptly, "the Trafalgar oil wells were set on fire, and the English members of the staff, with their wives and children, were butchered by a mob led by the local secretary of the Communist Party."

Grovermuller gasped. "God! There's not been a whisper over here – yet there's a Reuter's correspondent at Brezka, and also a *Times* man and a B.U.P. man, if I remember rightly."

"All in jail," explained Carpenter briefly. "Their reports were considered 'biased by capitalistic prejudice,' and they were clapped into prison. Nothing is likely to get out for two days at least. My agent out there was able to send a long message in code. Even the Foreign Office has as yet no information of the outrage."

Grovermuller rose to his feet. "It's gone eleven o'clock. I'll go and tell them to keep the main news page open for a big story."

Carpenter detained him. "Nothing of the sort. There will be no mention of this in the early editions. I do not want anything to appear until it is too late for the other papers to make any investigation and comment. The late editions will carry our full story. Whatever it costs us they must eventually reach every part of the country. Meanwhile our own Empire News Syndicate, which feeds virtually the whole Empire Press, will be sending out the same story. As soon as the presses stop running with the late editions of the *Mercury*, the early evening *Mercury* will be put through carrying the same story. We will overwhelm all our competitors, who will be unable to obtain any confirmation, and yet will not dare rush out a denial."

"*What* a scoop!" Heflin, the news editor, was heard to sigh.

"It will be more than a scoop." The Chief's lips framed this awful journalistic heresy without compunction. "It will be that final blow in our propaganda which will ensure success. But everything depends upon the nationwide distribution of the late editions."

Griffiths, the publisher, gave a hollow groan. He had been figuring rapidly on the back of an envelope and now regarded the result with horror. "It is impossible, sir," he breathed.

"You *think* it impossible," answered Carpenter with disarming suavity, "but it does not follow that it *is* impossible. Will you fetch Channing, your deputy? He may find means to do it. Meanwhile please make arrangements to leave the organization tonight. I will instruct the cashier to give you everything due under your contract."

Griffiths looked at him dazed. "I – really – of – course," he struggled. "It can be done of course," he gulped, "but the expense will be tremendous."

"Confound the expense," Carpenter shouted, his eyes blazing. "Have you no imagination? Don't you see that this is the greatest feat the press has ever attempted – to mould and drive a great nation by its own peculiar art? I have told you what you must do, Griffiths – it is merely up to you to do it. God, man, do what you like! Charter a special for every newspaper parcel. Hire every taxi in London. Book aeroplanes, speedboats, and hansom cabs. Take on who you like. Pay as much bill money as you like. Take on hundreds of thousands of street sellers. Every scrap of plant in this place is going to be used. The biggest printing staff any one paper has ever had has been engaged tonight. Every journal of

Affiliated Publications is being held up. Even our flat bed presses will be used at a pinch. A hundred thousand pounds in cash is in this building tonight in case you need to use it. Tomorrow morning, when the streets are flooded with our posters, 'Russia Declares War–'"

"You are going to put that on the poster?" said Grovermuller, incredulously.

"Certainly. The news story we shall carry, and my article, will assume the Brezka incident to be an overt act deliberately designed as a *casus belli*."

Charles, who was watching Grovermuller keenly, saw indignation flare in his eyes, saw this dapper personification of restraint almost bursting with suppressed comment and then subside, as with a sigh. Snatching a cigarette-case from his pocket, Grovermuller covered his confusion by tapping a cigarette brutally against the case and lighting it with twitching fingers.

Carpenter swept on. "Every adult will buy a copy of our paper. It will urge them to demonstrate; they will demonstrate. Mobs will sweep through the cities demanding Russia's blood. Already the Premier owned to me he cannot keep his Cabinet in hand. He knows nothing of the Brezka incident. Tomorrow it will be too late."

Andrews, who had been watching the Chief with a sardonic smile, now spoke. "But surely the Premier won't go under like that? Isn't there any card he can play? The wireless, for instance?"

"I have thought of everything," answered Carpenter with the utmost simplicity. "That was the object, six months ago, of the agitation which resulted in the passing of the Broadcasting Act, 1938, which, of course, now bans all discussion of any matters affecting foreign policy on the wireless. Nothing can be done." Carpenter, a lover of dramatic gesture, flung out his hand and indicated a chased and ornate Florentine dagger on the wall, attributed somewhat dubiously to Cellini. "If you gentlemen were to jump on me simultaneously and cut my throat with that, you would be able – perhaps – to upset my plans. Aside from that unlikely conjunction, War is as inevitable tomorrow as the dawn."

Carpenter's heroic gesture was shattered by a hoot. "God! Stabbing's too good for you, you devil!" The voice was shrill and quavering with emotion. The effect was somewhat similar to what would have been produced by lobbing a hand-grenade onto the carpet. Every chair grated. Every eye turned to where, at the other tip of the crescent, stood up Bysshe Jameson, his lean frame trembling with excitement, his sensitive pale face distorted, his red hair bristling.

Carpenter regarded his "star" descriptive writer without resentment. "I hope you haven't been drinking, Jameson," he observed. "In any case, it doesn't look as if your presence will be of much value to this conference. Kindly go."

Jameson rose to his feet. "Don't you see? He is mad – mad with conceit. Can't you stop him before he pulls the world down around our ears?"

Carpenter's restraint deserted him. His eyes blazed and he towered over Jameson – not so much physically as in personality. "Get out, you young fool," he barked. And Jameson, his cheeks hectic, shambled out.

The "Chief" was himself again in a moment. "Now, gentlemen, any more questions?"

"There's one thing I don't quite see," said Andrews. "How are you going to prevent the news getting out through the staff?"

"Naturally I have thought of that. Until the last moment the knowledge will be limited to those here present and three compositors. Nonetheless, until the vital editions are gone to press, no one, for whatever reason, will be allowed out of here without a permit signed by Mr. Grovermuller. At this moment every member of the staff is being instructed accordingly. Full overtime will be paid, and two sets of door-keepers are being posted at every exit. In addition, every phone call, ingoing or outgoing, will be listened to by two of my personal inquiry agents. Can you suggest any further measure necessary?"

"I certainly can't," admitted the City Editor.

"Very well. My magazine page article, together with full details of the Brezka Atrocity, has been placed on your desk, Grovermuller. Hubbard, look out any relative information you can find for the Editor. I leave the treatment entirely to you, Grovermuller. You know exactly what I want, and you all know the supreme importance of what you are doing tonight."

"Very good, sir."

Carpenter nodded. "I am now going to have a short sleep." The Chief's facility in dropping off instantly at any time into a deep sleep was as famous as any of his more intellectual gifts. It was mainly for this reason that his suite in the *Mercury* offices contained a bedroom. The bed was more of a divan, for the Chief never undressed, but, loosening coat and collar, flung himself on it, to pass for an hour or two into oblivion and awaken again with a clear head.

Carpenter looked at his watch. "It is now 11.25 p.m. If I am not awake before, I shall expect to be called at 2.00 a.m. to see the proofs. Till then, there can be no excuse for interrupting me. Good night, all."

— II —

"Half-past one," sighed Miranda Jameson, Woman's Page Editor. "Why the hell need I stay on? My page went to bed ages ago."

"My dear! We are watching history being made," answered Charles Venables reprovingly, perched on the corner of her desk.

"Are we? Well, I think history is all rather bogus. I feel rather foul altogether, in fact. I was up too late last night."

"Miranda, you're worried," Charles remarked sharply.

"What makes you think that?"

"Observation. The angelic brow is furrowed by two little wrinkles which I have never seen before. And the times you have warned 'Constant Reader' that *nothing* is so bad for the expression as worry!"

"How observant of you. But in fact I was concentrating on knocking this wretched tripe into shape."

"That also proves my point. I can see from here that it has already been sub-edited. Judging from the title, it is an article which appeared on your page two days ago."

Miranda threw down her pencil with a weak smile. "Acting does not appear to be my talent. Yes, Charles, I am worried. It's Bysshe, you know. A brother like that is enough to worry anybody."

The phone bell rang, and Charles got up. "For me, I expect. I've got to take all Grovermuller's calls while he is in conference." Wearily he lifted the mouthpiece. "Hello? Hello? *Who* do you want? Yes, this is the editor speaking. Himself? Oh yes! You like the bit I put in the paper last week about affectionate goldfish? I'm *so* glad. Not at all. Delighted! You've always read the *Mercury*? How perfectly splendid! *Goodbye*." Charles rapidly jiggled the telephone arm, scowling. "Here, exchange, you B.F.! That wasn't a personal call for Mr. Grovermuller! It was one of our blithering readers. Why the devil didn't it go to Enquiries? Yes, I've answered it." Charles replaced the receiver muttering.

"About Bysshe," he said, with well-affected surprise. "Is it vegetarianism? Has he burned down another butcher's shop?"

"No. It's serious this time!"

"Oh, a woman."

"No. That sort of thing will never be serious with Bysshe, though it might be for the woman. I'm afraid for his job here."

"He's doing splendidly on this descriptive stuff. Absolute genius at it."

"Exactly. Bysshe is making a career at last. And I can't tell you how important that is. He's always been too proud to accept help from me. I never minded him going in for vegetarianism, sunbathing, Buchmanism, or Gertrude Stein prose, but I hated to see him starving. Now that he's doing well, I'm terrified that he'll put his foot in it with the Chief and wreck his career. He told me only yesterday that by remaining on the staff he was countenancing war."

Charles sighed. "I'm afraid he's already put his foot in it."

"What?" Miranda started. "What has he done?"

Charles told her.

"That settles it, I suppose," she sighed. "Damnation! Why is he such a fool?"

"I don't know. The Chief's a queer soul. He's a journalist himself, you know, and he realizes we are a bit temperamental, particularly the best of us. He is quite ruthless about inefficiency; and if anyone's a slacker, he just exterminates. But he expects us to lose our wool occasionally, and go gaga temporarily. Quite probably he will treat Bysshe as if nothing's happened."

"Yes, but Bysshe won't," wailed Miranda. "I've told him if he's going to indulge in scruples he may as well abandon journalism; but it's useless."

"He's very difficult to argue with," commented Charles, from experience.

"I know. Bysshe has always been like that. But can't you point out how *useless* it is? Thousands of people are ready to take his place."

"I've tried all that," Charles answered. "But one feels quite helpless arguing with an idealist on practical grounds. One has so obviously got the dirty end of the stick."

Charles rose to his feet. "Anyway, after tonight it doesn't matter much. If the Chief's plans come off, it will be too late soon for any gesture of Bysshe's. My martial sword I shall gird me on, and sling my harp behind me!"

Miranda said nothing. Charles looked at her closely.

"Having disposed of Bysshe, and if you still feel in the mood to let me help you, don't you think you might tell me what's *really* worrying you?"

Miranda laughed. "What *do* you mean?"

"There's something more than Bysshe." Charles swung his monocle, gazing at it with fierce concentration. "Will you think me impertinent – of course you will – look here, old thing, is it Carpenter?"

Miranda flushed. Charles looked up in time to see this phenomenon. It was the first time he had witnessed it. Miranda might look frail, with blonde prettiness, but she was fond of describing herself as the toughest woman journalist in Fleet Street, and then some. Cynical, even among a sophisticated tribe, Miranda, more usually known to her colleagues as "Jamey," was not accustomed to blush. Doubtless this made the process as painful as it evidently was.

"Oh, damn it," exclaimed Charles penitently. "I oughtn't to have asked."

"It is interesting to know it is so obvious," answered Miranda.

"It isn't. It wouldn't have been noticed by anyone who wasn't too blasted nosey by nature, and who also liked you enough to watch you rather closely." Charles paced to the window and back.

"Damn it, I know you're hurt," he said savagely. "So am I. So you've *got* to listen while I tell you something about Carpenter."

"Need you?"

"For God's sake, be human," said Charles. The phone bell buzzed and he started visibly. "See that? I'm cagey enough myself tonight. Oh, quiet, quiet!" He seized the phone. "Who's there? No, this is not Mr. Grovermuller. He is in conference and I am taking all messages for him. The City of London Police? Why, is that you, Bray? This is Venables. I thought I recognized your voice. A phone message–" Miranda heard Charles pause and say in a surprised voice, "I say, you know, you can't take it seriously. Oh, all right, all right. I'll go up and see."

Charles turned to Miranda. "Hold tight, old girl," he said gravely. "Do you believe in Nemesis?"

She stared at him, surprised. "Why?"

"That was the police. They have had a phone message – an anonymous call. It informed them that if we go now to Carpenter's room we shall find him – dead."

"Good gracious, it's the usual practical joke. Some lunatic or slightly bottled medical student."

Charles looked at her in silence for a moment. He appeared to be reflecting.

"No," he said at last, with deliberate confidence. "It is not a hoax. It is the truth."

A Magnate
Is Murdered

BETWEEN ONE AND TWO o'clock in the morning is an hour of
unrest in Fleet Street. Printers' messengers scurry up and down
stairs, subs swear, comps clatter type on the stone, and bleary-
eyed and tired-out, late-duty reporters play poker, yawn and
swap scandal about the circulation of their rivals. It is at such
times as this that the oldest member of the staff, the dead sea
fruit bitter in his mouth, lectures the youngest member on the
futility and vanity of the profession he has chosen. There is only
one cure for such a feeling, but at this time they are closed.

Andrews, hurriedly summoned by Venables, laughed at the
absurd suggestion, but as the staff lift shot them dizzily upwards
his face was thoughtful. The outer room of the Chief's suite, an
office, was alight, but the Board Room in which they had met
this morning, and off which the Chief's bedroom opened, was
in darkness. Andrews switched on the light, and Charles, after a
moment's hesitation, knocked on the bedroom door. There was
no answer.

They opened the door. In the half-light they could make out
the recumbent figure of the Chief, one arm outstretched and
one by his side. On the wall a Dutch mirror winked and glowed

and winked again as the flashing sky-sign outside incessantly stuttered, reminding the heavens and the toiling races of men of the *Mercury's* net sale, "Greatest in the Universe."

Andrews drew in his breath sharply. "Are you all right, sir?" he said hoarsely. He bent over the figure, suddenly illuminated as Charles touched the switch.

Carpenter's sleep was of the kind for which there is no *réveillé*. A crimson stain spread ornamentally round a tear in his grey waistcoat. It was already brown at the edges.

Natural horror and professional instinct fought visibly in Andrews' face.

"My God," he said at last. "What a story!"

— II —

"Do you know anyone in the office or outside, of the name of Ganthony?" asked Detective Inspector Manciple for the fifth time, of the fifth person. This was Felix Carpenter, the murdered peer's younger brother, and his heir, who had hurried down within twenty minutes of hearing the news. Felix Carpenter scrutinized his fingers, the thin, powerful fingers of the executant musician – and Felix Carpenter was an amateur violinist of no mean ability.

"Ganthony," he echoed, as if the question was only now starting to sink into his consciousness. "No. I've never heard the name before to my knowledge."

Blue-jowled, impassive, with the inscrutable placidity of a Buddha, Manciple seemed in no way disconcerted by this universal ignorance regarding the object of his queries.

"A sort of King Charles' Head, this Ganthony," commented Venables. "Is there such a person, or did you make him up?"

Manciple turned to Venables without the slightest change in

his expression. "A man rang up Sir Colin Vansteen, the Home Office pathologist, at 1.45 a.m., and told him that Lord Carpenter was lying dead in his suite at the *Mercury* buildings. He gave his name as Ganthony. Something in the man's earnestness, and the circumstantial way in which he spoke, convinced Sir Colin that it was not a hoax. He rang us up at once."

"An extraordinary story, Inspector," commented Charles. "Do you expect anyone to know this Ganthony?"

Manciple's cold grey eyes swivelled expressionlessly towards Carpenter, then back to Charles. "I don't."

"You think it is a false name?"

"The idea had occurred to me," answered Manciple, with irony in his voice but none in his face.

"The obvious conclusion," went on Charles, a little dashed, "is that the telephonist was the murderer, and yet was for some reason anxious for the murder to be discovered. Anxious enough, at any rate, to risk his voice being recognized."

Manciple's eyebrows rose a trifle.

"Venables is our tame crime expert," explained Grovermuller laughingly. "He feels it is up to him to show his mettle from the start."

Manciple inclined his head. "I read about Mr. Venables in connection with the Garden Hotel Case," he conceded without the faintest hint of cordiality.

He paused a moment, closed his eyes, and appeared to be lost for a moment in thought. A certain strength of personality latent in the man kept the others silent.

"Distrust the obvious, Mr. Venables," he said at last, opening his eyes. He paused a moment to allow the force of this remark to sink in, and then rose to his feet abruptly.

"Now let us get down to business," he said. "At 11.25 p.m. you left Lord Carpenter. He announced his intention of going to sleep, and apparently did so. Between that time and say 1.45 a.m. he was stabbed. The weapon, so far as one can see at present, is this dagger, which was replaced on the wall, and which still, though wiped, bears minute traces of blood. There may or may not be fingerprints on it."

Manciple glanced round. No comment was made.

"Where does that lead to?" he asked, pointing to a door opposite the entrance to the Chief's rooms through which he had come, the only entrance for the staff.

"That is Lord Carpenter's private door," answered Grovermuller. "It leads to a lobby and then into his private secretary's room. Then there is another passage and a private lift, which only serves the street. The idea is that no one can get to the Chief who is not on the staff, without passing through the private secretary's room."

"Who is – ?"

"Jerningham."

"Is Mr. Jerningham there now?"

"I should think so. Try ringing the bell."

Manciple pressed it. "You will, of course, leave this to me, gentlemen."

Fresh and debonair, Jerningham marched in, looking slightly surprised when he saw the gathering. "Was it the Chief who rang for me?" he asked.

Manciple looked at him closely, much as one might study an inanimate object. "I am from Scotland Yard," he stated. "Lord Carpenter has been murdered."

Jerningham turned a creditable shade of white.

"Murdered?" he repeated, staring round the room.

"Stabbed," amplified the detective.

Jerningham crumpled heavily into a chair.

"Where have you been during the hour?" asked Manciple, in a

conversational tone.

"In my room."

"Has anyone been through it?"

"No one."

"You are certain?"

"Quite positive."

"Good." Manciple walked to the windows, and looked out. "These are, of course, impossible. Therefore the murderer entered and left by the staff door of the suite between 11.30 p.m. and 1.45 a.m. That is something gained. Now what about the entrances to the building itself?"

"Carpenter had given instructions that the entrances were to be guarded," answered Grovermuller. "Two people were on duty at each, and although anyone was to be admitted, no one was to be allowed out without my written permission. Practically no one left the building, except, of course, the van-drivers, who never actually enter it. They are in the yard."

Manciple's eyebrows rose again. "An unusual precaution, surely? What was Lord Carpenter afraid of?"

"A leakage of news. We had a vital and exclusive story."

"Ah, that may have some bearing on the case. We may want to go into that later."

"I should think it is unlikely. But the result is rather a godsend to you, isn't it?"

Gravely, Manciple agreed. "The murderer must still be somewhere in the building. I shall get my men to make me a list of everyone, and we shall know all the possible suspects. I estimate at a venture that this will narrow our search down to five or six hundred people. This, of course, is a godsend."

Grovermuller smiled weakly.

"I should like some member of the staff to go with me," went on Manciple, "to explain as far as possible who everyone is."

"Quite so." Grovermuller looked round. "Andrews, your page has gone to bed, hasn't it?"

"Ages ago."

"Well, will you see the Inspector round? I am sure you will be able to do the potted biographies better than anyone."

"Certainly. Come on, Inspector. I look forward to seeing sleuthing at first hand."

As they left the room, Grovermuller turned to Felix Carpenter. "Lord Carpenter —" the man started slightly, addressed for the first time by his new title – "I presume this incident has left me in sole charge for the moment of the policy of the paper, until the destination of the controlling shares held by your brother are settled?"

"Oh, certainly," answered Lord Carpenter hurriedly. "Nothing to do with me, of course. Nothing at all. I believe the shares in question are bequeathed to me, but I am quite content to leave everything to you."

"The point is more serious than you may imagine," persisted Grovermuller. "For the last year your brother has laid down a policy to which I have rigidly adhered. At the same time, I have strongly disapproved of it." The trace of a smile appeared to linger on Grovermuller's bland features, with the careful eyebrows and delightfully neat silver moustache, a face typical more of the solicitor's assured background than the journalist's turbulent surroundings. His phrase had quite adequately summed up the tactics whereby he had maintained his place at the top of the ladder. Always he had conscientiously adhered to the instructions as laid down by Carpenter. None knew what internal fevers of disapproval had consumed him. And now the days of acquiescence were gone for ever.

"I suppose you are referring to my brother's militaristic campaign?"

"Precisely. Tomorrow's issue, or rather today's issue, was to culminate the campaign. We have in our possession information from your brother's secret agents. Used as we intended to use it, that information would make war inevitable. It is now my intention, however – with your approval – to refer to this incident in the most guarded terms. This will prepare the way for a complete reversal of policy on the part of the *Mercury*. With the country in its present state, we may now be unable to undo your brother's brilliant work. But if the Premier plays his cards skilfully, and we make no mistakes, the thing might be done. Have I your support?"

The new Lord Carpenter's mouth closed in a firm line. For a moment the untidy artist showed a faint image of the biting determination which had distinguished his brother.

"I had the strongest dislike, loathing in fact, of this agitation for war. I hated the end and I abhorred the means. So far as I am entitled to influence the policy of the *Mercury* or Affiliated Publications, you have my full support. Throw their whole weight in the cause of peace."

"Thank you." The smile flickered again; and Grovermuller went downstairs to wreck the supreme achievement of his one-time chief.

Carpenter's form was now lying in darkness, covered decorously with a sheet. The crimson stain was completely brown. But the Dutch mirror steadily and incessantly winked at the proved boast of London's largest sky sign. Venables, absorbed in studying the former resting place of the dagger, was left alone in the Board Room with Carpenter's successor.

"Cunning little devil!" said Felix Carpenter unexpectedly.

—　　—

"Are you quite sure you don't mind being dragged along, Sir Colin?" asked Manciple. "You see, you had the first news of the murder, and it seemed an insult to coincidence not to ask you to act as police surgeon."

"Oh, certainly," answered Vansteen. "Where's the body? Not been mauled by over-zealous helpers?"

"In there," said Manciple. "In perfect condition – a real pleasure to find. We've seen all we want – which isn't much. You know we laymen don't know where to begin, even, where the medical side is concerned. So the stage is yours."

"Your modesty does you credit," said the pathologist dryly. Before he had been retained by the Home Office, he had come into conflict with Manciple on more than one occasion. "I haven't always found the layman averse to forming an opinion on a point of medical evidence."

Manciple's lips moved in what was presumably a smile. He studied the knight's aloof and distinguished features. "I blush," he said; "I have already formed my opinion. Carpenter was stabbed about an hour ago by rather a clumsy assassin – the wound is all over the place. This knife was used."

Sir Colin rubbed his hands. "Well, well. A snap judgement." He opened his case and pulled on a pair of rubber gloves. "You know my little ways by now, Manciple. I'll let you have my considered opinion tomorrow afternoon. It will be final. I'll stick to it till hell's blue. Till then – nothing."

The door closed on Sir Colin and his professional attentions to what had been Lord Carpenter. Charles, who had succeeded in remaining in the sitting room by a process of industrious percolation during the whole two hours that had elapsed, turned to Manciple. "As a matter of curiosity, how long is your list of suspects?"

Manciple took out a sheaf of papers from his pocket. After a hurried inspection: "Three hundred and fifty-six and a few more to come," he said, with apparent seriousness.

"I say, a bit of a tall order."

Manciple closed his eyes. "When you have had some constructive experience of criminal hunting, Mr. Venables, you will appreciate that it doesn't matter how long your list of suspects is, as long as one is certain the criminal is among them. When my men finish their preliminary investigations tomorrow, I expect the list to be reduced to thirty." Manciple opened his eyes with a slightly amazed expression, as if he had spoken more than he intended.

"And are you *certain* the murderer will be among them?"

The detective tapped a cigarette reflectively on its case. "Nothing is certain till the courts decide," he said evasively.

"Oh, be matey, chaps," wheedled Charles. "Have you any positive clues? Damn elimination. You know better than I do how useless it really is!"

Manciple looked at him keenly. Then without a word he walked to the table and took the Florentine dagger from the drawer in which it was locked. The silver, intricately chased with Cellini's reverent fertility of invention, gleamed palely and remotely in the glare of a light which Cellini had never allowed for in its fashioning.

The light trickled over the hilt and wavered uncertainly down the rippled steel of the broad blade, dappled with flecks of blood. The room vibrated faintly, like a hidden pulse, with the beating revolutions of the giant presses in the basement. In the streets vans backed and roared and whined. Charles screwed in his monocle and bent forward while Manciple, with stubby forefinger, pointed to two fingerprints, one on the hilt and the other on the blade, both cleanly outlined in fingerprint powder.

"The man who made those fingerprints," Manciple said simply, "will probably hang."

A Pathologist Is Uneasy

Sir Colin Vansteen joined the tips of his exquisite surgeon's fingers and studied them for a moment.

"You've put me in an infernally awkward position, old chap," he groaned to his visitor. "If it had been anyone else but you, I wouldn't have stood it."

A wintry smile illuminated the other's face. "I'm sorry. I haven't your experience of murders. I hadn't the least idea of what was the right thing to do."

"Damn it, it's no smiling matter!" answered the pathologist. "Here have I completely obscured the police inquiry with an illusive and most mysterious Mr. Ganthony – I, Colin Vansteen, Consulting Pathologist to His Majesty's Home Office."

"Why on earth 'Ganthony,' if I may ask?"

Vansteen led his visitor to the window of his Piccadilly flat. "I happened to look out of the window while I was telephoning the police and that is what I saw – G. Anthony, Florist."

"Are the police really searching for him?"

I think that cute devil Manciple guesses there's no such person. Heaven only knows when he'll tumble to the conclusion that I made him up." Vansteen moved his hand across his silver hair with a gesture of mock despair.

"I'm terribly sorry, Colin. But you know, I think, that it was not a personal matter. I shouldn't care a damn if I were the only

31

person to be involved."

"Oh, I've thought of all that, old chap. If it had been only you, I should have thrown you to the lions without compunction. Thank the Lord you rang on Carpenter's private telephone – the one line that wasn't listened in to. And if it does come out that you were associated with the affair, don't, for heaven's sake, let out that you were really a Mr. Ganthony!"

"No. Well, goodbye, Vansteen, and God bless you. I don't think you will ever be sorry for what you have done."

"Perhaps not," grumbled Vansteen as he saw the other to the door. "I certainly appear to have developed a brilliant gift for lying plausibly at the shortest notice. My next task is to prepare a report which will contain the maximum amount of information with the minimum of risk. And if there is an independent medical examination of the body – well, there may be trouble."

Left to himself, Vansteen was lost in thought for a time. Then he pressed his bell for his confidential secretary.

"Take down this, Browning, will you? Send it with the usual letter round by hand to Detective Inspector Manciple. Begin 'The Death of Lord Carpenter' and fill in the usual official bilge. Then follow on:

"'I duly attended at Mercury House at 2.05 a.m. on Tuesday, October 12th, at the request of Detective Inspector Manciple, to investigate the reported death of Lord Carpenter. The body was lying on its back on a bed in the middle of the room. The photograph initialled by me correctly delineated its position at the time I arrived. The right leg was fully stretched and the knee of the left leg was slightly raised. The right arm was resting beside the trunk and the left hand was placed behind the nape of the neck.

"'Death was the result of the penetration of the aortic ventricle by a knife or similar instrument. This had been withdrawn immediately after making the incision. The Florentine dagger I was shown by Detective Inspector Manciple would be capable of making the wound that caused death. The blood on this instrument belonged to the same group as that of Lord Carpenter's according to the Toscanini reaction (analysis report Sch. 5642/8 attached). The deceased was healthy, bearing in mind his age, with no organic disorders of any marked kind. His medical history is good. Death would have been almost instantaneous. I formed the conclusion that the deceased was stabbed while asleep, and died without regaining consciousness, and probably without moving markedly from the position he was in when stabbed. In my opinion death took place between 11.45 p.m. and 1.30 a.m. of that night. – Colin Vansteen, M.B., M.R.C.S.' That will be all, Browning. Include the detailed post-mortem in the usual way."

— II —

Meanwhile, the almost sacred wood of the *Mercury* Editorial Conference table reflected, with the meretricious glitter peculiar to Empire hardwoods, the neatly folded hands of Detective Inspector Manciple, which hovered like a benediction over the surface. Manciple himself, with the benign lack of expression of a Chinese sage, lectured his audience of three. Grovermuller's face was lit with a certain feline amusement; Carpenter's face showed nothing but baffled perplexity; Charles had succeeded in making his monocle spin, with a faint whirring sound, on the edge of the table.

"The Deputy Commissioner has asked me to keep in touch with you gentlemen, and you too, my lord, and let you know as much of my investigations as I consider consonant with their successful prosecution."

"Quite, quite," said Carpenter. "Naturally we don't want to know more than it is politic to tell us." His aloof air suggested that he would far rather have nothing whatever to do with the affair.

"A sentiment no journalist can agree with, Lord Carpenter," interposed Grovermuller pleasantly. "It is, in fact, the essence of our job to know more than is considered good for us."

Manciple plunged on like a destroyer, shouldering off the spray of their pleasantries without deflection. "In my opinion it is not consonant with the successful prosecution of my investigations to tell you anything—"

"Oh," said Carpenter, as if he were in a lift which had suddenly dropped four feet without warning.

"—However, as it was very obviously General Murgatroyd's intention that you should be told something, I propose to put you in possession of the main facts as I see them."

"Very good of you, Inspector," conceded Grovermuller.

Manciple cleared his throat. "Lord Carpenter was stabbed between 11.45 p.m. and 1.30 a.m. The dagger with which he was stabbed was a museum piece which hung on a wall bracket, on which it was subsequently replaced."

"It may interest you to know, Manciple," interrupted Charles, "that at the conference just before he went to sleep, Lord Carpenter referred to that dagger. He said jokingly that if anyone wanted to alter the policy of the paper" – Charles's eyes rested innocently for a moment upon Grovermuller – "they would have to take that knife and cut his throat. That remark provides a possible psychological link between the murderer and the weapon."

Manciple permitted himself the luxury of a faint cluck of approval. "Most interesting! I must get the names of the members of the staff at that conference."

"I thought you would want them," admitted Charles, "and in fact I have here the list."

"Thank you." Manciple gravely pocketed the slip of paper. "To return. The main clue we possess at the moment is that there are two fingerprints on the dagger, one on the hilt, the other on the blade, actually made over one of the flecks of blood. You will appreciate the significance of that. It means that whoever left those fingerprints, did so after the murder."

"Then surely your task is simple?" said Carpenter. "You have only to find the man."

"It is not necessarily so easy," answered Manciple. "A fingerprint is not like a telephone number. So far we have not identified them. However, we have a list of everyone who was in the *Mercury* building at the time. These have all been questioned with the result that there are twelve people finally on our list without alibis, each able therefore to commit the murder within the times mentioned." Manciple paused. "Now that I have gone so far, I see no grave disadvantage in reading out the persons I suspect at the moment. They are as follows:

Mr. Grovermuller, Editor.
Mr. Venables, Crime Expert.
Miss Miranda Jameson, Woman's Page Expert.
Mr. Bysshe Jameson, Reporter.
Mr. Jerningham, Private Secretary.
Mr. Hubbard, Librarian.
Mr. Hardy, Advertisement Manager.
Mr. Perry, Art Editor.
Mr. Andrews, City Page Editor.
Mr. Lee Kum Tong, Eastern Correspondent.
Mr. Heflin, News Editor.
Mr. Bowles, Head Reader.

"Really, Inspector Manciple! This is the most preposterous farce!" exclaimed Lord Carpenter. "Mr. Grovermuller is quite beyond suspicion."

"Also Mr. Venables is our crime expert," grinned Grovermuller sardonically. "It will hamper his investigations on our behalf if he was the murderer."

Charles said nothing.

"May I point out that my Chief's instructions were to inform you. He said nothing about consulting you," answered Manciple. "I must ask you to remember that the list I have read is quite provisional. It is, for instance, eleven to one, or at any rate only slightly less, against Mr. Grovermuller having done it."

"I am relieved I am not yet a favourite for the scaffold stakes," admitted Grovermuller. "I am rather staggered by the thought that one of the excellent people you have mentioned is a murderer. It comes to me with more poignancy, you see, because I know I am not the murderer. Therefore one of the eleven must be. I shall even feel uneasy about calling on old Hubbard in the library – wondering, you know, whether he may not plunge a paper knife into my vitals. In fact, as I've already hinted to him that we'll have to retire him shortly, it's possibly a real danger."

"I take it," suggested Venables, "that you have in mind some method of reducing your suspects to a convenient figure. Do you feel at liberty to tell us?"

"Certainly. First of all I propose to find out if the fingerprints on the dagger correspond with those of any of the suspects."

"And if they do?" Charles drummed reflectively with his fingertips on the Empire hardwood.

"Then, Mr. Venables, we shall endeavour to prove a motive. Finally, if the suspect's account of his movements is unsatisfactory, we shall have an excellent case."

"But what about Mr. Ganthony?" inquired Venables.

"Oh, Ganthony! He will figure as an alias."

"How awkward," murmured Charles, "if he turned up after you had made your arrest."

Drawing his silk handkerchief from his pocket, he wiped the table where his fingertips had been resting.

— III —

"Does that deep devil Manciple really suspect me?" Grovermuller swung round in his chair and faced Charles.

Charles snuggled luxuriously into the reposeful chairs which were a feature of the Editor's office. He tapped his knuckles reflectively with his monocle.

"I should say the hypothesis he is working on is that you did it, sir."

Grovermuller, his keen dark eyes fixed on Venables, seemed to withdraw into himself. He gently stroked his clipped moustache. "And you?" he asked.

"Yes, sir," answered Charles cheerfully. "My hypothesis tends the same way. Of course it is a purely evidential hypothesis – in no way based on personal opinion."

"You interest me. Continue. What is the evidence?"

"Oh, all indirect of course. Otherwise you would be more than a suspect. Your movements are entirely unaccounted for during the fatal hour. You have the easiest access to the suite. You are generally known, sir, to have been in conflict with Carpenter on a vital point of policy, and it must have been exceedingly unpleasant to be in conflict with so forceful a personality as the Chief. By his death you gain a fifteen per cent interest in the ordinary shares of the *Mercury*. It is rumoured in the office that you have been plunging on Lagonda Reefs and were oversold on a bull market."

Grovermuller stared at Charles, who added, "Manciple doesn't know that, I think, which is probably rather lucky. On the top of that, the Chief has often informed you before witnesses of the amount you would inherit by his death. Finally you have the calm and resolute temperament which would pull off this sort of thing very neatly."

"Thanks," said Grovermuller grimly. "You seem to have been investigating with great efficiency. May one ask if you consider it part of your duty here to put your editor in the dock?"

"Speaking personally, sir, I should rather put my News Editor there," Charles answered unctuously. "From the point of view of the paper, however, it would make an even better story if it were the Editor himself who was hounded down by the Crime Expert."

"I believe you're right. I am sorry to disappoint you, however. I did not murder Carpenter. I have often felt like doing so, but then so has every member of his staff at some time or other."

"Even I," conceded Charles.

"Exactly. So, strong in the conviction of my innocence, I propose to give you full rein. Only this morning's story was not one of your best efforts, you know. You must do better than that."

"Mr. Heflin has already indicated that. He put it rather more forcefully. 'Any more junk like that, Venables, and you go out on your ear,' were his exact words."

"Grovermuller smiled. "He would. By the way, do you believe my confession of innocence?"

"Not very strongly," admitted Charles. "You could hardly say much else at this stage."

"Let me suggest something else for your consideration. If I had the calm and resolute temperament you give me credit for, would I have been so foolish as to leave my fingerprints on the dagger?"

Charles for some reason looked embarrassed. "I don't know. It's the sort of stupid thing anyone might do in the rush of the moment."

— IV —

Miranda Jameson, absorbed in cutting down an article on "Unappreciative Husbands" from 3,000 to 250 words, did not hear Charles come in. With unobtrusive steps he made for the only comfortable chair and sat down in it. Miranda, turning to retrieve the paste-pot from the table behind her, perceived him with a start.

"Good heavens, what are you doing here?"

"Looking at you: a delightful occupation."

"You must be rather hard up for an occupation."

"Not at all. I consider it a point of national importance to decide why it is that black hair, of fairly normal length, framing a face with a freckled nose and the customary number of eyes, etc., should irresistibly impel me to –"

"Stop," interrupted Miranda firmly. "If I thought you were serious I should be rude. Besides," she added as an afterthought, "my nose isn't freckled."

"Freckled," repeated Charles firmly. "But how divinely modelled. How exquisitely chiselled. Though why it should be complimentary to carve a nose with a chisel I don't know, speaking as one who has done some sculpting."

"Don't you think you had better reserve this for Lady Viola?" answered Miranda, slashing the typescript before her with ruthless efficiency.

"I've just been jilted," answered Charles. "Well, a month ago to be precise. I went five diamonds when we were vulnerable, and I regret to say that, impossible though it may sound, our opponents,

39

who had doubled us, got a little slam. The ensuing conversation was too painful to be described. It was all very shameful, and the result was to leave me free of attachments, eligible, and, at the present moment, at the peak of the rebound."

"I don't blame her," laughed Miranda. "However, in that case you can go on. You had got to the bit about my nose."

"Yes. Brow with the marmoreal whiteness of subcutaneous Parian. Eyes piquant and yet thoughtful, in whose brown depths—"

"Wait a moment. My eyes are blue."

"Undeniably. The heroine of the novel from which I happen to be quoting had brown eyes, however."

"Good gracious, was it all second-hand? And you call yourself a journalist!"

"I do, but Heflin doesn't. I hate to think what he called me. Where do news editors get that manner: is it a gift?"

"No, it's only since Edgar Wallace. However, he's always been very nice to me."

"He would be. But let's forget Heflin. Why have you been avoiding me all day?"

"Avoiding you?" Miranda laughed, not very successfully.

"Avoiding me, you know you have. I don't want to butt in, but are you sure I can't help you?"

"No; it's very sweet of you. But I'm quite tough enough to carry on alone. Sweet of you to offer."

"Not at all, granted as soon as asked," murmured Charles. "Hello, here's Bysshe."

With tousled red hair, and the roving bright eyes which are the peculiar property of genius, fanaticism, and racing-car drivers, Bysshe slouched into the room.

"'Lo, Andy. 'Lo, Charles. Lazy devil. What's the latest line on the murder business?"

"Slowly and surely the steamroller of Scotland Yard surges towards its objective."

"Oh. Am I its objective by any chance?"

"No, the objective is not even in sight. The bloodhound of the law, however, detects a strong smell of Grovermuller wafted round a bend in the road."

Miranda looked at him anxiously. "What did you mean, exactly, Bysshe?"

"Only that Manciple and his confounded minions have been badgering me as to what I was doing between 11.45 p.m. and 1.30 a.m. Not only that, they have been asking everyone else."

"Where were you at the time, anyway?" asked Charles.

Bysshe looked uneasy. "That's the devil of it. I was wandering aimlessly round the corridors."

"Did you know anything about this, Charles?" asked his sister.

"I knew Bysshe was one of twelve possibles. So am I. So are you. There's no need to worry yet. Hello, here's Hubbard. You seem to be having quite a reception here tonight!"

Hubbard did not often emerge from his library. He lurked there like a kobold in his mine, and there those who desired the wisdom of forgotten decades sought him. Hubbard was almost domiciled in his library. Once, fifteen years ago, he had buried his mother, but had turned up in the evening, in his funeral garments, to dispense obituaries with philosophic indifference to their grim symbolism.

Owlishly he peered round through his horn-rimmed spectacles. "Ah, Venables. Perhaps you can tell me what the police are up to. Two of them have been cross-questioning my staff and frightening my typist into hysterics."

"Cheer up, Hubbard," Charles answered reassuringly. "I was just telling Jameson that everyone in this room is a candidate for the scaffold, including myself. Other suspects include Grovermuller and, I am glad to say, Heflin." Charles paused for a moment and repeated it ecstatically. "Gorgeous, isn't it, Heflin!"

"All I can say," remarked Bysshe, his eyes lighting up, "is that if I knew which was the murderer, I would shake him by the hand. Carpenter was vermin. He has been exterminated, and that ought to end the matter."

"Really, Jameson," said the librarian nervously, "I don't think you ought to say that. I think it is very rash to abuse Carpenter publicly like that."

"Very rash, whoever it is abusing him."

They turned suddenly at the familiar accent. Inspector Manciple was in the doorway, smiling.

"Do you always creep into rooms like this, Inspector?" asked Miranda. "It must be great fun for you."

"I knocked," said Manciple good-humouredly, "but you were so deep in conversation, I fancy you didn't hear me. I am sorry I interrupted you. It is more a matter of form than anything else. Would you be so good as to each give me an impression of your fingerprints?"

The detective treated them to a smile of bland encouragement, which made his heavy face seem for the moment convivially cheerful. "Strictly speaking, since I believe I already have the fingerprints of the criminal, I should warn you that this action might incriminate you. On the other hand," he chuckled, "it would be still more incriminating if anyone refused, eh?" Still smiling, Manciple laid on the table the inked pad and sheets of stiff white card.

For a moment there was dead silence. Then Miranda, white and rather strained, spoke. "I consider your request an impertinence, Inspector." She folded her hands precisely, and placed them in front of her with an air of finality. "I refuse absolutely to comply with it."

Again there was a dead silence. Manciple's eyes moved to Bysshe. He flushed and spoke hotly. "I agree with my sister. The request is absurd. It places us on a par with criminals. I refuse to submit to this interference of officialdom. I propose to uphold the liberty the law allows me. I refuse!"

Blinking, but determined, Hubbard wheeled into line with the other two and brought his own guns to bear. "Mancini has exposed the weakness of the fingerprint system. The odds against duplication are high, but they are finite. The odds against winning the *Mercury* £10,000 crossword are high, but it is repeatedly won. No fingerprints have yet been discovered duplicating existing ones – therefore the time must be drawing near when the duplicate will be discovered. The position of any innocent person possessing duplicates of a guilty set would be terrible. No would believe his innocence. I refuse to take the risk merely to make your task easier."

Slowly Manciple's look of encouragement had dissolved. So far as it was possible for his stolid features to express any emotion, he now looked baffled.

"God bless my soul!" he exclaimed. "In all my experience –" He turned to Charles. "Mr. Venables, you at least appreciate how unwise, and how very obstructive this attitude is. Can you not persuade them to change their minds?"

Gaily Charles plunged into the fray. Someone more familiar with his moods than was Manciple would have been needed to detect the constraint in his gaiety.

"I am sorry, Inspector, but I agree with them entirely – on artistic grounds. Consider – where is the technique of criminal investigation if it depends on the crude matching of fingerprints? Where are your psychological values? Where is the subtlety of move and counter-move? Where is the slow unravelling of motive? The chess-like ranging of possibilities against alibis? I will strike a blow for the æsthetics of our much-misunderstood art. I refuse to have my fingerprints taken!"

Manciple got up to go. "I see you have had all this arranged. That's what comes of having to talk beforehand." He looked bitterly at Venables. "You are unwise to work against me, even if you can't work with me."

Newspaper Cuttings Behave Oddly

"WOULD IT NOT BE as well to indulge in a little mutual frankness?" asked Charles.

There was electricity in the air, even after Manciple had left the room. Venables' question, if anything, added to the overcharging of the atmosphere.

"Shall we begin with you, Hubbard? Will you let us into the secret of your real objection to letting your fingerprints being taken?"

Hubbard's eyes glittered behind their wide lenses with the ardour of a fanatic. "I have told you! I disbelieve in the system. Bertillon has hoodwinked the police of the world – not a very difficult matter. Any rational man, studying the possible variations of the fingerprint as classified, and allowing for a margin of error due to smudging, I say every rational man" – Hubbard stabbed the air with the emphasis of a bony forefinger – "cannot fail to see the fallibility of the theory. The chances of ambiguity are a matter of everyday possibility. I refuse to countenance the system by giving my impression."

Charles looked at him keenly. "You interest me, Hubbard. I had no idea of the range of your erudition." He turned to Bysshe.

"Do you want to say anything? I think we shall be able to help each other better if we all lay our cards on the table."

Bysshe passed his hand over his forehead. His eyes were full of foreboding. "It may be dangerous for me to put my cards on the table. Still, here goes. I've an idea at the back of my head that when I was looking at that dagger a day or two ago, in the Chief's room, I may have touched it and left my fingerprint on it."

Charles rubbed his chin thoughtfully. "If that is the literal truth, it will be quite safe to tell it to the police. The fingerprint which worries Manciple was made after the murder. But be quite sure of your time, you know."

"Why, what do you mean?" asked Bysshe sharply.

Charles ignored the question and turned to Miranda. "And you?"

She cupped her small chin on her hands and stared at Charles reflectively. "Do you know, I don't think I shall tell you. Not for the moment at any rate. Why don't you tell us yours?"

"Certainly," said Charles, returning her glance coolly. "If the police were to get my fingerprints, I should be arrested."

— II —

"Inspector Manciple!"

"Yes, Mr. Jerningham?"

"I say, did you or your people collect any newspaper cuttings when you searched the Chief's room?"

"Cuttings? No. Never saw any."

"Well, here's a funny thing. Before I left the Chief immediately after the conference, he was reading some cuttings Hubbard had given him. They seem to have disappeared."

"Curious. Do you remember what they are about?"

"Oh yes. They were all from the Russian file. Accounts of

previous Bolshevist atrocities and so forth. There can hardly have been anything of importance among them."

"On the contrary," pointed out Manciple, "if the murder were in any way connected with the Russian war plan, the cuttings may have contained evidence which would have put us on the right track."

"Oh yes, of course," said Jerningham vaguely. "Well, anyway, they've gone."

Manciple pondered the matter of the cuttings more than once during the day; of course, there mightn't be anything in it, but often investigation turned on the smallest trifles. His inquiries hit upon no one who had seen them. Eventually they brought him to Venables.

"Hello, Inspector," said Charles, with the utmost cordiality. "Have you found an owner for your fingerprints yet?"

"No," answered the Inspector without graciousness. "Still, one can guess." His eyes lingered on Charles's long white fingers.

Charles observed the gaze.

"I say, have you ever played 'Up Jenkyns'?" he remarked suddenly.

"Eh?" The other stared. "No."

"It is a parlour game; popular among our grandparents. You have to guess in which one of several closed hands a sixpence is concealed. You are not allowed to make a mistake."

Manciple, suddenly betraying a sense of humour, laughed heartily. "I see what you mean, Mr. Venables." He winked. "Well, I've a pretty shrewd idea in whose hand the sixpence is concealed. Don't think I'm afraid of making a mistake either. I happen to be waiting for confirmation which will support the purely circumstantial evidence of the print."

"I suspected that was the position," Charles smiled graciously. "I hope we are not going to be on opposite sides of the fence all through the case."

"I hope we are not going to be on opposite sides of the prison bars at the end of the case!" said the Inspector, chuckling. "Joking apart, Mr. Venables, I do not see there is any need for us to be at cross-purposes even now. I may be able to help you. At the moment you can certainly help me."

"The mouse and the lion. Well, what is it?"

"Come into my den, and I'll tell you." He led Venables into the little office which had been put at his disposal for the duration of his investigations.

Charles looked at it enviously. "You officials have a pull. Here you are in this snug dug-out, and I have to share my office."

"Sit you down," said the detective hospitably. "A cigar?"

"By Jove, the old country does you proud." Charles crackled it appreciatively.

"Not my country. A client of mine."

"A client of yours? How do you mean?"

Manciple grinned. "I call him a client. He was hanged. He left me these and hoped I'd smoke myself to death. Sardonic beggar." He selected one with deliberation.

"To his fragrant memory." Charles puffed an oblation. "All I need is some '87 port."

Manciple winked again. With an expert and practised gesture he shot open the drawer of his desk. "Not exactly '87 port, but very good sherry." He produced two glasses and filled them with the amber fluid.

"Manciple, I thought you were less than human. You are more than human. Godlike!" Charles gazed sentimentally into the sherry as he gently rotated the glass to release the mellow fragrance of its bouquet. "This is ambrosia. Tell me your trouble – if you can have a trouble with this sherry nestling in your desk."

Manciple told him.

"Yes, they might be important," admitted Charles. "Unfortunately I never saw them." He was silent a moment. Then he spoke again. "You know, that's given me an idea – or perhaps it is the sherry. Could it possibly be true?" Charles hit his knee ecstatically. "It's an idea. It's good enough to be true. Look here, leave the search for those cuttings to me for a little while. If I can find them, I may be able to confirm my brain wave. If not, one possibility less."

"I'll certainly leave it to you," said the other gloomily. "As I can't find them, you're welcome to try yourself. I envy you," he added, "being able to derive a clue from them without even seeing them. I was proposing to wait until I found them."

"How cynical a man you are – for a detective," lamented Charles. He rose to go. Then as Manciple made to sweep the glasses back into the drawer he checked him. "Wait, I have still a heel-tap. I must drink a toast."

He raised the glass. "To the acuteness, the persistence, the histrionic powers of Scotland Yard, which recognizes even the importance of being amiable." He drank.

Manciple, watching him, said nothing.

"You know the custom of us old Liburnians when we drink a toast." Venables' eyebrows rose at the other's silence. "No? No lesser health sullies the consecrated crystal." With a sudden gesture, he shot out his hand. The glass described an arc of silver, shimmering out of the open window, to fall from five storeys on to the paved street well below.

Gravely Charles drew a sixpence from his pocket. "Woolworth's," he explained. "It may have only been threepence. If so, put the change in the Court poor-box. Excuse the theatricality of my gesture. I wished to emphasize that I saw through your amiability as clearly as you saw through mine."

49

At the door he turned.

"By the way, do not try to collect the bits in the hope you will still get a complete fingerprint. I shall probably crunch 'em up with my heel as I go out."

— III —

"By Jove, Hubbard!" exclaimed Charles, "you have made history in Fleet Street."

The little man smiled weakly. "Yes, it's the first time I've been away on sick leave since I joined the *Mercury*. Extraordinary – a sudden attack of influenza. I keeled over in the tube and had to be taken home in an ambulance. Right as rain next day, but the doctor forbade me to go out."

"You don't look any too well yet."

"I don't feel it. As a matter of fact the doctor told me I wasn't to stir out of my house today either. I just couldn't bear the thought of being away, so along I came. Just as well I did, too," he added, with a dry emphasis.

"Why? Anything wrong?"

The librarian plunged into a sea of denunciation. "Mr. Grovermuller," he exclaimed, his voice piping with indignation. "He actually sent Jerningham down here while I was away to find a cutting. He told him, apparently, 'to scratch about until he found it'. Scratch about! In my system!" The librarian's utterance became choked with rage. With a trembling hand he indicated the tiers of polished metal boxes which represented a life's work.

"Dear, dear," said Charles sympathetically. "Tell me now, are matters too disarranged to give me what you've got on the Russian militarist movement?"

"The Russian militarist movement?" repeated the librarian

slowly, swaying gently from side to side as his eyes ran up and down his shelves. Then suddenly he darted into their intricacies like a thrush in search of a worm on a garden lawn. After a minute or two he emerged with a compact sheaf of cuttings. "There you are," he said proudly.

"Thanks," said Venables. "Are they all here, do you know? Thought possibly some might have been bagged for the Russian stories we've been running."

The other peered at him closely. "Well, now you mention it, the Chief had some the day before he died. I took them up to him myself. In fact I thought I gave him the lot. Evidently I was mistaken."

"It doesn't matter, anyway. I've got what I want here."

Absorbed in a plan of the office buildings which was pinned in front of him, Manciple looked up with a frown of concentration as Charles entered his little room. The frown vanished as he saw his visitor, but it could hardly be asserted that it was replaced by an expression of cordiality. "Well?" he asked.

"Push out the cigars, there's a hero," answered Charles. "I've run out of cigarettes. Don't be reluctant. I deserve your gratitude." He deposited the cuttings on the Inspector's desk.

Manciple picked up the cuttings and rapidly scanned them. "Yes, these are they," he remarked grammatically. "May I ask where you found them?"

"I'm afraid I shall never make a good detective," answered Charles. "I can't think of anything but the obvious things. As they were from a file of cuttings, I went and looked for them in the files, and there they were!"

Manciple snorted. "Oh, were they? And does that convey anything to you?"

Elbows on the table, Charles regarded him solemnly. "Gosh, lots. I know who stabbed the Chief now, I think."

— IV —

"Look here, Venables, you seem to have got on the wrong side of the police. You shouldn't do that, you know. It makes you almost worthless to us."

Very pleasantly, as Charles admitted, but none the less decidedly, Grovermuller was putting him on the carpet.

"I'm sorry, sir. At the moment, it's inevitable."

"What's the trouble?"

"I refused to let them have my fingerprints, you know."

Grovermuller gave a genuine start of amazement. "What the devil –"

"I know," interrupted Charles sympathetically. "The same thought is going through your head as quite obviously passed through Manciple's mind when I refused. 'This bloke can hardly have the effrontery to refuse his fingerprints if he is really guilty – therefore he must be being deliberately obstructive, the blighter! Thinks it's clever, perhaps!'"

"Some such thought did occur to me," admitted Grovermuller with a smile.

Charles shrugged his shoulders. "Well, sir, I can only ask you to give me the benefit of any doubt you may have for four days longer. Then I shall be able to be perfectly frank!"

"Four days? Why? Oh, in four days' time the Anglo-Russian Treaty will have been signed – if it ever is signed." Grovermuller stared keenly at the other. "That opens up interesting possibilities. But perhaps it isn't fair to question you about them. I will wait another four days. Meanwhile take a word of advice. Don't go out of your way to put Manciple's back up."

"Right, sir. Will you think me frightfully impertinent if I ask if I can give you a word of advice in exchange?"

The Editor smiled. "It depends on the advice."

"This then. I'm a little nervous about your personal safety in this building. Be careful. You're all right with more than one person. But don't go sleeping in your office with the door unlocked. And so forth. You might find it unhealthy."

— V —

In the Assembly Hall at Geneva the Russian and British delegations sat in dignified isolation. The others bustled round them with the air of people who expected two of their number to break out any moment into noisy vituperation, know it will be their duty to stop them instantly, and regret the necessity. Peace may be peace, but a good fight is a spectacle. At a signal from the President, Lord Vanguard rose to his feet. Balancing gold pince-nez on a shapely nose, he spoke with precision in his native tongue.

"...My Government can only look on the Brezka incident as an act of wanton aggression. The evidence proving the participation of the Russian Government in the outrages has been laid before the Committee of Thirteen. No satisfactory apology or explanation has yet been received by my Government. The safety of the life and limb of a country's nationals, the inviolable sanctity of inter-state contracts – these, gentlemen, are no light things, nor can they be treated lightly." Lord Vanguard was performing his part admirably. That practically none of his hearers understood English in no way flattened the deep sincerity of his utterance or robbed his perorations of their rotundity. The Russian delegate listened to his speech with a set smile and then, as it was translated into French, changed his expression to one of horrified concern. He sprang to his feet voluble, gesticulatory, denunciatory...

The other delegates read, slept, listened, or whispered behind sheafs of papers... The journalists swapped telephone addresses and solved crosswords. Anglo-Russian shares collapsed behind a bear onslaught... Sterling slumped... The Angel of War beat his scarlet vans uncertainly over the blue Genevan lake.

"Are you running a story, too, about the Russian business?" asked Altrincham, leader writer, wearily, of Andrews, editor of the City page.

"Of course," answered the other. "What else is there?"

"Cheer up. It can't go on for ever. Somebody will murder someone else, or we shall definitely declare war. Anything as long as I don't have to write any more leaders about it."

Andrews laughed. "My dear fellow, your leaders are miracles of skill. Nobody reads leaders, otherwise you could claim the credit for the amazing way the Premier is wheeling his Gadarene swine round again."

"You underestimate the power of the Press," answered the other. "We've been of some use, although Sanger of course has been the master. Even now it's touch and go. If another incident joggles the tightrope, the nation will plunge into the abyss of war."

"For God's sake, don't quote from your leader," groaned the other. "I say, are the police going to discover who did in the old boy? It's a bit awkward, because it's certain it's someone in the office."

"Yes. It makes us such fools in the eyes of the public too, with our own pet detective on the staff. He isn't making any headway at all apparently. In fact I heard a rumour the other day – of course I don't believe it – that he's under suspicion himself."

Andrews wagged his head solemnly; "I don't want to be unkind, but I think Venables is a bit of a B.F. Charming youngster of course, but one of the Chief's mistakes. The Garden Hotel business must have been just a lucky break."

Thus too, but in brusquer tones, Heflin the news editor. Once, five years before, Heflin had seen a news editor in an American film. Up till then he had taken a simple pride in being the rudest news editor in Fleet Street – no mean achievement. But the poignancy of insult, the brilliant scintillations of sarcasm, the sweep and soar of abuse which had been exhibited by this actor had, Heflin recognized at once, made his own tantrums childish by comparison. For a time the film had sobered him, but insidiously the amazing conception was germinating in his breast and slowly Heflin began to remodel himself on his ideal. The horn-rimmed spectacles came first. Then, after some months of assiduous practice, he was able to describe an unassisted circle with one end of a cheap cigar, retaining the other end in his mouth, while talking down a telephone. Then he developed a telephonic style of unique brilliance. With a dove-like coo he would inveigle some unfortunate correspondent who had failed to get a story into a charmingly ingenuous explanation of why he had failed. Then suddenly he would unmask his batteries and, howling like a dervish, would abuse the hapless newshound until he dropped the receiver from his trembling grasp and tottered out into the cold night air.

"I say, Venables, old chap," said Heflin with a benign air, "any developments on the murder yet?"

"Nothing publishable," answered Charles.

"Slow business of course, this crime investigation, isn't it?" went on Heflin sympathetically. "One can't expect it to conform to the rush of a daily?"

"No, I suppose one can't," agreed Charles.

"No!" ejaculated Heflin, with a squeal of rage. "Of course not! Why the devil should one bother about a wretched rag like the *Mercury?*" Heflin's face went bright purple, the cigar tip rotated rapidly, and the veins stood out on his forehead. "We tame Sherlock Holmeses can't be expected to conform to the depraved popular demand for sensationalism. And of course, *of course* we can't be expected to hint even about what we're doing till we've solved the whole case and handed everything over to the police. And that may take a week; or a year; or" – with a tremendous yell – "NEVER!"

"By Jove," exclaimed Charles, inserting his monocle in his eye, and gazing at his news editor with an air of bright surprise calculated to infuriate. "You read my mind like a book. You've an almost feminine intuition."

Heflin snorted with rage. "Are you going to get me a story today or aren't you?"

Charles sighed. "I'm sorry, but I've got a worrying afternoon before me. I'll do my best, but I'm afraid this evening I shall be in no mood for writing."

"What is it? Grandmother died, or something?"

"Far more serious. I'm having another fitting of my light blue hopsack lounge suit. Merriam and I – Merriam is my cutter – built great hopes on it. He thought he was going to achieve something really great – something worthy of his genius this time." Charles shook his head dejectedly. "I fear it is going to be one of our failures." With dignified haste he left the room. A strangled cry and the dull thump of a heavy object striking the door indicated that he had been only just quick enough.

"Of course, the Heffle-bird is quite right," admitted Charles to Miranda a little later. "My stories have been complete tripe. But what can one do? The only things I have discovered are all things I certainly daren't write about."

Miranda looked at him absent-mindedly. "Go back to society gossip," she said.

"Never! I have tasted of the flesh-pots of Egypt. Besides, I could only write about society gossip in the dubious and patronizing tone one uses of arrested criminals."

"It would go rather well," answered Miranda. "You know – 'the alleged society beauty, Miss Vavasour-Cooper.' Cheer up. No journalist's job is all roses," she added with a bitterness that made Charles look up.

He decided not to notice it. "The real truth," he went on reflectively, "is that there is no scope nowadays for the crime expert. You've the law of libel, obstruction of the police, contempt of court, all up against you. Carpenter ought never to have revived the past. Anyway, I've made a private vow to solve this case or bust. If I bust, I bust. If I solve it I'll push off and go in for something restful."

Miranda sighed. "You're a born journalist obviously. We all resolve to quit every month. We never do."

"Nonsense. You've been reading *The Street of Adventure*," he said accusingly. "You know perfectly well you've never thought of leaving your job before. Neither have I."

"I loathe it all," answered Miranda firmly.

"Why? You used to like it. You're a first-rate journalist, and you know it. You're earning more than I am probably. You're bound to get on. Why this melancholy?"

"Yes, I'm clever," said Miranda bitterly. "I write clever little stories. I can produce an article on anything under the sun. I know what Human Interest is. I know how to make my stuff Sexy without being Salacious and Sentimental without being Sad. I know whether Typists make Good Mothers and how to prepare a Dainty Meal for Two for Sixpence. I've interviewed the Queen of Kossovia on Immorality and a Shop Girl on Being a Queen. I'm bright, and I'm cheery, and I'm a good mixer. And I loathe and detest the whole blasted game."

"Steady on, old girl!" said Charles, alarmed. "What's gone wrong? Can't I help? If not in a professional capacity, in a personal one. Frightfully personal if you like. Listen, I –"

He turned as the door opened. It was Manciple, and he came up to Miranda without speaking to Charles.

"I must ask you to go with me to the Yard," he said gravely, "in connection with the murder of Lord Carpenter."

The Editor Regrets

"I CAN'T VERY WELL refuse to go, I suppose," said Miranda. "Anyway, I want Mr. Venables to come with me."

Manciple hesitated a moment. His acquiescence, once granted, did not seem in any way unwilling. "Certainly," he said. "Come along, both of you."

In his office at Scotland Yard Manciple seemed possessed of a new reserve of quiet assurance. He saw that both his visitors were settled and then lowered himself into his chair with casual and hospitable ease. He smiled indulgently on Miranda as he propounded the first question:

"Why did you not tell us that you visited Lord Carpenter after 11.30 p.m. on the night of his murder?"

Miranda looked at him with coolness and a certain wary interest. Charles, without any great success, was endeavouring to gaze carelessly out of the window. Trams banged, cars hummed, sirens on the river whined in the silence that followed Manciple's question.

"Come, come, Miss Jameson," Manciple went on sternly. It was plain that had this been an ordinary prisoner he would have gone on to point out offensively, "you have a tongue in your head, haven't you?" As it was he contented himself with – "you may as well tell us – you were seen leaving the suite."

"Who by?"

The Inspector smiled tolerantly. "I am questioning you, you know."

Miranda looked straight ahead. "I saw him, of course," she said. "It's not surprising I was seen. I didn't take any trouble to hide it." She stared suddenly at Manciple. "It had nothing to do with the murder of course."

"Then why not tell us?"

"Because the matter we discussed was a private one."

"Surely you must allow us to be the best judge of that?"

Miranda flushed faintly. "On the contrary. I cannot imagine any people less qualified to judge of the decencies of ordinary social intercourse."

"It is no good being rude," replied Manciple wearily. "This is my duty. Cannot you see that it is your duty too? In this interview of yours with Lord Carpenter, much must have taken place which, although it seems immaterial to you, may be vitally useful to us. Won't you help us by giving us some measure of confidence?"

The danger signal still glowed in Miranda's cheeks. "Very prettily put – I apologize. I still see no reason for altering my mind, however."

Manciple rose to his feet. "Very well then, Miss Jameson. If you refuse to guide us in any way, we are forced to rely on our imagination – aided by a certain amount of help from other sources."

"Indeed. How interesting for you."

"This then is what our imagination suggests." Standing in front of her, he wagged a massive forefinger to emphasize the points as he made them. "We picture you as carrying on a liaison with Lord Carpenter..."

Charles jumped to his feet. "Look here, Manciple," he protested. "You have no –"

Miranda's voice, dry and hard, cut across his protest. "Quiet,

Charles! I am anxious to hear the Inspector's imagination at work. It is all so delightfully characteristic – even down to the word 'liaison'. Go on." There was a smile on Miranda's face as she encouraged her interrogator. Charles's eyes, straying from her face to her hands, gripping the arms of her chair, saw her knuckles whiten.

Manciple continued.

"On the morning of the day in question, you found that Carpenter had become infatuated with a blonde typist in the Advertisement Department – one Irene Hubbard. The friendship – since you dislike the word liaison – between you and Carpenter had been a friendship between intellectual equals. He was captivated not so much by your undeniable good looks as by your restless and brilliant mind – at least so he was clever enough to make you believe."

Miranda still smiled.

Charles wiped the cold sweat from his forehead and spoke. "Look here," he pleaded, "why the devil do you listen to all this nonsense? There's not the least reason in the world why you should."

"Will you be quiet, Charles! I'm sorry I brought you. If you can't keep quiet I'll have you put out of the room. Carry on with your reconstruction, Inspector."

Still with an air of benign speculation, and swaying gently on his feet, the Inspector went on. "It was, as I appreciate, infuriating for you to discover that this marriage of true minds had been disrupted by a tow-headed little chit who made up for her conversational deficiencies by hitching up her skirts a little higher. On that night you go to Carpenter and tell him so. We imagine that at this stage Carpenter might cease to be the tactful lover and become the bored cad. He told you even – the man was capable of it – why he preferred the tow-headed chit. I do not underestimate your character in any way, Miss Jameson. In my opinion you possess no uncommon measure of resolution. I do not detect in you any measurable alloy of softness. At the moment I am merely daydreaming like a novelist – I shall soon be told the truth in your sworn statement – and so, in my random way" – his voice at last lost its suave tone and became menacing – "I found no difficulty in imagining that you paid him a second visit that night, a visit inspired by fury but reinforced by reflection; that without hesitation you went to the dagger where it hung, seized it –"

"This is outrageous," interrupted Charles, white with rage. "Miranda, the man has not the slightest right to examine you in this way. You must allow yourself to be protected against it."

Miranda's voice was not of the timbre that calls for protection. It was icy and dead. "I will do nothing of the sort. At last this begins to grow interesting."

"– and used it," went on Manciple, as if there had been no interruption. "You then replaced it and carefully wiped the handle. It then might have occurred to you to make the identity of the murderer as elusive as possible. You remembered that all outgoing telephone calls would be listened into that night by the Chief's orders. The Chief's own phone would, however, be immune. It therefore occurred to you to ring up the police, disguising your voice as a man's. A little reflection decided you that it might be dangerous to ring up the police. There was the danger that even while you were talking a Flying Squad tender might be on its way. Your mind – anyone's mind – would turn naturally from the police to Sir Colin Vansteen. You looked his name up in the telephone directory. He need not be ashamed of having thought that it really was a man speaking. After all, Miss Jameson, you are an actress of no mean ability for an amateur, and brilliant in men's parts." Manciple smiled with self-satisfaction.

"We have spoken to people who have seen your Portia, and also your Olivia in *Twelfth Night*, so that we can understand Sir Colin's mistake. Having evoked this mysterious Mr. Ganthony out of the blue, you had nothing to do but return to your office and wait for the police to arrive."

Suddenly, and quite without warning, Miranda laughed. She waved Charles away as he sprang to her side. "It's all right. I'm not hysterical. But that bit about my imitating a man's voice!" She paused, and when she spoke again there was no laughter in her voice. "Inspector, you are wrong. I paid no second visit."

"No doubt," Inspector Manciple said reasonably, "but if I am wrong, why not tell me what is right?"

Miranda shook her head.

The inspector regarded her silently for a moment as if making up his mind. Then he left the room. "Please wait here till I return," was his parting injunction.

Miranda turned to Charles defiantly. "Well! Now you know what sort of ideal heroine I am."

"Why go on hurting yourself and me?" said Charles in a low voice.

"Is that what you think I brought you here for?"

He smiled ruefully. "It's not been a cheerful party, has it?"

For the first time her face softened. Fiery lips quivered perceptibly. "Don't you see? I – well there's no one I would rather have know the truth than you. It was a sort of confession by proxy, I suppose."

"I'm grateful," said Charles. "But didn't you know that I'd guessed ages ago? You didn't conceal it as well as that, you know. You're not very good at concealing things."

Miranda did not answer. Manciple found her lost in thought, with Charles strolling aimlessly about the room.

"Well, Miss Jameson," he said as he seated himself. "Are you really going to leave it like this? Aren't you going to tell us a word about what happened that night?"

"I am quite resolved to help you as little as possible," answered Miranda coldly. "I'm taking a week's holiday tomorrow, somewhere where the sun is shining, and you'll have to settle your case without my help. Nothing will persuade me to give evidence in this case. When it comes on I shall be out of England."

The Inspector pressed a bell. "Sergeant," he said when it was answered, "Miss Jameson is detained as a witness." He surveyed the two. Miranda said nothing. Charles made as if to speak, then checked himself. "Miss Jameson is the last person known to have seen the late Lord Carpenter alive," he added.

— II —

"Would you recognize the voice again?" persisted Manciple.

He was sitting in Sir Colin Vansteen's consulting room. Gravely, with the keen and practised regard of the experienced physician, Vansteen listened to him.

"I don't think so, Inspector. You know how difficult it is to recognize even familiar voices when you hear them over the telephone for the first time."

"There was no trick of speech, no peculiar inflection? Remember it is not positive identification we want. We recognize that to be hopeless. We want something that out of four or five possibilities, would indicate a probable."

"I am afraid I am sure of nothing, except that it was a strange man speaking."

"Are you sure of that?" asked the Inspector, looking at him keenly.

The pathologist started. "What precisely do you mean?" he asked stiffly.

"I mean," explained Manciple, "could you be certain it was not actually a woman, disguising her voice?"

A smile flickered for a moment on Vansteen's classic features. "I couldn't be certain even of that," he admitted.

Manciple strolled to the window and glanced out. "Nothing is certain in this case," he muttered. He relapsed into gloomy silence, broken suddenly by an exclamation.

"What an amazing coincidence!" he said.

Vansteen joined him at the window. "See!" pointed Manciple. "The name of your mysterious conversationalist was Ganthony. The name of your fruiterer and florist across the road is G-ANTHONY!"

"Very curious," said Sir Colin dryly. The eyes of the two men met. They regarded each other in silence. Sir Colin lifted interrogative eyebrows. "It can hardly be anything more than coincidence, can it?"

Manciple hesitated a moment before replying. "No," he said at last. He rubbed his massive chin. Then he smiled cheerfully. "Well, it's just as well you're such a friend of ours. If this had happened to anyone else we might have thought there was something fishy about it." They laughed together, and Manciple, still grinning, made his goodbye.

Left to himself, Sir Colin mopped a torrid brow. "I really cannot stand much more of this," he murmured weakly to himself; "not at my age."

Meanwhile Charles was phoning. "Yes, Venables of the *Mercury* speaking. I say, Manciple detained Miss Jameson today. Oh yes, it's legal enough – in the circumstances he was quite justified. But you know really it has nothing to do the murder, and she's not the sort of girl this sort of thing is pleasant for. I've no right to ask your help, of course – it's rather like blackmail – but could you do something about it? Miranda Jameson, the name is. I say, thanks most awfully."

Charles hung up his receiver with a smile; "It's a bit hard on Manciple" he thought.

— III —

Perry came upon Venables sitting in his own semi-private office. Semi-private, because he shared it with the *Mercury* poultry expert, a fellow with a suburban reputation for literary gifts as a result of being "on a paper." To do him justice, he dressed the part – tall, cadaverous, with a bow tie, velvet coat and wandering hair. His office was generally scattered with dead carcasses of dejected fowls sent in by readers to find what they died of. Repellent as most people found this, Venables asserted that it gave him a "homey" mortuary feeling. Producing a bottle of formaldehyde from the expert's desk, Venables expertly quenched the odour of the latest dejected victim, and waved Perry to a chair.

"Polly Peony?" inquired Perry.

"Slim, sad and six-and-twenty. Sweetie of the Maharajah of Mandustan. The Maharajah was discovered by an hotel chambermaid neatly transfixed to the divan with a hatpin through the heart. It was Polly's hatpin, as she at once admitted. In those days hatpins were hatpins. There was an affable smile on the Maharajah's face, but she explained that he was trying to murder her and she did it in self-defence. She told a most heart-rending story of his nasty habits – burning slaves with hot irons, kicking dogs to death, and collecting albums of naughty photographs. The atmosphere she built up of being an English violet defiled by the wicked heathen was going wonderfully well until it was rather spoiled by the prosecuting counsel, who produced a perfectly good set of naughty photographs with

Polly as the subject. Accused then broke down and was helped weeping from the box. Unfortunately prosecuting counsel went too far. When she said in her evidence that she was a clergyman's daughter, he winked at the jury, and remarked slyly, 'That is generally the case.' Storm of tears from Polly and actually a poor wretched country parson was dug out from Somerset and admitted, dithering and distressed, that Polly was his daughter, and there was still a home waiting for her if she had learned her lesson and shunned the primrose path. 'Forgive her,' he said, 'for she has loved much.' Sensation in court. That was before the days of women on juries, and Polly was acquitted."

"What a mine of information the man is!" said Perry. "All I wanted to know was how far I could hint that very considerable suspicion did attach to her. We're including the case in our 'Famous Trials' series, and I'd like to put her photograph with the caption: 'Was she a murderess – or only a simple bewildered country lass?'"

"Put what you like," said Charles. "She retired to the Somerset vicarage and was photographed in a sunbonnet feeding pigs. She soon got tired of this, and moved to the Riviera, where she started a series of houses of dubious fame with the proceeds of the Maharajah's jewels. After twenty years she made a fortune, and returned to London as Madame Durand. Hardly anyone knew her history; she became a patron of the arts, founded and endowed the French Theatrical Association, and died full of years and honours in her house at Surbiton two years ago."

"Good, thanks awfully." Perry, having secured the information for which he had come, still showed no particular inclination to move. "By the way, there's a ghastly rumour about your having a row with Heflin. What's the truth about it?"

"Well, look here, if I tell you. Will you promise to keep it to yourself?"

"Certainly," said the art editor eagerly.

Charles looked round furtively. Then he bent forward. "I accused him of murdering Carpenter. He fell unconscious to the floor and lay there in a dead faint for two hours; then he tried to cut my throat with a pair of scissors. It's a miracle I'm alive today to tell the tale – but you know what office scissors are like."

"Oh, all right, don't tell me if you don't want to," said Perry with hauteur. "I was only passing on the current office gossip." Languidly leaning against the mantelpiece, and looking like a ready-to-wear tailoring advertisement, Perry still was curious. "It's all confoundedly mysterious. I suppose you suspect someone, you secretive devil. What about Miss Jameson – fishy, eh?"

"You have your elbow on a set of diseased giblets," pointed out Charles.

Perry hastily stood upright, then he repeated his question.

Without raising his eyes from his pad, Charles answered him. "I do suspect someone."

"Is it a secret, or can you tell one?"

"Certainly. I suspect you."

"Come on, be serious and tell who you think it is?"

Charles leaned back in his chair and surveyed the other through his monocle. "I repeat: I suspect you."

"You must be wandering, old boy." The other smiled patronizingly.

"On the contrary," said Charles incisively. "On the morning of his murder the Chief had a private interview with you. He gave his precise opinion of your abilities as an art editor in his familiar style. He was fed up with you for missing a photograph of the Taunton miracle, when three witnesses swore they saw a girl turn into a swan by breaking a bewitched girdle cake over the local wishing well, as prescribed by a mediaeval formula. Quite naturally, the Chief being what he was, there were words."

Perry's lounging figure gradually became rigid. He still smiled, but his eyes were wary.

"You threatened him," Charles continued calmly. "He kicked you out of the office." Perry flushed. "That morning he dictated a note to his cashier reducing your salary by fifty per cent."

"How the devil do you know all this?"

Charles smiled sweetly. "I am endeavouring to show you that, although it is evidently your opinion that I am mooning helplessly about, I am really getting on quite well, thank you. To continue. At the present moment you are deeply in debt. Hence the motive. In addition you have a violent temper. Larry Dodman once playfully baptized you with a mug of beer in a local hostelry. If his skull wasn't so thick that he recovered from your crack over the head with a beer bottle after being three days unconscious, you would have been in the dock for manslaughter."

Charles leaned back in his chair and looked at Perry smilingly. Perry's face was as white as the flower in his buttonhole, but he still attempted to stare back with an assumption of calm.

"No one in this office," continued Charles, "can vouch for your whereabouts between 11.30 p.m. and 12.30 a.m. But the letter from the Chief cutting your salary has disappeared from the file."

"My God, Venables, you're wrong, I swear," said the other. He dropped into a chair. "How the devil did you find out about the letter?"

"You removed the carbon copy and destroyed it. You forgot that a carbon copy is produced by a carbon-paper. Provided it's not been used too much, a carbon-paper can be read. That carbon is still in existence – in fact in my desk. That, and a few investigations natural to anyone of my prying nature, rounded out my little story."

"I swear I didn't do it, Venables. Honestly I didn't. I swear I was never near the place."

Charles drummed meditatively on the table with his pencil's point. "I'm inclined to believe you, Perry, my lad. All the same, how did the letter disappear?"

"I fixed that with Jerningham."

"Oh, ho!" Charles thought for a moment. "Yes, that lets you out. It explains a lot. We must have another talk later. Meanwhile, of course, we'll keep the carbon business dark. All very natural."

"Thanks awfully," said Perry, rebounding into cheerfulness with relief. "As a matter of fact – when the police started nosing round I was thoroughly scared. I went to Grovermuller and told him what Carpenter had said he would do. I thought it might safeguard me against its coming out later and looking bad. Of course I didn't tell him about pinching the letter. I never thought they'd get on to that."

"Not much of a safeguard. If I had been you and *had* murdered Carpenter, it would have been the first thing I should have done. That would have occurred to Manciple."

"Grovermuller was awfully decent. Said it would be quite all right. He said Carpenter's wanting to reduce my salary was reason enough for him to confirm me in the old figure."

"Just like him. When was this, by the way?"

"Oh, before I came to you."

"Left him alone, I suppose?"

"Yes," answered Perry, surprised at the question. "You know what he is, lurking in that room at the end of the corridor. Anybody would think he had nothing to do with the paper, instead of running the show."

Charles looked at his watch. "Five past twelve. Damn the man." He picked up the phone. "The Editor's room at once!" He turned to Perry. "It sounds silly, but I'm scared. There's a murderer in the office, and I've a hunch that they might have an eye on him."

The phone bell tinkled. "What, no answer?" He turned to Perry seriously. "Come on – let's go there. This looks fishy."

The Editor was sitting with his back to them as they opened the door. Only the forward stoop of his shoulders and the hue of his lurid cheeks indicated that someone had been attempting to strangle him to death.

Charles rapidly loosened collar and tie, freed the tongue in the clenched jaws, and then put his head to Grovermuller's chest. "He's not breathing," he said.

A Chinaman is Helpful

DINED AND WINED, MANCIPLE settled himself into the most comfortable armchair in the smoking-room of the Deputy Commissioner's Mayfair flat.

Murgatroyd, the D.C., smiled as he saw him critically examine the cigar offered him and slowly light it up. "I think you are about the only officer in the Force who really appreciates the cigars I give away here," he said.

"It is always worthwhile to discriminate – whether in cigars or human beings," Manciple answered quietly, unfolding in the benign afterglow of a Tokay that was like sunlight in the blood. "It all helps in our game."

The two smoked in silence for a time, while the cigar smoke rose vertically from their chairs. Then Murgatroyd spoke.

"I'm speaking unofficially of course. Was it necessary to grill that girl in the way you did when you believe she is innocent?"

"All the more reason," replied the other. "It is only human nature for a guilty man to be dumb. Our law recognizes it. In her case it is mere pride that is keeping her silent. She is putting her own unimportant feelings before the task of bringing a murderer to justice."

"Is that altogether a fair point of view?" suggested Murgatroyd. "After all, Carpenter was a pretty rotten kind of skunk where women were concerned, and a girl is entitled to some reticences."

Manciple smiled – a genuine smile which illuminated the carefully-planned façade of his countenance and made his stolidity human. "Even speaking unofficially, that is no viewpoint for an officer of the law. But – supposing one takes it. I made the girl uncomfortable for an hour. As a result she will recover all the sooner. Drastic treatment is specific for her kind of complaint. And she has the appropriate comforter close at hand."

"Venables, I gather."

"Yes – hopelessly – poor devil."

"What do you make of him?"

"Clever, certainly. Too slap-dash, too thin-skinned, and too unprincipled to make a first-rate detective. And yet might he not make up for all that by intuition – or is it luck? It doesn't matter which it is really. You remember Napoleon never asked his Marshals whether they were far-seeing, experienced or deeply versed in the arts of war. He asked them only if they were lucky. I sometimes feel our C.I.D. should be staffed on the same principle."

Manciple smiled wryly. "In that case Venables would be chosen and I should not. But I must admit that at the moment I find him very puzzling."

"I gathered he was on bad terms with you."

"Only officially. Personally I generally find myself sympathetic. Both of them know much more than I can make them tell me. I can guess part of it. If my guess is correct, they cannot really help me much."

"Are you on any line yet that is proving fruitful?"

"Yes, one. That's all I can say at the moment."

"What do you propose to do about Miss Jameson?"

"Detain her for a day or two. It will spur Venables into action at any rate."

"Isn't that a little ruthless?"

"Very. I often am in my job."

"Soulless beast! Well, I've talked enough shop. Do you remember that eighth hole at St. Comyn's where you once holed out in two? Well..."

— II —

"Nothing," panted Charles, "is more apparently useless than the Schafer method of artificial respiration. In fact to me it always seemed designed to defeat the very object it is intended to secure. Still, turn him over and try again."

After five minutes' hard work Charles and Perry turned Grovermuller on his back again. "Thank the Lord," exclaimed Charles, "he's breathing! When is that confounded doctor coming?"

The doctor and Manciple arrived simultaneously. After a stimulant and a rest Grovermuller was able to talk. The terrible blotchy colour in his face had given place to pallor.

"My throat," he murmured. "Diabolically sore. I feel as if my head has been twisted round three or four times... That, of course, is not possible... The vertebrae... The vertebrae..." He relapsed into silence and his eyes clouded.

Manciple leaned over him, recalling his wandering attention with an urgent gesture. "You were strangled. Who was it?"

Grovermuller stared at him. Then he slowly shook his head. "Don't know. Took me from behind," he articulated.

Manciple's face reflected his disappointment. "Just my luck," he said gloomily.

Grovermuller struggled at one last effort of speech before he relapsed into the vague and drowsy inanition of reaction. "Venables knows – who it is," he said, and then lost interest in the investigation.

Manciple looked at Venables inquiringly.

"I warned Grovermuller to be careful several times," explained Charles. "I feared he might be attacked by Carpenter's murderer."

"Does it help you that your theory has been proved correct?"

"It hasn't been. It's proved quite wrong, and I'm suffering all the humiliation of failure."

Manciple looked at the other keenly. "I'm sorry, I don't follow you."

"I hate to go too deeply into my fantastic speculations. But you see I never anticipated an attack like this. A poisoned cup of tea, I thought most probable. Or a struggle with a masked assailant in a corridor. Or a shot from a revolver missing him, with the bullet visibly embedded in the panelling. I was even prepared to find it in his arm or his leg. When I found him strangled and as good as dead if we hadn't found him, the bottom fell out of my theory with a resounding crash."

Manciple had followed his elliptic explanation with the facility of a fellow craftsman.

"A pity," he said. "It was a very ingenious idea of yours to give him those warnings. What an amazing coincidence that he should really have been attacked. It certainly rules him out as a suspect." He looked at Charles keenly. "At the same time I should be sorry to believe that the man who attacked Grovermuller is Carpenter's murderer."

"Why?" asked Charles.

"It will make our task immensely difficult. I can conceive no motive for murdering Carpenter which will apply equally to a similar attempt on Grovermuller."

"So we're both puzzled."

"Certainly."

Charles confessed his bewilderment again to Grovermuller

next morning when he called in to see him on the way to the office.

"I am really only on the fringe of the investigation," he said.

"But surely you had an inkling of who was the murderer when you warned me?"

There are some subjects about which it is impossible to be frank. One cannot confess to another that one seriously suspected him of homicide. Charles skated gracefully past.

"That! Oh, merely a logical deduction quite independent of the identity of the murderer," answered Charles vaguely. "Or call it a guess if you like."

"It was damned lucky for me, anyway. I'm grateful to you."

Charles endeavoured to sweep the coals of fire from his reluctant head. "Nonsense. What a fool I should have looked if another murder had occurred in the office. No, the painful truth is that I'm hardly advanced at all. And Manciple's in the same boat, except that he has the disadvantage of suspicions I'm free from."

"Such as," asked Grovermuller, whose throat still made him economical of words.

"Suspecting me, for instance. I know he's wrong there by knowledge. And Miss Jameson," Charles grinned cheerfully. "I know he's wrong there by faith. The root of the trouble is, that when a man like Carpenter is killed, it is very different from the murder of Jones of Tooting. It is impossible to tell what enmities he may have stirred up, what dark avenging forces he has unloosed. And yet until you have probed to the motive, you have never got to grips with the investigation of the murder."

"Any sign of a motive?"

Charles pondered his answer carefully before he gave it. "There are two possible motives in this case – women and politics. It might be either and it might be both."

76

"The former probably. Inspired swine the man was!"

"He was," agreed Charles fervently. "He seemed to have a genius for throwing women over in a way most calculated to break their hearts. I feel compunction about bringing the murderer to justice. In fact at the moment my main interest is not to do that but to clear Miss Jameson."

"Sorry they detained her."

"Oh, they let her go late last night."

Grovermuller looked surprised.

"Yes, they didn't want to, but I wangled it. I've a friend at court. Manciple may be a bit peeved."

"My God," groaned Grovermuller, "I don't know if it's the after-effects of strangulation or the normal result of criminal investigation, but my head is spinning." Looking frail and older than usual, Grovermuller passed his hand over his forehead. "Remember, as long as the murder is unsolved the *Mercury* looks an ass. The Russian business has distracted public attention a little – but even so... Go away and do your best now, and oh, by the way, see that I'm not strangled again!"

— III —

As was his way when his mind was perplexed, Charles wandered thoughtfully in to talk to Lee Kum Tong, the *Mercury's* Oriental expert.

Lee Kum Tong was young enough and old enough to bridge the gap between the old China and the new. He was among the last batch of students who immured themselves, each in his own little hut, at those examinations so poetically described as the "Forest of a Thousand Cedars," there to wrestle with the ancient wisdom of his country's classics and the diabolical perversity of his country's language, in order to prove his fitness to govern his country's uninstructed millions.

Time was when the totally unsuccessful candidate, disappointing his parents and degrading his ancestors, would expunge the stain by casting his unworthy body from a commodious precipice. Lee Kum Tong was unsuccessful, but the new thought of new China was stirring in him. He survived, came to Europe, and acquired the strangely complex and yet fundamentally simple academic apparatus of Western civilization. He was in sympathy with the new China and an acknowledged authority, perhaps a unique authority, on all the East and its fermenting millions. He could write like a journalist or like a don. He could speak like an undergraduate or, if his company obviously expected it, like a stage Chinese. Normally he avoided the sententious and flowery wisdom of the classics. Phonetic writing and simplified grammar would soon rob Confucius of that sacred authority with which he spoke to Lee Kum Tong's fathers. But his speech was rich in that proverbial wisdom of China, common alike to peasant and mandarin, and expressive of the humour, the penetration, and the cynicism of China.

"How goes it, Venables?" he said, as Charles strolled in. "You look depressed."

"I feel depressed. The more I find out about this business, the less informed I am."

Lee Kum Tong regarded him calmly through his massive horn-rimmed glasses, and stubbed a cigarette reflectively in its tray.

"Those who speak, do not know. Those who know, do not speak. This was current knowledge in the T'ang Dynasty."

"No doubt, but it hardly makes my task easier."

"How should a detective expect otherwise? A gem is not polished without grinding, nor a man made perfect in his profession without trial."

"I can stand the wisdom of the East," said Charles, gazing

bleakly out of the window through his monocle, "but I cannot stick its sarcasm."

Lee Kum Tong grinned, with the easy cheerfulness of the Chinese. "Patience. The scraps of fur from the left hindquarters of many foxes will in the end make a robe."

"The whole trouble is I've enough for two robes."

"I gather the police suspect our honoured Jamey. What do you think?" There was a childish concern on his face as he put the question, too childish to be natural.

"Absolute nonsense, Lee!" Charles, overlooking it, wagged an emphatic and Anglo-Saxon forefinger. "She is more innocent than I am."

"But also more rash. We have a saying that it is injudicious to lace one's boots in a melon field, and imprudent to adjust one's hat under a plum tree."

"You knew, then?" Charles stared at him in surprise. "You are an amazing person, Lee. You seem to know everything that goes on in this office, or for that matter in this country – and yet you never seem to ask a question – or show the slightest curiosity. How do you do it?"

"This is the wisdom of heaven – not to speak and yet to obtain a response. You flatter your unworthy friend. I am only as the mud bank in the Yangtse's mouth, receiving what the waters secured with effort after many moons."

Charles, knowing Lee's eccentricities, did not press the matter further. He wandered into an analysis of his difficulties. "I'm particularly puzzled here," he ended, because of the *kind* of man Carpenter was. He was, in his way, a great man, and therefore nobody knows how many enemies he may have made." Unconsciously Charles echoed Manciple's own complaint.

Lee gravely shook his head. "Why should he have made them, my dear Venables? Do not, I beg, repeat these rules of thumb. We say in our country, 'the poorer a man is, the more devils he meets.' How rarely are great men murdered? How often are the lowly and humble struck down? I confess I cannot see why you are puzzled. Carpenter's hatred of Russia was his chief trait. Hate begets hate. If you cannot find the murderer with that line to guide you, you are like the lazy wayfarer in the reign of To Yan Tsen, who, when the beneficent works of the Sun of Heaven were pointed out to him, lamented that the signposts had no tongues."

"There's nothing in that line, so far," answered Charles thoughtfully. "I've probed as deeply as I can."

"One flea will not raise a coverlet. Persist." Lee grinned smugly.

Charles looked at him with sudden interest. "So you're on to something, you sly devil. Why didn't you tell me before? No, that's too good an opening for your proverbial wisdom. Tell me now."

"If I tell you, will you believe me?"

"Certainly."

"Then you are less than wise." Lee Kum Tong nodded his head pleasantly. "Trust not the word of your aged friend. Of ten bald men, nine are deceitful, and the tenth is dumb. You must see for yourself."

"This sounds interesting. So you have nosed something out, have you? What exactly are you on the track of?"

"You will see. Can you come presently?"

"At once if you like."

"No. You must change your clothes. If you meet men or devils, you must act as they do." Lee smiled shrewdly.

"What kind of devils are these?"

Lee spread his yellow fingers eloquently. "Poor devils!"

"Good, I can live up to that easily. If you have this information, though, why didn't you tell Manciple earlier?" Charles asked with affected casualness.

"You are working with him?" Lee's question was equally casual.

"No, against him most of the time!"

Lee's shrug expressed complete understanding. "Two of a trade never agree. Why should I tell him?"

"If he does find out you knew something you haven't told him, he's liable to be unpleasant."

"Bah, why this fuss over the death of one man." Lee spoke airily, the history of a house that had disposed of thousands of slaves like chickens was in his blood. "The importance is exaggerated, simply because Carpenter was this and that. Let a dog bite a learned man and no one cares; but if a gnat sting a mandarin, sympathizers block the outer courtyard with their importunate chariots."

Charles smiled. "I am sure I appreciate your jettisoning your philosophy merely in order to help me."

"I am only human. Observe closely the woman who sells fans. You will note that from time to time she shields her head from the sun with her hand." His eyes glittered behind their spectacles. "I anticipate we shall have some fun today."

"I have an uneasy suspicion you may have had a hand in this," Charles said. "Notice my Western candour. I trust this little trip is not intended to throw me off the scent."

Lee returned his searching glance with simple surprise. "My desire is only to learn. I know nothing about criminal investigation, but today I shall be a detective. The humble flea can only hop two paces, but in the tail of a noble steed it can travel a thousand miles."

"I am quite defenceless against the Chinese form of leg-pulling," confessed Charles. "When shall we meet?"

"In two hours' time outside the Spotted Tavern, Commercial Road."

— IV —

"Me think you lookee velly fine." Lee, in a dirty blue serge suit and pointed but cracked patent leather shoes, tucked his hands in his sleeves, bowed and smiled a toothy grin.

"Where on earth did you learn to speak like that?" enquired Charles.

Lee smiled. "From a small book one of the messengers left in my room," he confessed, "entitled *Nick Diamond's Million Dollar Mystery*."

"Well, quit fooling and tell me exactly what I am supposed to be."

"Come inside." They seated themselves in a quiet corner of the Spotted Tavern's tap-room. "We will drink the wine of the country," explained Lee, and fetched two bitters.

"Now," he said with a new briskness. "Let's have a look at you. Hair convincing. Tie still a little new, but it will pass. Shirt excellent. The coat is brilliant."

"I bought the coat on the way down." Charles regarded it with pride. It was antique, shiny, and stupendously frayed.

"Trousers." Lee shook his head. "No. Exaggeration is to be avoided. Those pieces of string tied round the ankles, those are too much! Besides, they are not fashionable now in these parts."

Shamefacedly Charles removed them.

"Good, now I shall tell you what you are. You are an aspiring member of the working classes – a resentful, intelligent wage slave. You attend evening classes; you read *Das Kapital*; you are an earnest patron of your local lending library; you are intelligent. Yet you are still no more than caretaker's assistant in a newspaper office, to wit the *Mercury*."

"I begin to see daylight. Go on."

"Naturally you are a Communist. Naturally you seethe with

discontent. 'Ha, ha!' I – cunning little Chinese – say to myself, 'here is a man who may be useful. He helps clean out offices – he may find papers. He snoops round at night – he may overhear conversations. We will bring him along.'"

Charles smiled understandingly. "How the devil do you get on to this?"

Lee's eyes, which had been fixed on the door, gave a perceptible flicker. "Another time," he said, "here is Comrade Perkins."

Comrade Perkins caught Lee's eye and came up to them, staring at Charles inquiringly. A bulky fellow, with a mane of dark hair, and hands like huge hams, he looked like a film Cossack jammed into an East End ready-made.

"'Ello, Lee," said Perkins. His glance roved round the half-empty glasses. "I'll 'ave ze same."

"This is my friend, Bill Vane," explained Lee, indicating Venables. "He is one of us. He's employed at the *Mercury* and may be useful."

Perkins nodded understandingly. "Is 'e British?"

"A British subject," Lee assured him gravely.

"Goot!" Perkins wagged his head approvingly. "Ve British are ze salt of ze airth. Ve must stand together. Goot!" He raised his mug of bitter. "To England and ze Revolution. May it be soon!" They drank the toast.

"Comrade Perkins had a Russian mother and a British father," explained Lee without a smile. "He was brought up in Berlin."

The huge Communist slapped his chest. "I am British-pukka sahib," he muttered to Charles, gazing darkly at Lee. "Zese dam' Niggers: Vell, ve must use zem. Zen, ven ve 'ave the Revolution, ve fling zem aside." He flung out his huge hands and spoke in a droning chant.

> "Be vith us at ze break of day,
> Lord of our Nordic Soviet.

Guide us upon our conquering vay,
Lest we forget. Lest ve forget!"

"Kipling," he added, "my favourite author."

"Can't say I remember it," said Bill Vane politely.

Perkins frowned. "Zen it must be 'Sapper' – also my favourite. No matter." He drained his mug and rose to his feet. "Let us go. It is time."

They went down a narrow street infested with grubby children and second-hand clothes shops, and then shot abruptly up a narrow alley. At the end was a café, "The Savoy. Proprietor S. S. Ferenov." Inside, three or four tables were set beside a counter piled with dingy cakes, depressed tomatoes, fly-frequented slices of ham, and faded cigarettes. Perkins nodded to the pasty girl of fourteen or so leaning against the counter.

"They're all 'ere, the 'ole blinking lot," she said sulkily.

Perkins turned to them. "Vait 'ere a moment," he said, and went through a door.

The girl looked curiously at the Chinese and his young companion, and watched the latter edge up to a cigarette advertisement, scowling. The Chinese joined him.

"Don't look behind" muttered Bill Vane, gazing interestedly at the advertisement while he pointed out its beauties to his companion with his forefinger. "That navvy over in the corner reading the *News of the World*."

"What about him?"

"Only that it happens to be our news editor, Heflin."

Russians are Mysterious

IN A LITTLE WHILE Perkins came for them. "You are not velcome," he said. "Zey are annoyed I bring you." With which encouraging words he led them into the room.

The labourer that was Heflin, his eyes following their movements over the top of his paper, still saw only their unrecognizable backs – or if they were recognized he gave no sign.

The inner room into which Perkins took them was the living room of the café. A cloud of smoke made the air foggy. The room was furnished with respectable but dowdy relics of Victorian luxury except over the mantelpiece, where a hammer and sickle banner drooped forlornly.

Three men and one woman were seated round the mahogany table. The woman, thirty or so, with the broad face and the bright eyes of Russia, looked keenly at Charles. Her thin, white-faced neighbour was immersed in some papers. A large bearded individual on her other side stared at him dreamily, while a little monkey of a man jumped to his feet excitedly.

"Comrade Perkins, why did you bring these people in? Who are they? We are fed up with your foolishness. Comrade Lef Paulovitch," he said, turning to the white-faced man, who looked up from his papers wearily, "what shall we do about Comrade Perkins? He is a bourgeois."

Comrade Perkins drew himself up to his full height and frowned menacingly on the little man. "'ow dare you, you Russian scum! I 'ave taken my Lenin course at Moscow. 'Ow dare you call me bourgeois. Bah, kulak!"

"Shut up, both of you," said Lef Paulovitch quietly. "Stefan, you know Perkins is a useful member of this Cell. Stop abusing him."

The little monkey relapsed into his chair, muttering. "The most anti-revolutionary sentiments are encouraged now. We are, it seems, to welcome reactionary..."

His muttering was interrupted by the girl. "Now then, father, you know Lef Paulovitch is right. We must all pull together, or we shall never get anywhere. Isn't that so, Nicolai Petrovitch?"

The large bearded man sat up a start. "Yes, certainly, Anna, that is very true, what you say. Each for each and all for one. How shall we bring about the revolution and the World-state if we quarrel like children? Comrade Perkins and you, Stefan Stanislasovitch, my heart is heavy that you quarrel." His voice boomed as he gestured eloquently. "We must unite, or how shall we wage-slaves be strong enough to overthrow capital. Consider what Marx said..."

"We will consider what Marx said another time, Nicolai," interrupted the man addressed as Lef Paulovitch, and who was or had assumed the role of the leader of the party. It transpired later that his surname was Rogin. "There is business before us at the moment. Perkins, who are these two?"

Charles, who had been dimly struggling with the conjectures aroused by his surroundings, met Rogin's penetrating gaze. He waited with some interest for the introduction.

"Zis is my goot frien' Comrade Lee," Perkins explained, pointing to the Chinese. "Comrade Lee 'as credentials as an agent of ze Chinese Government." He winked meaningly at his hearers. "I'ave known 'im for many years now. Comrade Lee, 'e knows of our interest in ze Carpenter business. Zerefore ven 'e introduce me to 'is sister's brozer-in-law, Bill Vane, and tell' me 'e vork in ze *Mercury* office, I ask 'im to bring 'im 'ere."

"Quite right, Comrade." Rogin, in his precise voice, almost devoid of accent, addressed himself first to Lee. "It is true that you are an agent?"

Lee bowed. "Humblest of the servants of the servants of China, I pick up unimportant crumbs of information. I am considered only sufficiently useful to be worth, once a year, the too-generous thanks of the Deputy Assistant Under Secretary for Foreign Affairs, Ho Lung."

Rogin raised his eyebrows. "Ho Lung, eh? Do you know anything about me?"

Lee nodded. "Ho Lung mentioned to me, as a matter to be remembered, that should it be necessary for the servant of China to seek aid from the servants of Russia, one Rogin, who lived above the café of Stefan Stanislasovitch Ferenov, would give ear to this." Lee produced from the pocket of his greasy suit a small square of vellum on whose surface in vivid colour a dragon and an eagle, soaring in amity, lifted jointly between their claws a giant hemisphere.

"This is enough. Welcome, Comrade Lee. We shall ask no further questions. Sit at this table." Rogin, smiling thinly and peering through his pebble glasses, motioned Lee to a seat beside him. Then he turned to Charles, who leaned against the sitting room wall with a fine gloomy air.

"Bill Vane, are you a Marxist?"

"I have read *Das Kapital* twice," said Charles, with simple pride.

"Are you a worker?"

"Of course. Didn't Comrade Perkins tell you? I'm a caretaker at the *Mercury*."

"You manage to keep your hands in good condition for a worker," said Anna suddenly. She leaned forward with a smile and grabbed his hand, lifting up the tips. "A bourgeois' hand! A gentleman's hand!"

Charles assumed an attitude of sulky ill-humour. "I don't do rough work," he said. "I am an intellectual. I study. Later I shall teach. I shall write."

"Quite right," said the large bearded man. "The revolution has need of all types."

"Down with intellectuals," spat out the little monkey, who had been watching with intent, shrewd little eyes. "They are bourgeois at heart. Scratch an intellectual and you find a reactionary."

Anna, who had been watching Charles's face closely, released his hand. "I was only teasing," she said. "Bill is proud. Also rather foolish. Go on, Lef."

Lef, without forsaking his casual air, went on. "Do you believe in the revolution?"

"I do," answered Charles, feeling rather like a bridegroom. "I believe in revolution, the rule of the workers, and the abolition of capital. I am anti-religious and class-conscious."

"Bill Vane is a member of the Communist party in good standing," interrupted Lee. "You need not be in the least afraid."

Rogin nodded. "Quite. But one must ask these questions."

He spoke to his companions. "We have some matters to discuss which are too difficult to be discussed among us all. You understand what I mean. Therefore, comrades, please sit in the café and leave us alone." The words were spoken authoritatively, and the three men filed out without questioning it. Charles and Lee were left alone with Rogin and Anna.

Rogin waited till they were gone. "Now we can talk sense.

You must not laugh at them though. All are excellent men. Nicolai, the man with the big beard, speaks magnificently, like an angel. You or I could twist him round one finger, but he can twist the hearts of ten thousand men. Anna's father is a brilliant agitator. He can set the most contented factory even of ox-like Yorkshiremen ablaze with discontent. Perkins, too, though you may laugh at him, is a fine fellow. He is a sincere Communist, and yet he is in his fancy a kind of illiterate knight-errant. What do you make of that? You smile. Well perhaps a revolution needs its knights, however quixotic."

Rogin leaned back in his chair. "Seriously, though, Anna here and I are the brains of this cell. It is on us Moscow depends. I – no fool, not easily deceived by passion – and Anna, who has a man's brains and a woman's intuition." He looked at her kindly, but with the benign air of a professor praising his prize student. "Enough of this. You are wondering why I am interested in Carpenter. Carpenter, that enemy of Russia (you might say), is dead. That, then, is surely enough."

Rogin rose to his feet. He began to pace rapidly up and down the little room. "It is not enough. I must know more." Suddenly and apparently inconsequentially he went off into a tirade. "Do you think it is pleasant for me to be wasted here, a petty agent occupied with petty affairs? Don't you think I know that with my brains I could be Commissar, Director, what you like? Lebedeff is in charge of agricultural mechanization. Very well – what has happened? Sabotage – peasants eating their seed grain; decline in production, abandonment of collectivization." His voice rose an octave. "Incompetence. I tell you if I were given power I could remedy it in a year. I know group psychology; I know agriculture. Lebedeff knows neither. How can he succeed? My knowledge is unique; it is gladly and freely available. And it is wasted."

Anna, who had been watching Charles's expression and Lee's expressionless face, interrupted. Her light, low tones appeared specially designed to soothe the lean, eager Communist.

"Yes, Lef, that is all very well, but you are worse than the ones you have sent out."

Lef subsided into a chair. "You are right – as always – Anna. Pardon me; we all naturally think we are worthier than we are treated." His tones became precise and businesslike. "Comrade Vane, we wish to know – for reasons of our own – how far the police have got with the investigations of the Carpenter affair."

"Nowhere," answered Charles shortly.

"Come, come, that is an exaggeration! They must suspect someone!"

"They suspect several people," Charles replied sulkily.

"What do you mean?"

Prompted by the questions of Rogin and Anna, Charles gave an account of the investigations into the Carpenter case which was in substance true. Bill Vane had picked it up, it appeared, by overhearing Manciple's telephone conversations with headquarters, by means of gossip, and from the notes found in Manciple's waste-paper basket. His reconstruction was artistic and convincing.

"Excellent. Comrade Vane, you are most helpful." Lef looked at Anna. "Do you think we can risk it?"

She nodded. "I think so, but let us go into it with the others."

Rogin turned again to them. "Thank you very much, Comrades. Your information has been most helpful to us and our cause. Now we must say goodbye. As soon as you know any more, let us know."

Rogin saw them to the outer room. Charles glanced quickly round the café. Nicolai, Stefan and Perkins sat round a table, but otherwise the room was deserted. The labourer who was Heflin was gone.

Again in the open air, Charles spoke to Lee. "Is this a comic opera you have let me into?"

"It is quite real. Remember Heflin."

"How the devil did you guess he would be there?"

"I was as surprised as you were."

"What does it all mean, though?" asked Charles. "First, what is your relation to this Communist outfit? How did you know them?"

"As you saw, I, the impartial Oriental expert, Lee Kum Tong, am also Lee, a little East End Chinese, who is an agent, spy perhaps is truer, in the service of the Chinese Republic. This secret, by the way, you must keep."

Charles nodded. "Of course."

"Well, in the course of my duties I come across a Communist cell which is particularly interested in finding out all about the police investigations into the Carpenter murder. I say to myself, 'This is interesting. Russia in the east is my country's ally; we must not call in the police. I will call in my excellent friend, Charles Venables. Then we shall find out. This has its dangers perhaps, but if the current is not rapid the fish do not jump.' Then, as a bounty from Heaven, we have the mysterious News Editor thrown in. Lee's heart rejoices within him. Lee Kum Tong perceives difficulties."

Charles looked at the Chinese suspiciously. "Lee, I believe you are pulling my leg. You must know more than you say you do."

"'The yellow bird said to the owl,'" quoted Lee Kum Tong sententiously, "'*When will the rains end?* The owl, who did not know, said nothing. *O wise bird!* said the yellow bird, *you are not so foolish as to blab your knowledge to us silly songsters.* Thus the owl's silence gave him his reputation for wisdom.'"

— II —

"Miranda!"

Miranda Jameson started guiltily and quickly turned over the sheets of a manuscript in front of her. "What is it, Charles? I'm busy."

"You've been crying," he said gravely.

"Well?"

Charles laughed bitterly. "Well? Oh, don't let me interrupt you, if it amuses you. Can I lend you a handkerchief? Or do you prefer to drip on to your desk?"

"Don't be a brute. Is my nose red or shiny?"

"Both. Frightfully," answered Charles seriously. "I rather like it like that."

"It was a mistake to weep," said Miranda. "It's ages since I've done it, being naturally tough, and I didn't find it such fun as I've been told. Added to which it is difficult to do it in the neat way one sees in the films. One gets all puffy and messy in real life." Miranda drew her powder-compact from her bag and removed the traces of her indulgence thoughtfully. She accepted a cigarette.

"Now, old thing," said Charles, lighting it, "I am going to speak to you very seriously. Consider me as an elder brother, you know the kind − middle-aged, professional, wise, and full of more or less useful advice for the women of the family. My advice is this. Why not tell the police the whole story?"

Miranda hit her lip. "I don't know *why*," she said. "I just know I can't."

"After all," went on Charles, looking away, "they guess it."

"That makes it worse."

"I see." Charles nodded his head. "Still, is it wise?"

"Of course it isn't. It isn't wise and I haven't been wise. I've been the worst kind of fool. I want to forget it. I can't, I won't, stand the thought of appearing as 'the woman in the case' at a public trial, with the public giggling and the papers playing it up and – oh, can you imagine it?"

"I'm afraid I can – whether you give evidence or not."

Miranda gave a cry of exasperation. "I don't know which is more infuriating, your being so understanding or so logical. I don't care what you prove to me, I'm not going into the witness box."

Charles shrugged his shoulders. "Slap in the face for elder brother for being so sympathetic, blast him, and so right, damn him. All the same, young lady, be as hoity-toity as you like, but do you realize it may not be the witness box you'll be asked to step into?"

"Oh!" Miranda thought this over. "Am I under suspicion?"

"I'm afraid so. It's not very surprising, is it?"

Miranda looked straight ahead of her. When she spoke it was with the cold, hard voice that Charles had heard at Scotland Yard. "Perhaps I had better tell you exactly what happened."

"I think it would be better, you know, if I'm really to be of any help to you."

Miranda continued to look at a spot five feet high on the distempered wall opposite her. "It was all true, what Manciple said, you know. That's why I couldn't answer him."

"I saw that."

"I suppose I was hypnotized by Carpenter. I'm cured of that now. But I'm not well." She was silent for a minute and then she said suddenly, as if on her defence, I think he was a great man, a genius. But I suppose he was what you would call a bounder."

"I should," Charles said shortly.

"He was fascinating, you know. With that fascination that comes of ordering things and people all your life – planning things and seeing they are done – ruling human nature, watching it obey you – a compelling fascination. And he was clever. When he liked, there was a glitter in his mind – oh, call it superficial if you want to, but it was dazzling." Quite abruptly she appealed to Charles. "Do you think I was really in love with him, or do you think I imagined it?"

"I'm no judge," Charles answered a little unsteadily. "I haven't that freedom from prejudice which is so necessary – oh, *go on!*"

"So it went on. I never dreamed for a moment that things were different. That's the worst of being conceited. It makes you blind. I found a note on my desk one morning in the usual way. He asked me if I could see him that evening at about 11.30 p.m. in his suite. This was the first time he had ever made an appointment with me at the office. I went, of course, and then he told me – what Manciple said." The going was a bit sticky, but Miranda pushed on. "Ever since then I've known exactly how mean and torturing humiliation and jealousy and misery is. Oh, Charles! Haven't I been punished enough for being such a fool, without every moron who can read the headlines of a newspaper having the joy of sitting in judgement on me?"

"The swine!" Charles looked older as he got up. "Tell me, though, the second visit?"

Miranda looked at him surprised.

"There wasn't one."

"The police have been told so – evidently by someone who saw you on the first visit and claimed to see you on this."

Miranda shook her head. "No," she said firmly, "they're mistaken."

Charles thought a moment. "That's interesting. There may be something in it. One thing more. Why did you object to giving up your fingerprints?"

"I–" Miranda stopped suddenly and looked confused. "I don't

think I ought to tell you that."

"Another slap in the face for the elder brother, damn his impertinence," said Charles bitterly. "Well, don't tell me if you don't want to."

"Don't be offended, please. Will you believe me if I tell you it hasn't anything to do with me personally?"

"I'll believe anything you tell me."

— III —

Oakley looked like a small and dyspeptic monkey, but a monkey which had surprisingly been trained to wear a morning coat and grey slip with address and distinction. He was, despite his appearance, one of the most brilliant and supple solicitors of the day, now in the full tide of success. He hopped rapidly round Venables as he welcomed him and seated him in a chair.

Then he sat down and looked at Charles with a simian leer over the tops of his glasses. This, however, proved to be his habitual regard. "The present Lord Carpenter," he said, "has asked me to give you all the information I have – yes – in connection with this unfortunate affair." He removed his glasses and carefully polished them before making his next remark.

"Are you connected with the police?"

"No." Charles stressed the unofficial nature of his visit. "I am investigating the case on behalf of Lord Carpenter," he said, with not complete accuracy.

"I see." Oakley gave a short, dry little laugh. "The family detective meets the family solicitor. Well, what can I tell you?"

"First of all, let us be completely frank."

"Certainly not. Frankness is a barbaric vestige. A fault, young man, chiefly of the young."

Charles smiled. "Then I won't shock you by complete candour.

What I wanted from you was this: If I am correctly informed you were something more than Carpenter's solicitor, you were also his financial adviser – in a measure his business adviser – and in possession of complete knowledge of his personal affairs?"

The lawyer nodded. "Yes. It is as much as a business adviser as a lawyer that I am consulted. Most solicitors are. That's why we're such bad lawyers. I'm a bad lawyer. That's why counsel exist. Take their opinion but act on my advice. Go on."

"Well, what I want is for you to give me a candid, unbiased opinion – out of your intimate knowledge of the man – as to what he really was. I want the sort of opinion that will be a touchstone to me in my investigations."

Oakley leaned back in his chair and closed his eyes. "A very unprofessional question! Carpenter, then, was brilliant, a genius–"

"At what?"

"At gauging the public taste, stimulating it, leading it, mobilizing it; at building up an organization with an aggregate circulation of millions which would exhibit his gifts with the minimum of advice and assistance from him; finally at making that organization pay."

"Was he liked?"

"By women almost invariably – because he wanted to be. By men, no, because he liked to bully and humiliate them. Yet he was able to evoke in men a genuine loyalty, for men can be loyal to impersonal things. The snowball of Affiliated Periodicals gets real loyalty from the men who push it down the slope of Carpenter's contriving."

"I see, go on."

"He was, I should say, completely and innocently unscrupulous – I mean both as to the letter of the law and the accepted code of honour among gentlemen."

"Did you like him personally?"

Oakley opened his eyes with a start. "I? I thought him the most unmitigated swine that ever I had met."

Charles blinked. "I should hate you to be completely frank. Can you think of any plausible motive for this affair?"

"Plenty – Women," Oakley joined his thumbs together – "Money" – he touched the forefingers – "Politics" – he mated the remaining fingers and regarded the tips with disapproval. "As to the first, women – there was the main trouble. Any bother about money generally arose from it. I shared his confidences on the score of both. As regards politics –" The lawyer shook his head gravely. "He was playing with fire, Mr. Venables, and I told him so. In these days even a newspaper magnate will find it difficult to engineer a *coup d'état* without being seditious or treasonable."

"Do you think–?"

"I think nothing," Oakley interrupted hastily. "I only stated a fact. Now is there anything else?"

"Can you think of any monetary transaction – had Carpenter any considerable amount of money on him on the day of his murder?"

"Now precisely why do you ask that, Mr. Venables?"

"Guesswork – based on his psychology, as you have told it to me, and certain rather puzzling happenings."

"Well, you have guessed correctly. I handed over to him at noon £5,000 worth of bearer bonds."

"Quite negotiable?"

"Oh, absolutely."

"Would it surprise you to learn there is no trace of any bonds in Carpenter's office?"

"Not at all," replied the lawyer blandly. "It is just what I expect. If I understand Carpenter aright, there was a lady to be consoled – and I take it, since the bonds have gone – she is consoled. I gather that another–" Oakley was about to embark on an explanation, prefaced by a "man-to-man" wink, when his professional intuition enabled him to read the storm in the other's face. "Oh, perhaps you know the lady in question?"

"Yes," said Charles shortly, collecting his hat and stick, "and as she does actually happen to be a lady, I know that you are mistaken as to the destination of the bonds. That explains a lot. Thanks awfully for the information, and good morning."

"Anyway," grumbled the lawyer to himself, when he was alone, "he probably murdered Carpenter himself, judging by the look on his face when I mentioned the girl."

A Secretary is Frank

"HAVE YOU TOLD OUR excellent Heflin that you met him dressed as a navvy in a low café in the East End?" asked Lee Kum Tong.

"No," Charles answered, "I haven't. And if you ask me why, I confess I don't know. The longer I leave it the more difficult it is to let it drop conversational-like. But there you are."

"Your inaction," smiled Lee, "is masterly."

"I hope you haven't been inactive," the other said hopefully.

"No. A chance day is better than a chosen day. Perkins asked me to go with him to a meeting of the cell yesterday evening. I went and saw Rogin take some documents out of the safe. The combination was simple."

"Good. What was it?"

"Nonetheless, the palest ink is better than the most retentive memory." Lee extracted a slip of paper with a few figures on it and handed it to Charles.

Half an hour later Charles was handing the same slip to Antinous Brown, the son of a charwoman at the British Museum and the godson of an expert on Greek sculpture. Hence the name. Brown believed his patron saint was St. Anthony, and his intimates called him Tony. A month or two ago Charles's investigation into a murder trial had brought to light evidence which saved Brown from an awkward situation. It was true Brown at a pinch could have proved an alibi, but as the alibi happened to be the opening of a safe in a shop twenty miles away, with burglarious intent, Brown was intensely relieved not to need to make use of it.

"Count on me, ole man," Brown had said, as one artist to another. "If ever you're in a jam and I can get the dockerments, you gimme the wire."

He fingered a lavish supply of whisky sitting in Charles's best chair, and gave a snort of disgust.

"Ere, wotcher tike me for?" He waved the slip of paper indignantly. "You ask me along for a safe-cracking job, and glad enough I'd be to do it for you, and then, blimey, you give me the blinking combination."

"Well, I thought it would make it easier for you."

"Easier?" Antinous Brown's voice rose in contempt. "Of course it's easier. 'Oo said it wasn't? But why ask me? A blinking insult, that's what it is."

Charles, having wounded his artistic pride, did his best to soothe him. He pointed out that his skill would be needed on the doors.

Brown snorted. "Probably damn big Chubbs you could open with an 'airpin!"

And also he would be needed to guide Charles and his friend, Lee Kum Tong, in the art of burgling.

"Wot, you coming too, *and* a Chink!" Brown put down his whisky and rose to his feet. "Look 'ere, this ain't a joke. We'll get caught sure as 'ell with a couple of amachoors messing and mucking arahnd."

It took a quarter of an hour for Charles to pacify Tony Brown, but he succeeded. At two o'clock that night a short and stocky figure, moving with the ease of practice, walked up to the door of Ferenov's café. He seemed to fumble with the lock for a minute or two, and then it opened, and he passed inside. Five minutes later a young labourer and a Chinese strolled casually up to the door, opened it by the simple process of turning the handle and disappeared inside.

In the inner room of the café a torch played fitfully over the open safe, the contents of a desk, and a filing cabinet. The young labourer, in ordinary life Charles Venables, straightened himself with a sigh of satisfaction. "Here it is," he said, putting a sheet of paper into his pocket. "I was afraid for a moment it wasn't here. Let's beat it now."

"Thank Gawd for that," said Antinous, who had been working himself up to a state of jumps as the minutes dragged on, and Charles imperturbably and unhurriedly turned over papers. "We've been long enough on this as it is."

"Haste is the weakness of devils," said Lee. "Leisure is the ornament of men. I also would like to turn over these papers."

Brown gave a hollow groan and sank into a chair. "Shall we make some tea?" he said sarcastically, "and perhaps have a little dance and a sing-song?"

"Don't get nerves, Tony," said Charles, "Lee won't take long."

"Oo's got nerves?" answered Brown indignantly, turning on Charles. As he did so, he swept the torch off the table and gave a shrill cry.

Lee was meanwhile running through the papers rapidly. With a nod of content, he abstracted six or seven and swept the others aside. "We can put these back," he said.

Charles paused in the act of shutting the safe. He regarded Lee with admiration.

"I wondered why you were so anxious to come with me. Now I see."

Lee smiled affably. "Your own country, poor as it is in homely fable, tells of the monkey whose deplorable cunning induced the cat to abstract chestnuts from a hot place for his own vile benefit."

"Monkeys!" wailed Brown. "For Gawd's sake come on."

They opened the door and filed out. Charles was closing it behind him when a caped and helmeted figure detached itself from the shadows and went up to them.

Brown gave an exclamation of disgust. "That's done it. A cop. Watching us all the time, I expect."

The policeman shone his torch on their faces. "A neat job," he said. "Did you get what you wanted?"

"Yes, thank you."

"Good night, sir."

"Good night, officer."

Antinous Brown giggled hysterically as they walked off. "A copper. 'A neat job!' Blimey – pinch me, someone."

— II —

In the magnificent Hall of the Ambassadors at Leningrad, Malakoff and Mr. Pepys met for the fourth time. In artful perspective, mirrors echoed the weary figures of the Russian commissar and the British plenipotentiary. Under the clear light of the early morning, the Imperial double-headed eagle showed here and there in the plaster-gilt efflorescence, phantasmally surviving its obliteration beneath the Hammer and Sickle.

Pepys, a flush on the Mongolian cheekbones inherited from a Russian mother, rose to his feet. "You are asking the impossible! We are prepared to give any sanction to maintain the integrity of your frontier which will not conflict with our present obligations; beyond that we cannot go. Count on our goodwill."

"Yes – but can we leave a point so vital to Russia's existence" – the commissar's ironic smile flickered – "to your goodwill? Carpenter–"

Pepys, whose complete lack of scruple made him the ideal

man for Moscow, bent closer. "Carpenter has been mysteriously murdered." He paused, and the commissar and the Englishman looked into each other's eyes. "That," said the latter, "should guarantee our goodwill..."

"Ah!" A look of admiring comprehension dawned on the commissar's face. "Your country is in earnest. Dense of me not to realize it. Even more than before, I admire your marvellous English policemen..."

— : —

The First Lord of the Admiralty ended the conference. "It is agreed then that the autumn manoeuvres of the North Sea Fleet be advanced one month. Plans will at once be prepared for manoeuvres, having as their hypothetical theatre the Baltic Sea."

The Premier's warmest supporter in the Cabinet protested indignantly. "It means war if the Fleet is mobilized."

"Supposing we have war without its being mobilized?" snorted the First Lord.

The cool voice of the Attorney-General cut in. "Let Trodger play with his ships. Remember he'd never seen the sea until he became First Lord. He's got the same disease that makes old men play with model yachts by the Round Pond in Kensington Gardens."

Sanger, as usual, was thinking of something else. He rarely listened to what took place at Cabinet meetings."I wonder why we haven't heard from Pepys," he said...

— : —

"My dear sir," pointed out the bank manager, affably tapping the desk with his pince-nez, "this security – the Old Jewry Russian Oil Fields Trust – is quite unacceptable as collateral for an overdraft. Yes, I know their splendid record, *but*..."

— : —

"Can the Prime Minister really weather the Brezka incident?" asked the oldest lobby correspondent. "The old fox has done wonders, of course, but the whole party is shoving the wretch on from behind."

"It all depends on Pepys," said Hartigan, with the confidence of the very young. "If he gets those terms agreed upon, the Premier can hold the old gang. If not – War. The R.A.F. for me. I shan't be sorry..."

— : —

"Oh boy, oh boy, oh boy," said the first Baron Fitz Vanbrugh (née Reuben). He chucked his wife under her third chin with a pudgy and bediamonded finger.

"You naughty boy!" said his lady. "What have you done?"

"I got the option on fifteen mills today," answered Fitz Vanbrugh. "We can turn out four thousand miles of khaki a month when the war begins. And how!"

There was a reminiscent look in Lady Fitz Vanbrugh's eyes. "Oh dear, all those bothersome war charity committees again."

— III —

Meanwhile, Charles Venables, a humble Gallio, neglected to read the papers and cared for none of these things. The problem of the murder of the newspaper peer was absorbing. And it was exasperating.

"How are you getting on, old chap?" Bysshe strolled aimlessly into Venables' room and passed lean white fingers through his flaming red hair with a gesture of weariness as he sat down.

"I'm not getting on, confound it. It's as bad as being ill. When you're feeling rotten and want sympathy no one asks you how you feel. When you are well and bounding with vigour, everyone stops you and asks you if you're any better yet."

Bysshe played with a pen on Charles's desk. "Does it really matter who did the dirty dog in? Can't you let it rest at the coroner's verdict, 'Murder by person or persons unknown'?"

Charles looked at him carefully. "I would if the police would," he answered. "First of all, I've got to clear your sister, you know."

Bysshe groaned in answer. "Damn that feller, Manciple. He's got his knife into us both. As for Jerningham..."

Charles was interested. "Oh, what has Jerningham done?"

"Why, didn't you know? The little blighter told Manciple about Andy originally. I heard him being questioned again about it the other day."

"Oh, that's very interesting."

Bysshe looked up. "Does the portentous tone mean anything? Or is it the professional manner? Like the doctors who say gravely, 'Ah yes, of course,' while they speculate rapidly whether they should diagnose angina or just indigestion."

"It means," answered Charles, "that there is a hot time coming for Jerningham."

Debonair and point-device from patent leather toes to patent leather hair, Jerningham looked up with an easy smile when Venables entered.

"Banzai, O sleuth! What of the hunt?"

Charles accepted a cigarette and lit it with deliberation. "The hunt has just encountered its second check. Can you help me? I gather you've been a fount of information to the police."

"I loathed doing it," said Jerningham with a shudder. "Really, Manciple has the delicacy of a rhinoceros. What a pity the C.I.D. is recruited from the ranks! Yet what can one do in a case like this? After all, he was one's employer, and one has a certain loyalty, hasn't one?"

"Undoubtedly one has," answered Charles seriously. "By the way, are you staying on?"

Jerningham shook his head. "I'm thinking of throwing up work for a little." He gave a deprecatory grin. "One has a minute income of one's own."

Charles nodded solemnly. "Yes, I suppose it is minute. It's impossible to get a *safe* five percent now. But a good prior mortgage stock should bring you in £200 a year on your £5,000. You did say it was £5,000, didn't you?"

Alarm flamed in Jerningham's eyes, was suppressed with an effort, and was only betrayed by his tongue, flickering for an instant over dry lips... "I didn't mention any sum."

Charles's voice became menacing. "No, you didn't. Someone else did. But I'm right, am I not? *That's what the bonds fetched, wasn't it?*"

"I don't know what you are referring to," said the other precisely. His shaking hand rose to his mouth and paused halfway at his tie, which he straightened with ostentatious casualness.

"Rot!" Charles answered with calculated brutality. You know perfectly well. I've got the numbers of the bonds – and you're caught."

Jerningham wobbled into a chair. "My God, what a fool I was. It was an impulse of the moment, Venables! I swear I didn't steal them; not deliberately. I saw them lying on the table and put them in my pocket in case anything happened to them. Then when the Chief was killed I didn't dare..."

"Another lie," Charles commented coldly. "This isn't the first time you've robbed Carpenter. Perry caught you once, and used the knowledge as a lever to make you destroy a letter about him."

Jerningham passed abruptly from whining to defiance. His eyes ceased their shifting and narrowed to pin-points. "I deny it," he screamed. "I deny everything."

Charles contemplated his defiance calmly. "Complete denial is not of much value. The only thing that saves a murderer from the scaffold is a really ingenious defence. You'd better start constructing it now, before they get you muddled."

"The scaffold!" the other squeaked with a sudden horror. He regarded Charles in silence for a moment. "Why I – you don't think I had anything to do with the *murder*, do you?"

Charles blew a cloud of smoke from his mouth, expelled it, and regarded Jerningham with a judicial air. "That's better. You have the air of injured innocence to perfection. Now get an ingenious explanation for the nasty facts, and half the battle's won."

"Don't torture me, Venables," pleaded the other. "They can't say I did it, if I didn't."

"Your main trouble is that the motive and the opportunity both fix it on you," pointed out Charles. "That was careless. Is it your first murder?"

"I'm not the only one. I can think of a much better motive," whined Jerningham. "What about Carpenter's affair with – Miranda Jameson?"

"Pity you haven't a chin," said Charles chiefly to himself, for his fist had caught the private secretary very hard on the "mark." He looked for a moment dispassionately at the figure writhing on the floor and then lifted the telephone.

"At this stage we will have Manciple along," he said, still to himself. "Nothing weakens the moral fibre like a smitten solar plexus, and Jerningham will be positively spouting truth for the next hour or so."

Manciple arrived, surprised but uncommunicative.

"Your witness," said Charles affably, "is at last about to tell the truth."

"I thought he was lying to me," answered the detective briefly. "What's made him truthful?"

Charles explained.

"Then you write about the police's third degree methods!" was Manciple's bitter comment. "Anyway, are you sure it is the truth now?"

But there was plainly no doubt of it. Jerningham's initial revelation was shattering.

"It was her idea," Jerningham had begun. His two listeners exchanged a glance of interrogation.

"Whose idea?" asked Manciple sharply.

"Lady Carpenter's," explained Jerningham.

Hurriedly Charles searched his memory. He recollected now – at the funeral! Tall, dark, over forty, and with the port of a Juno, but a Juno whom yet younger deities had displaced, leaving her face marred with the wreckage of a former beatitude. Then there had been whispers and scandal, because Carpenter, except for one paltry legacy, had passed her over in the disposition of his vast fortune.

"She came to see Carpenter that night – to have it out with him. She's a strange woman," Jerningham had said reflectively, and Charles, remembering those glowing eyes, could believe him. "It was a bitter quarrel they had," Jerningham went on. "She'd done with him, she said. His public humiliation was unbearable. A private *ménage*, kept quiet in a gentlemanly way, she didn't object to. But she would not submit to promiscuous office amours. They shamed and humiliated her."

There was a storm of passion. At last she threatened him. She would leave him at once, as publicly and scandalously as she could devise.

Charles appreciated that Lady Carpenter, as a woman of intelligence, had chosen an effective threat. Carpenter's latter days had been made not a little ridiculous by a social scramble. His marriage to a Burgh-Carrington had been an open-sesame operation on obdurate doors. Maliciously she rubbed in her threat. She would run away with a negro comedian, or she would divorce him, citing a staggering array of co-respondents.

He in his turn had used the threat which so often had been his weapon in their sordid history of quarrels. She was unprovided for in his will; there was not even a marriage settlement, for when she married him for love (both smiled ironically at the retrospect) he was a handsome but very struggling young journalist. The allowance he made her was contingent on her good behaviour.

Divorce was out of the question. Had there not been that affair with young Graeme, in the not so distant past? A bulky dossier bearing that name still reposed in his detective agency's secret files.

So it went on, in the unintelligent and unedifying way of quarrels. At last, to his surprise, she had offered to sell her compliance, within reason. Those bonds on the desk – for they had figured also in the bitter wrangle – and she would forgive him this once.

He would have needed subtlety to guess the reason for this bargain. With the money she had decided to inflict the last humiliation on her husband. She proposed to run away with his secretary. Yes, admitted Jerningham miserably, the affair had been dragging on for some time. Moreover, Lady Carpenter – recollect that the Burgh-Carringtons were part French – had not allowed her *tendresse* for the handsome young man to blind her to his character. The money would be essential to ensure his running away with her. At least, so Charles read between the lines of Jerningham's halting confession.

Did he love her? Charles hesitated. It is easy enough to say *gigolo* in these young man-old woman affairs and be done with it; but life is not always as easy as that. There is a certain strain of weakness in a man that comes out like that. To be adored by wealth and rank, to find feminine experience and brilliant intelligence enticingly submissive; this has a certain fascination for a nature a little bruised about the self-esteem by contact with a rough and ready world. Lady Carpenter like other ageing and unhappy beauties, had a personality that might be overpowering. Then there was the glamour of her position and her influence. Finally (and Charles inclined to give this last reason greatest weight) there was a sweet flavour of revenge in making a fool of an employer who had casually indulged in the luxury of making a fool of him.

They had gone away together.

"You left the room?" said Manciple in a tone of mingled horror and incredulity. He looked at Charles, who showed no surprise. But the policeman's horror was natural.

The starting point of all their investigations was that the murder must have been committed by someone *inside* the office. The sole entrance to the exterior world – through Jerningham's office – had been guarded by Jerningham.

But now, if Jerningham had been lying, even this, their carefully constructed theory, had been built over an abyss, into which, before Manciple's eyes, it plunged without a sound.

He sighed, but otherwise remained stoically silent.

Yes, Jerningham went on, they had gone to Lady Carpenter's house and made a few hasty plans. Then he had returned to lock up the bonds and, to his horror and dismay, the bell had rung. He had gone into the Chief's office and seen that sudden ominous conference and heard the horrifying news – Carpenter had been murdered.

Charles rose to his feet. "Lady Carpenter now, I suppose?" he said wearily.

Manciple looked at his collaborator without enthusiasm, but he made no objection. They shared a taxi to Lady Carpenter's house, and Charles paid for it.

A Detective Is Arrested

MANCIPLE, CHARLES FOUND TO his delight, had a faint air of not looking forward to his interview with Lady Carpenter. It showed in an added grimness in his manner; still greater inexpressiveness in his heavy face.

Lady Carpenter had a manner. No doubt it had been largely acquired as a result of going round with a husband who (in his early days) had been a social interloper. It was a manner admirably calculated to envelop two people in one aura and sweep both along, gloriously and impressively, the length of a crowded reception room. The foundation of it, however, was natural. It was based on what had been a lovely figure, and was still tall and regal, and on a black-browed, firmly-modelled face, of the kind that even in middle-age retains its impressiveness, if not its grace. Here was nothing of the fat forlornness of the gigolo-hunter. Carpenter was equal to this sort of thing; but Charles began to feel sorry for Jerningham, as helpless as the spider in the grip of the female of the species.

"We are anxious, my lady, to get from you some information which I believe you have for us."

Lady Carpenter nodded. "Certainly." She indicated chairs. "You are both from Scotland Yard?"

"This is Mr. Venables, of the *Mercury*," explained the Inspector. "He is investigating your husband's murder at the wish of his brother." This was, of course, why Manciple had allowed Charles to come with him without protest. Charles was "on" the case almost for the family – so Manciple's manner indicated. And so Manciple hoped that Lady Carpenter might talk more freely than at a merely official interview.

Lady Carpenter, however, looked at Charles with extreme coldness. The young man dropped his monocle, caught it vaguely as it swung on his lanyard, and simpered deprecatingly, but did not fail to notice Lady Carpenter's eyes rest on the lens and her mouth curve faintly in a smile that might have been contempt.

"What can I do for you both?" she said.

Manciple cleared his throat, shuffled with his boots and pulled a notebook from his pocket. He had lost any air of unease, and Charles recognized with admiration his gifted performance as a thick-skulled, thick-skinned officer of the law.

"On the night of your husband's murder," he began, "you saw your husband."

"Who told you that?" asked Lady Carpenter, suddenly sitting bolt upright.

The detective stared at her with ox-like calm. "Mr. Jerningham, of course, told us the full story," he said. His manner gave no hint of the pressure which had been put on the unfortunate man to extract the information.

Charles, familiar with the tortuous technique usually necessary to secure an admission during an interrogation, was surprised at the sudden change in the atmosphere. Lady Carpenter's eyes blazed. For a moment she struggled with her fury, and her face looked evil and horrible. Then without another moment's hesitation she threw Jerningham to the lions.

Charles, who had started by feeling sorry for the woman, felt a revulsion of feeling. Hurt, she turned on the thing she loved as instinctively as a tigress.

"It is true," she admitted. "I went to see my husband to warn him about Jerningham. I had reason to believe the man was untrustworthy. And I caught him in the act of appropriating some bonds." She looked at the detective calmly. "What sort of story he's told you, of course, I don't know. I warned him I would tell my husband next morning. And next morning—" She shrugged her shoulders. Her face, which might, in its strength of line, have compelled an adventitious beauty under the influence of love, now, because of that same strength, was hideous with hatred.

Charles guessed at that moment the events sequent on her husband's death. Lady Carpenter's desire to run away still stronger – Jerningham's frightened refusal – a sordid and unhappy quarrel.

"By the way, Lady Carpenter," he said suddenly, and quite untruthfully, "your maid said you told her to pack on the night of the murder."

Her eyes met his with cold ease. "Yes, I did think of spending a day or two with some friends in the country."

"I see," commented Manciple. "That explains it. Now at what time on the night of the murder did you see Lord Carpenter?"

"About twelve. A little after, I think."

"And you left him?"

"Half an hour later – quite that."

"And he was perfectly all right then?"

"Of course. He said he was just going to lie down for a short sleep. I gathered he expected to be wakened up soon after."

Manciple closed his book with a snap, put it away, and leaned back. "Now, Lady Carpenter," he said briskly and genially, "have you any objection to putting your fingerprints on record?"

The smile died instantly on her lips. "The suggestion is outrageous," she exclaimed. "Why – as if I were a common criminal!"

Icily Manciple broke into her protest. "Legally I cannot compel you. Do you refuse?"

"I wish to know your reason."

"Do you refuse?"

Her eyes blazed and the manner came into full play. "Don't try to bully me!"

Manciple was silent for a moment. All three heard the clock steadily ticking. Lady Carpenter watched the detective, her lips compressed. Then he leaned forward, and without the slightest change of manner, spoke again.

"Do you refuse?"

"Very well," she answered with heightened colour. "You may take them."

"It will serve my purpose if I examine them," said Manciple. "The right hand if you please."

The slim white hand, with the firm fingers that betray race more surely than any other feature, lay for a moment in the detective's massive palm. He scrutinised the tips beneath a glass in silence for a moment. Then he looked at her gravely.

"Lady Carpenter, you are in a very serious position. We have evidence to the effect that you were with your husband on the night of the murder. You had a quarrel. Please do not interrupt me. Now on the hilt of the dagger which stabbed your husband, I find your fingerprints. Every morning the dagger, like the other weapons in the room, was carefully cleaned and the hilt polished. Therefore you must have handled the knife that day."

Lady Carpenter looked at the Inspector appraisingly for a moment. "Well, what are you going to do?"

"I am going to ask you for a franker and fuller statement than you have seen fit to give us so far."

"And if I refuse?"

"I can only remind you that such matters as the quarrel

are matters of evidence where we may be mistaken. But the fingerprint is material evidence. It cannot be challenged and confused. It cannot," said the Inspector, almost lyrically, "be accused of malice, or prejudice, or forgetfulness. It is a fact."

"Let me think it over."

Manciple nodded and relapsed into his chair in an attitude which suggested his readiness to prolong immobility eternally.

Lady Carpenter rose to her feet and walked to the window. She stared out of it for a moment, and then sat on a settee at the end of the room. She interrupted her brooding to look up suddenly at Charles. "Come here a moment, please, Mr. Venables." Obediently he sat on the settee beside her.

"I know your father, I think." She looked at him appraisingly. "Not such a fool as you try to look, are you?"

"Better, as I understand it, than not looking such a fool as you are," answered Charles with caution.

She nodded. "Are you with me or against me?"

He considered for a moment. "Neither," he said.

"Oh, the impartial investigator?"

"Not even that, I'm afraid. Only that I do not yet know enough to decide."

"Then I shall throw myself on your chivalry."

"Such of it as I have," Charles answered in a low voice, "is already engaged in the service of another lady."

Lady Carpenter sensed his meaning with the keenness of a woman. "I understand. But your – client and I are, you know, in a measure companions in misfortune." It was sensitively put, and dissolved his latent antagonism.

"Tell me," she went on, "what sort of position am I in?"

"About as awkward as it could be."

She nodded, "And what do you advise?"

"A step as unpalatable and obvious as any doctor's prescription

– complete and utter candour."

Lady Carpenter considered for a moment, her ample white brow furrowed with thought. "Very well," she said at last, and, rising, walked back to the detective. "Inspector," she told him, "get out your notebook."

Her statement was brief and given without hesitation.

"I visited my husband on the night he was murdered. We quarrelled – bitterly, violently, as we have quarrelled before. At one moment something he said so infuriated me that I took up the dagger from the wall, and threatened him. I almost believe that if I had the opportunity, at that moment, I might have stabbed him. But the moment was passed almost before I was aware of it. I found myself standing rather foolishly brandishing a dagger. I replaced the knife.

"The quarrel ended – as others have ended – amicably. I left him alive – and on good terms with me. Secretly I was planning to break with him for ever." She paused and shrugged her shoulders. "Someone spared me the trouble."

They left her, Manciple non-committal, a veiled anxiety in her eyes. They paused outside.

"I can't offer to share your taxi," grumbled Manciple. "I could justify it if I were going to take a statement, but not now I've got it."

Charles smiled cheerfully. "And as there's no story in this, I can't justify one either, so we'll split a tube train between us."

They had walked halfway to Bond Street station before either spoke. "Of course she didn't do it," said Charles at last. "She's capable enough of knifing him in a rage, but she's just as incapable of stabbing him in his sleep."

"I don't mind that," groaned Manciple, with guarded amity. "What is fretting me, is that I'm back where I started now, because there is no need for it to have been someone in the office.

I'd like to see that little swine Jerningham swing," he added with venom, "for leaving his wretched little office that night."

There was another pause before Charles spoke. "Well, I think this lets Miss Jameson out. Jerningham's story of her second visit was just a frame-up in case anyone got to know that a woman had seen Carpenter after twelve."

"Yes, it lets her out," answered Manciple without enthusiasm. "And it lets everyone else in. The Lord knows who may not have come in by that private entrance."

"Anyone!" agreed Charles.

— II —

Charles stopped to borrow a match from the Very Youngest Reporter. "Great larks," said that fair-haired babe, "our dear Heflin hasn't turned up today.

"Well, I'm damned," he added, as, matchbox extended in his hand, he saw Charles flying up the corridor.

Charles arrived in Grovermuller's room, breathless but unruffled.

"Heflin's disappearance may be serious," he explained to the Editor.

Grovermuller looked startled. "Bless my soul," he said, "have you been reading the detective serial in the *Mercury*? I mean, dash it all – 'disappearance' and 'serious'! Just because Heflin hasn't turned up!"

"Did you know anything about Heflin's double life?"

Grovermuller burst into a laugh. "No, I don't, and don't want to. Our staff's matrimonial troubles–"

Charles interrupted him rudely. "I can see you don't know anything about it. Odd. However, I can tell you it's serious. Just a moment while I phone him at home."

No, Mr Heflin was not there. He had left home about eight, as he always did, and had not been back since. As a matter of fact, he rarely did come back. Almost invariably he went on to the office about twelve or one, without going home again.

It was then three.

"I can't stop to explain now, sir, but you must take my word for it that it is serious. I'm going to try and get Heflin out of his mess. I want you to stand by here, and if I give you any sort of message, however silly it may seem, act on it."

Grovermuller looked at him dubiously, then nodded. "Very well," he said.

Charles shot downstairs to Lee Kum Tong's room. The Chinese listened gravely to his story.

"The yellow bird chases the locust," said he, "and in all ignorance the locust chases the cicada."

An hour later a shabby Chinese and the young working man who was his companion entered the café of Ferenov. It was empty. A few bluebottles buzzed dizzily round the room; a tired lettuce curled drably in the sun, and there was a pile of unwashed cups on the counter.

Charles went quietly to the door of the inner room. There was a hum of voices. He knelt, his ear to the keyhole, while Lee, with negligent abstraction, leaned against the jamb of the street door and stared up the street.

It was easy to make out the voice of Rogin, shrill with fury.

"Are you mad?" he screamed. "You'll have us all hanged! How dare you take such a step without consulting me! You comic opera villains, you've as much brains in your collected noddles as I have in my little finger. Yet you act like this, without a word to me."

"I tell you what it is," said a voice which Charles placed as that of Ferenov, the acidulated little monkey of an agitator. "You're

119

streets ahead of us when it comes to brainwork, but you're soft. You're bourgeois. You can't face action."

"True," boomed the bearded mystic. "You are afraid of blood, Rogin. The blood of martyrs is the seed of the Church. Ha, ha, so the Capitalist told us. We know better. The blood of the bourgeois is the seed of the World State. You're soft, Rogin, my comrade."

"Bah!" Rogin shouted, beside himself with fury. "On behalf of Moscow, whose representative I am, I disown you. I am not responsible for your action! I refuse to have anything to do with you! You are mad! I expel you from this cell!"

There was an undistinguishable murmur, above which Anna's voice rose clear and decided. "Rogin, you are talking like a fool. It is not Moscow we are thinking of now. It is nothing to do with Russia. We are not acting for the World State. We are saving our own skins. Nicolai, and you, father, and you, Comrade Perkins, you are fools too."

"Ze fellow was no gentleman," said Perkins' sulky voice. "Ee was a dirty Irish spy."

"You are fools, because there was no need for violent measures. We could have saved our skins without violence. But we have gone so far now, we can't draw back. Rogin, you must leave it to the other to do the job as efficiently as possible. I know you've got a weak stomach, but you must be calm."

Charles rose to his feet. Then signalling to Lee, he whispered in his ear for a moment. The Chinese grinned and nodded. They crept quietly out of the café, paused for a moment, and then walked noisily in. Without hesitating, Lee went straight up to the inner door, and rapped on it loudly. After much whispering it was unlocked.

Charles gave a quick glance round as he followed Lee in. Rogin, pale, with the sweat standing on his forehead, looked at the newcomers with a nervous expectation. His hand trembled as he pointed to a seat. The big bearded man's face was flushed with argument, while Ferenov looked maliciously at Rogin's evident fright.

"Friends!" he said, as if to soothe him.

Perkins, leaning against the mantelpiece, glared sulkily at Anna. Ferenov's daughter seemed unaware of any tension in the air. She looked calmly at Lee and Charles and welcomed them with a smile. "We did not expect you," she said.

Lee indicated Charles. "He has important news for you," he said.

Anna's eyes met his with a veiled kindness.

Charles looked carefully round the room, collecting eyes with the skill of a hostess. Then he leaned forward dramatically.

"You've a spy here!" he said.

Anna's look of surprise was the only convincing one. "What on earth makes you say that, Bill?"

"I know it. I've positive proof – with my own eyes." Charles dropped his voice. "When I came here before, I saw a fellow reading a paper outside. Dressed like a worker, he was, looking as if he'd never earned more than thirty shillings a week in his life. I got a light for my cigarette from him as I went out."

"Well?" asked Perkins impatiently.

Obviously enjoying himself, Charles continued: "Well, when I got to the *Mercury* next day, as sure as I stand here I recognized one of the nobs of the *Mercury*, Mr. Heflin, the news editor, as that same labourer!"

The Russians exchanged glances. "Impossible," said Anna, "it's just a likeness."

"No, oh no it isn't! I know what I'm talking about," went on Charles, with the perky self-satisfaction of the Cockney. "When I was cleaning the windows in Mr. Heflin's room, before he came in, I had a dekko in his desk. In one of his drawers I found a bit of paper with the name of this place written on it, and all your names! What price that?"

Anna looked at him coldly. "Well, what about it?"

"What about it?" Charles broke out into a shrill excitement. "Well, you're a lot of cabbages, you are. Are you going to sit down, you silly mugs, and wait for the police to come and jail you? You damn well deserve to, that's all I can say."

The girl shrugged her shoulders. "What can you do?"

"What can you do?" Charles looked round meaningly. "Why, I bet Lee here could do something if you asked him. He doesn't fancy going to jail for being concerned in Communist propaganda, or me either, for that matter." He narrowed his eyes and looked at Rogin. "There's no bourgeois conscience about me. What about you, eh? If you can't get rid of him here, near the river – and him in disguise – you're a fine lot."

Lee laughed. "You should know whether you want to go to prison or not, Bill."

"That's a fact," Charles said, with a creditable snarl. "I've had enough of their blasted prisons, and their slaves of policemen, lying and perjuring the working classes. There's no justice or mercy for the likes of us; and well I know it."

Charles's tirade evoked a murmur.

"There you are, you see, Rogin," said Ferenov, "even these two outsiders, with much less to lose than we have, have got more guts than you." He turned to Charles. "We were only testing you, comrade. We had already found out all you have told us – and we are perfectly capable of dealing with our friend."

"That's the stuff!" said Charles approvingly. "What are you going to do? Settle his hash and drop him overboard?"

Rogin groaned. "It is madness. I shall have nothing to do with it."

"Here! What does he say?" Charles pointed an indignant thumb at the white-faced and pallid Communist. Are you going to let him get away with that – splitting to the police, perhaps?"

Ferenov shook his head. "He won't say anything. He's too frightened of being implicated himself."

"Where is he now?" asked Charles.

Ferenov winked. "Not very comfortable!" He went to a cupboard door and flung it open. Bent double in it, bound and gagged, the limp body of Heflin sagged wearily.

His eyes fell on Charles and Lee with an expression which mingled hope and incredulity. Charles masked it from the others in the room by stepping between. Leaning over Heflin, he kicked him conscientiously. "——I" he said.

They closed the door.

"Where are you going to get rid of him?" asked Charles.

Ferenov mentioned the place.

"Is it necessary to tell them everything?" asked Anna, her eyes on Charles.

He laughed carelessly. "Oh, don't get suspicious. I asked because I'm going to help you, and see you do the job thoroughly. I know you Russians, I've been let down by you before."

"Ee is right," said Comrade Perkins solemnly. "Ve British must stick togezzer."

Lee, who had been watching with an impassive face, now spoke. "You will certainly make a mess of it if you do what you say. At night that spot is regularly patrolled by the police. Don't you know the river?"

"Not very well," admitted Ferenov.

"There's a place by the Isle of Dogs which is perfect for your purpose. There is a road running right down to a wharf. Neither has been used for years, for the river is silted up there. The patrol boat sweeps past the mouth of the inlet, but the wharf cannot be seen. It will be easy to run a car to the wharf, put Heflin in a boat, and dump him overboard to drown like a rat, without being seen."

"There you see, Anna," said Ferenov, "Lee is right. He can help us a good deal. You yourself were saying it was a pity we did not know the river better."

Charles interrupted the discussion. "Anyway, what I say is, it's hours yet before it'll be dark enough to do the job. What about drinks all round? It's going to be a cold night, and the stuff'll put a kick into us."

"A good idea," boomed Nicolai. "Come along, Rogin, some of Ferenov's vodka will brighten up your gloom."

"Vodka," said Charles, with enthusiasm. "Now I haven't never had any of that stuff."

The spirit disappeared rapidly. Lee spoke in a warning whisper to Ferenov, but it was too late. Charles was visibly elated, and insisted on singing comic songs in dubious taste in a gusty tenor. By one o'clock he was gloriously tight, and it was unanimously decided to leave him behind. Charles extended himself on the sofa, and broke abruptly into snores.

Unfortunately he came to after they had returned in a battered and ancient four-seater. They were going to carry Heflin, extended on a stretcher, but still bound and gagged beneath the sheets, out to the car, when Charles staggered out. Singing loudly, he tottered into the street and cavorted round the car. He eluded one or two attempts at capture, and a policeman rapidly advanced on them, attracted by the noise.

Still singing, Charles staggered up to him. A look of recognition was exchanged between them, for it was barely forty-eight hours since they had bidden each other good night.

With a cry of vinous pleasure, Charles embraced the policeman alcoholically. "Ring Grovermuller, Central 23000," he whispered, clinging to him, "and tell him to arrange for the Flying Squad to be hidden under a tarpaulin in an old truck at Gunter's Wharf before 3 a.m. He can get it done, where they won't believe you."

"'Ere, wot the 'ell are you playing at?" said P.C. Robinson, a man of quick perception. As he placed Charles on his feet, he repeated the phone number, the address and the time. "You ought to be locked up, you did." He addressed the anxious group of Russians. "'Ere, you put your friend in bed, or 'e'll spend the night in a prison cell."

With which words, P.C. Robinson stumped heavily off. Rough hands seized Charles and locked him in the inner room of the café, together with Rogin, who seemed indeed almost as prostrate with fear as Charles with alcohol.

There the police found them when they returned from Gunter's wharf, having caught the little band preparing to launch Heflin into the Thames, gagged and bound, with a few lengths of lead piping tied to him *pour l'encourager*. The bearded Russian had fought like ten men, with the strength of a madman, as Charles had foreseen.

"Had I been Bulldog Drummond," he explained to Heflin, "Lee and I and P.C. Robinson could have dealt with them easily, for what can a system lowered by vodka do against a right arm nerved by beer? But it would have been too shame-making if we'd been all laid out."

Comrade Perkins was the only captive to speak. "You un-English bounder!" he said to Charles, with infinite contempt.

— III —

"Fanny wants to know how to remove blackheads," said Charles.

"How disgusting," remarked Miranda abstractedly.

Laboriously Charles wrote it out. *"Fanny, Peckham, S.E., wants to know how to remove blackheads. How disgusting!"*

Awakening from her brown study, Miranda restrained him in alarm. "Don't be silly, that's not the answer. Really you are more of a trouble than a help. Just put down 'Stock Answer No. 232.' Miss Brown will know."

"Oh, I see." Chastened, Charles turned to the sheaf of letters. There was silence for a moment, and then Charles appealed again for help.

"Here's a point of etiquette which is quite beyond me. Listen. *The boy I am walking out with (Alfred) said he had to go and visit his mother on my afternoon off, so I went out with another boy. We went in the Park and there I met Alfred bold as brass with another girl. I told him I would never speak to him again, but Alfred said I was as bad as he was* (smart of Alfred that), *but I say he was in the wrong. Please what do you say, and am I right in telling him (Alfred) that I don't love him any more; what I feel is, a girl has to stand up for herself.* I say, that's a hell of a problem, isn't it?"

"It is beyond me," agreed Miranda. "It is quite obviously a matter for Aunt Agatha's soothing style. Will you mark it for the attention of Mr. Johnson?"

"Done. Is Aunt Agatha that pale and pimply youngster?"

"Yes. He has a penetrating insight into the human (feminine) heart and a delightfully maternal style. Are there any more of these wretched queries? It's too bad of Mrs. Forester to get ill just when I'm short-handed."

Charles gazed fixedly at the pile of letters in front of him. "There's one more," he said quietly. "It's from a young man."

"Fire away."

"It seems," explained Charles, "that he loves a girl who thought she loved someone else. She was let down badly, and she can't seem to recover from it. Should he wait, and leave it to time, or should he force her to see that the world hasn't changed, that—"

"Don't." Miranda's voice was decisive, but its harshness was the harshness of self-control retained only by an effort. I can't stand kindness. Treat me just as if I were – normal."

Charles got up and looked out of the window.

"Don't think I don't appreciate it. You are helping me tremendously."

"I'm a useful ornament to have about the house, I suppose," Charles answered, with a tincture of bitterness. "Useful to hang one's hat on, and maybe leaned against in an emergency."

"Don't be nasty, Charles. It's not only myself. I'm worried about Bysshe – frightfully worried."

"Picture of faithful friend floundering heavily to the rescue. But, woman, am I thy brother's keeper?"

"It's serious, Charles – this time. Listen."

But Charles did not listen, for at that moment a diminutive page-boy precipitated himself into the room. "Detective Inspector Manciple wants to see you, very important," he announced with a conspiratorial air.

"Throw him in – and mind he doesn't arrest you," answered Charles. "He was speaking to me about a sixpence which was picked up by someone to whom it doesn't belong."

The small boy's jaw dropped. "Oh," he said uncertainly. "I thought finding's keepings. Anyway," he added with apprehension, "it was a shilling."

"Oh, it's all right with shillings, they have to be dealt with by Superintendents. He can't touch you."

Detective Inspector Manciple hesitated for a moment in the doorway. Another man waited behind him. He made no direct answer to Charles's suspiciously cheery greeting.

"I have a warrant for your arrest," he began expressionlessly, "on the charge of wilfully murdering Arthur Viscount Carpenter" –

the formal wording came patly off his tongue. "Anything you say may be used in evidence against you," he concluded.

Charles looked at him closely. "Tell me, when you found that the fingerprints on the blade were different to those on the hilt made by Lady Carpenter, did you guess whose they were?"

Manciple made no reply.

"Confoundedly careless of me to leave my paw marks on the actual snickersee!" explained Charles. "By the way, I hope you found my fingerprints in the tumbler on my desk? I made as good a set for you as I could."

Manciple's companion smiled, but the detective himself ignored the question. He pulled out a notebook and wrote for a moment. "I have warned you," he reminded Charles.

"Oh, that's all right; thanks a lot," answered Charles. "I deserve to be arrested for being so careless. I shall look a fool, shan't I?"

"Would you care to make a statement?" said Manciple in his most seductive tones.

"'Will you come into my parlour?' said the spider to the fly," quoted Charles. "No, I should hate to."

Miranda, her face white, had watched the scene. She drew him aside for a moment. "Charles," she said in a low voice, "what have you done?"

"Only made a fool of myself." He read her mind. "Only a fool."

Bewildered, she looked at his smiling face. "I shall never forgive myself if—" she turned away abruptly. "Oh, I suppose I oughtn't to press you even. I've no right."

"Now, now, Andy," said Charles seriously, "don't go getting wild ideas in your head."

"It's so amazing." She shuddered. "So *possible*. But I know it isn't true. It isn't, is it?"

"No, it isn't." He looked at her again, but now her eyes were inscrutable. "Well, *au revoir*. You can bring me my lunch in a red spotted handkerchief if you like."

"Goodbye, Charles."

He returned to Manciple.

"Can I see the Editor before I go?"

Manciple hesitated for a moment. But he belonged to a service which was accustomed to accord special privilege to the Press.

"Five minutes," he said grudgingly.

A News Editor
is Suspicious

"IS THIS A SETTLED policy?" asked Grovermuller, looking at Manciple over the tops of his glasses. "Do you propose eventually to arrest the entire staff of the Mercury?"

"We hope that this will be the last," explained Manciple with a wintry gleam of humour.

Charles helped himself to one of the Editor's cigarettes absent-mindedly, and dropped into a chair. "Frightfully sorry," he mumbled, "to be arrested like this."

"Not at all!" said Grovermuller. "Perhaps I should apologize"

Charles looked up quickly. "Oh! So you were the witness who saw me leave the Chief's room?"

Grovermuller nodded.

Charles reflected a moment. "Yes, and then, of course, I attempted to murder you in order to distract your attention from myself by rescuing you."

Charles turned to the Inspector. He slowly expelled a cloud of smoke from his mouth. "I hadn't thought of that," he said at last. "Manciple, I congratulate you – you appear to have a cast-iron case."

Twirling his monocle in his long fingers, Charles regarded

the detective benevolently, as if congratulating a successful subordinate. This, however, failed to provoke him to reply.

"By the way, am I still on the staff of the *Mercury?*"

"Most certainly," said Grovermuller. "We are arranging for your defence at once."

"Awfully decent of you; but a little premature." He took out his pocket-book, tore a leaf from the diary and scribbled on it. Folding up the sheet, he handed it to Grovermuller, who was watching him with a faintly surprised look. "Keep this, and act on the advice in it."

Grovermuller took the scrap of paper. "If it's reasonable, I will. You're rather puzzling sometimes, Venables. If a word of advice will not be resented, I suggest you will do best, in your own interests, to say as little as possible."

"Very true, sir," said Manciple, suddenly springing into life.

The prisoner rose slowly to his feet. "The manacles," he said, "and the 12 h.p. Tumbril."

— II —

Oakley faced Venables in simian wonder, as a monkey might stare if you flashed a bright light in its face or suddenly produced some startlingly gaudy object for its edification.

"Your attitude is inexplicable, Mr. Venables," he said. "You cannot, I suppose, imagine it is helping you?"

For half an hour Oakley, at Grovermuller's request, had attempted to get at the strength of the defence. Charles, as agile as an eel, had politely but skilfully evaded all leading questions.

"There are several possible answers to the charge," admitted Charles, "but I do not think discussion at this stage would do much good. Action is needed." He rolled the word on his lips with the unction of a chairman at a shareholders' meeting. "Yes, action," he repeated, glancing slyly at Oakley.

The solicitor laughed for the first time. "Action! What sort of action do you suggest?"

"I want you to take a letter to a confidential destination," Charles answered. "I should be very surprised if it does not procure my release."

"I should be surprised if it did!" As he made the reply, Oakley's feelings underwent a certain change. Although he had had little experience of this sort of thing he had many friends at the Criminal Bar. They agreed in giving as the one common hallmark of the murderer an overwhelming self-confidence. Always the murderer believed he would never be caught, or if he was caught he could bluff judge and jury, or if he was sentenced, at the last hour, the sympathy of the public or some secret influence would pluck him out of the jaws of death with a reprieve.

"You are a man of sense, Mr. Venables," said Oakley in his most impressive tones, "but even men of sense are inclined to lose their perspective in a dilemma of this sort. Think again. How can any influence you may possess be exerted in your favour in a capital charge?"

Charles shrugged his shoulders. "I am afraid it is useless for us to argue. I have expressed my own feelings on the matter."

"Very well," Oakley said with a trace of temper. "You seem to me to be treating this affair with deplorable levity. I shall deliver any letter you give me, but unless you care to be franker with me than you at present consider fit, I shall feel forced to tell Mr. Grovermuller that you do not appear to desire the services of a solicitor."

Charles acknowledged the rebuke and drew his chair up to the small table in the corner of the interviewing room. The lawyer frowned at his nails while the scratching and spluttering of an official pen accompanied Charles's fluent epistolary style. He sealed the envelope with decision, and then handed the letter to Oakley.

"God bless my soul!" exclaimed the solicitor, as he read the superscription. "Do you think he can do anything for you?"

"He can and I hope, will," answered Charles, "but the letter must get to his hands, and his hands only."

"Surely his confidential secretary–" began the other.

"His own hands only," repeated Charles with emphasis. I believe you – or Grovermuller – can ensure that. I must specifically ask you to promise that this letter is not delivered on any other terms."

Impressed in spite of himself, Oakley promised and took his leave. As he was conducted back to his retreat Charles thought deeply.

"I wonder if I *have* got myself into a jam?" he said at last.

"We shall have to do what he asks, I suppose," grumbled Oakley to Grovermuller after telling the story of the solicitor's visit.

"We certainly must," the Editor answered, caressing his short grey moustache reflectively. "That young man has given me two surprises already, and is quite capable of giving me a third."

"As the principal witness for the prosecution, you do not seem to have quite the correct attitude towards the prisoner," smiled the lawyer.

— III —

The arrest of Charles Venables had given Manciple more anxiety than any other in his career.

"How goes it?" the Deputy Commissioner had asked him when he came in that morning.

Manciple had looked at the Commissioner with a diffidence

which, in a less positive man, would have been described as shy.

"I have a *prima facie* case against Charles Venables," Manciple had answered.

"Charles Venables! What? Not the *Mercury's* investigator?" Murgatroyd roared with laughter. "Manciple, you're pulling my leg!"

"I'm perfectly serious," said Manciple. He closed his eyes for a moment and for the hundredth time ran over the main features of the case. "It seems watertight to me. But I warn you that he's an acute and slippery customer. I cannot imagine any circumstances in which he would have been so injudicious as to leave the clues we have picked up."

"No, Inspector, I cannot allow that last remark. Murderers are notoriously careless."

"Criminally careless," agreed the detective with a smile. "Here then is the case."

"First of all, Venables was seen leaving Carpenter's rooms at 1.20 a.m. on the night of the murder. The witness – who is particularly trustworthy – did not think Venables saw him. He is not certain, however, and it is significant, first that Venables attempted to throw suspicion on this witness, secondly that the witness was murderously assaulted. Venables curiously enough predicted that he would be assaulted – no reason given – and miraculously enough knew exactly when the assault had occurred."

"Yes, allowing for a subtle mind on the part of Venables, that is interesting. What did your witness think of Venables' appearance?"

"'Intensely worried' was his own description."

"Is this the only positive clue you have connecting him with the murder?"

"No." Manciple looked distinctly happier as he reached the

nucleus of his case. "On the blade of the weapon, made over an actual smear of Carpenter's blood, was Venables' fingerprint."

"Good God! How does he explain it?" Already the Deputy Commissioner's sceptical expression had changed to one of keen interest.

"He doesn't explain it. But − and this is the most conclusive feature in my case − he refused to give his fingerprints on request."

The Deputy-Commissioner thought for a moment. "Didn't one or two other people do the same?"

"True," admitted Manciple. He pulled out a battered diary and skimmed over the pages. "Here is what actually happened." He briefly summarized the incident. "You see," he concluded, closing the book, "the only person who doesn't give a serious excuse is Venables."

"Extraordinary! I can't make out whether the fellow's amazingly subtle or amazingly rash." Murgatroyd drummed with his fingers on the table as he rapidly revolved the salient facts in his mind. "Where's your motive?" he asked at last.

Venables is in love with Miranda Jameson. Carpenter had an affair with her; you'll remember it came out in that earlier statement I showed you."

"Jealousy, eh? Sound enough. You can prove it, of course?"

"Certainly − on his own admission."

An hour later a warrant for the arrest of Charles Venables was issued.

— IV —

"Now what the devil have you two and Charles Venables been stirring up between you?" grumbled Grovermuller.

Heflin's brawny bulk still looked shaken from his experience.

Lee Kum Tong, however, was bright, unruffled and smiling.

"The road to the Imperial Palace winds among the haunts of brigands," the Chinese explained. "In the quest of Truth, Charles and I encountered Bolshevists – and Mr. Heflin... Much to our surprise," he added.

Heflin's explanation was longer. "I was one of Carpenter's investigators into Communist activities in my spare time," he began.

"What, Heflin!" exclaimed Grovermuller. "You, our news editor, are really an inquiry agent?"

Heflin looked sheepish but unrepentant. "That's neither accurate nor fair. As you know, I'm a journalist. As you may not know, I also happened to work for MI5 during the War, not without success. Oh, I suppose every agent is inclined to overvalue his work – it's the effect of functioning alone and unassisted – but I still feel if full use had been made of the channel I opened up with Rasputin that disastrously sudden collapse might have been less complete. And again, if my warning that the Bolshevists were certain to come out on top – but there, these regrets are based on fallacies. I only mention them to show why I acted for Carpenter as a spare-time investigator.

"It was quite spontaneous, really. I came across a White Russian I had known in Leningrad. He told me of the existence of a certain Communist cell in the East End. It is a special type of cell. I need not go here into its place in the Communist system. But it's not a cell that the ordinary Communist can join, and it is destined to play an important part in the 'liquidation' of the British Capitalist state.

"I told Carpenter this. He was wildly keen for me to join it and gain all the information I could. 'Heflin,' he said to me once, 'as a news editor you are good, but replaceable. As a spy, you're unique!'

"This, however, was in one of his moments of enthusiasm. I can't say, truthfully, that I was very successful. Disguised as a labourer, I went in my spare time to the café which furnished a pretext for members to meet without suspicion. I heard a great deal because I understood Russian, and when they were speaking that language they were freer than otherwise. But they didn't often speak it.

"The situation was tantalizing. I gleaned useful hints. I furnished the material for one or two investigations. My one coup was obtaining a line on the Brezka incident. If it had not been for me, there would never have been a secret agent of Carpenter's on the spot at Brezka, ready to smuggle the news of the atrocity through a censorship. So it went on until Carpenter was killed."

Heflin's eyes narrowed, and he banged his fist on the table. "Venables is no more guilty than I am. It is fantastic. The line to follow is as clear as a signpost. It sticks out a mile. It points to Russia, with every emphasis of circumstance. What was Carpenter? An enemy of Russia! What was he planning to do? Persuade England to make war upon Russia! What prevented his doing this? His murder! If there is an undistributed middle in this, I'd like to know it. The whole deduction is so logical that you hardly need a clue or a schedule of the movements of the accused."

Grovermuller stroked his moustache reflectively "That's all very well," he said, "but it has been pointed out some time ago that you can't indict a nation. An individual, whether his name ended in 'son' or 'ski,' walked into Carpenter's room at a certain time, abstracted a dagger, and stuck it into him. It is unfortunately necessary to find who, when and why, and nationality hardly enters into it. The police have been able to reconstruct the crime with entire plausibility, with Venables as the murderer. Nothing is missing, not even the familiar fingerprint on the sharp instrument. The motive is quite adequate, and the behaviour of the accused is suspicious. Can you find an individual who will fill the bill more adequately?"

"I can't – yet. I must have time. All I can say is this. I have been investigating ever since the murder, and I am, I know, on the right track."

"I can't quite see the point of your no doubt very competent investigations," said Grovermuller, with some waspishness. "Carpenter is dead; I am your immediate chief and the new Lord Carpenter your employer. You have not done me the honour even, of confiding in me as to your investigations. We had on our staff a very efficient detective, who has proved his efficiency by saving you from the consequences of your own investigations. Apart from that, your obvious duty was to tell Scotland Yard your suspicions and what grounds – if any – you had for them."

"At least you are speaking straight," admitted Heflin. I will be equally so. I did not confide in you, because of a widespread feeling in the office, in which I share, that you were exceedingly glad to see the last of Carpenter, and exceedingly uninterested as to who did it." Heflin's voice was calm, but his hand was shaking with passion.

"I forgot, of course, that you were Carpenter's public pet, and apparently, private sneak," began Grovermuller with a contemptuous smile.

Heflin sprang to his feet. "You little time-serving cad!" he exclaimed. "Carpenter was fifty times the man you are. He was a genius. The sort of stuff that is moulded once in fifty years. You were only fit to lick his boots, and, by God, when he was alive, that's about what you did. And now – when he's dead – you think you're a brave little man to dance on his grave."

Grovermuller turned brick red. Heflin's face was within a

few inches of his own. He made a protesting noise, and then Lee Kum Tong, who had not said a word since his first remark, placed his hand firmly on Heflin's shoulder.

"The messenger of death will turn back when the mandarin repents, but the spoken word can never be recalled," he said soothingly. He looked at Grovermuller. "If any of us were forced to disclose the habits of our leisure hours, we might justly chew the bread of fury," he reminded him. Slowly but firmly he forced Heflin hack into his chair. "These personal compliments are interesting, and the exchange of them is usual among superior persons. None the less, they must eventually end, and when the cocoon has been unravelled, we come to the worm. Heflin, what did you find out that makes you think your Communist Cell has anything to do with Carpenter's murder?"

Heflin, pacified but still simmering, turned to Lee. "Oh, lots of things. First of all a general air of tension. Again and again I caught Carpenter's name in scraps of conversations. Once I heard Rogin say, 'Ought we to write the whole story to Moscow? Suppose the police got hold of it?' Anna, who is the most ruthless of them, laughed. 'Then, my dear Lef, we should swing. But why should the police get hold of it? Use your wits. Carpenter's murder will make us commissars. It's worth a risk.' That's all I could hear, but another day I overheard Lef say gloomily to Anna, 'The papers in that safe might hang us all. I wish to God we'd never taken the risk.'"

Lee's eyes opened in amazement. "This is surprising. And no doubt you tried to get the papers?"

"Yes," admitted Heflin, "and they caught me trying to get them." He turned to Grovermuller, his anger forgotten in his anxiety to drive his point home. "Don't you see that their attempt to kill me when they had realized I guessed their secret is a confession in itself? Murder breeds murder. That's why they took the risk.

That's why they are all in jail at this very moment."

"It is convincing. What do you propose to do?" Grovermuller asked distantly.

"Tell the police. Put the whole story in their hands. Get them to search the café and question the prisoners. Above all, make them release Venables."

"I don't agree with you. I advise you to say nothing to the police," said Grovermuller.

"You damn well would," sneered Heflin. "You want to see Venables stay in prison. I don't."

This time, Grovermuller was unaffected by Heflin's scorn. "You know Venables' writing, I suppose. Well, this is a message he gave me, just after he'd been arrested."

Heflin unfolded the paper. He read, in Charles's sprawling calligraphy, the following words:

Heflin has a wild theory that the Russians murdered Carpenter. For heaven's sake don't let him go and tell the police about this. They might believe him. He can tell them he was investigating Communist activities for the Mercury.
That's all they need know.
This is important. – C. V.

Puzzled, Heflin read the message again, then looked sulkily from Grovermuller to Lee. "I can't understand it," he said. "Is the fellow mad – or are we fools?" He thought a moment. "Well, Venables saved my life." He laughed cynically. "Fancy a journalist saving his news editor's life! Will anyone in Fleet Street believe it? But there it is. I suppose I must do as he asked."

He was silent for a moment; and then he looked sharply at Lee.

"Look here, your part in this needs a little explaining. What were you and Venables doing among these Communists? How did you get so friendly with them? How did you find they'd got hold of me? How did Venables find out why I was spying on them?"

Lee Kum Tong looked at Heflin with a deprecating and foolish grin. "Your questions require to answer them more wisdom than your humble friend possesses. I suggest that an explanation of all these matters should come from the learned Venables" – he paused and blinked owlishly – "when he is ready to give such explanations."

Heflin, who would have stood no nonsense from a European, questioned Lee no further. Such is the value of the fictitious reputation for inscrutability, built up for the Chinese by six generations of imaginative sinologues.

— V —

The discharge of his mission had possibly inspired Oakley with some respect for his client when, early next morning, he had another interview with him. At any rate, he was considerably more cordial.

"The gods are working in your favour, young man," he beamed. "Nowadays, it seems, they help those who refuse to help themselves."

Venables looked up, a vague trace of alarm on his face. "Oh, what's happened?"

"A very curious story," the solicitor replied. "Let me see now, where shall we begin? It starts, really, with an altogether unnecessary amount of agitation displayed by Miss Jameson's brother when you were arrested."

"Unnecessary? Of course I have no very high opinion of myself, but I think a little agitation is only right and proper."

Oakley laughed jovially. "Well, let us say excessive. The next thing is that the brother – Bysshe, you know – does not appear at the office. Inquiries are made and we find out that he's fled the country – there's no other word for it – simply gone, no one knows where. He rang up his sister, said goodbye, refused to say where he was going, and then – vanished."

At the climax of his story, Oakley was surprised to find Charles regarding him gloomily.

"Is this your good news?" he said.

Oakley looked surprised. "Really, I'm a little put out that you, a detective, don't see the implications at once. Still, a day or two of prison might blunt anyone's wits. Now here's the point. Bysshe Jameson has almost as much motive as you for murdering Carpenter. He has no alibi as to what he was doing when Carpenter was murdered. And now he's gone."

There was a baleful glint in Venables' monocle as he regarded Oakley. "I must be frightfully foolish," he said. "I'm sure you'll excuse me. You know when you first came in, I got the foolish idea you were attempting to get me *out* of prison. I didn't realize your job was to get people *into* prison."

Oakley flushed. "You are a very headstrong young man. If you would listen to me, instead of going off at half-cock, you would realize that the case against Bysshe is inherently unsound. *But*, and here is its value, it is of enormous importance in its psychological effect on a jury. In the hands of someone like Freeth-Jones it will turn the scales. In fact it will unsettle the police so much that they'll think twice before they proceed with the charge."

"I don't anticipate they will proceed with the charge in any case," answered Charles coldly. "I certainly dislike your suggestion and must ask that in no circumstances do you tell the police anything about Bysshe's disappearance. Let it be thought he's gone on holiday."

"My dear Mr. Venables," answered Oakley soothingly. Internally he vowed that this was the last time he had anything to do professionally with a murderer. "It is absolutely vital that they should be seized of these facts."

Charles got up. "I refuse to permit it," he said icily.

The solicitor's voice rose an octave. "I conceive it my duty to do so."

"Very well," answered his client. "Please accept my thanks for what you have done for me up to now. I will arrange for someone else to take on the thankless task of looking after my interests from this moment. Any steps you take hereafter of the nature indicated will be purely gratuitous. Naturally I cannot stop you if you choose to be a kind of legal busybody."

Outraged, the solicitor seized his dispatch case. "Busybody!" A crushing retort rose to his lips, never to be uttered, for at that moment Manciple entered.

"This is a private conference between solicitor and client," growled Oakley, his leashed indignation snapping at the first trouser leg that presented itself. "What do you want?"

Manciple bore the rebuke calmly. There was a slightly dazed look in his eyes and dumb amazement in his voice when he spoke.

"Mr. Venables, I have received a peremptory order from my superiors to release you without explanation. You may go as soon as you please."

A Deputy
Commissioner is
Astonished

GROVERMULLER TURNED IN HIS chair as Charles entered the room. "Good God!" he exclaimed with a perceptible start. "What are you doing here?"

"Don't look so alarmed," remonstrated the other. "I haven't escaped. I am released without a stain on my character, and the charge against me is withdrawn."

"Well, I'm damned."

"The correct response," pointed out Charles, "is 'Congratulations, but I always knew you were innocent.'"

"What made Manciple change his mind so suddenly?"

"Manciple has not changed his mind, that's the joke. Neither has the Deputy Commissioner nor the Commissioner. They all think I'm the perfect little murderer. But the powers that be have ordered them to release me, and here I am. Shocking miscarriage of British justice; not at all the clean potato in fact, but there it is and here am I."

Charles seated himself in an armchair. "Did you act on my note?"

Grovermuller glanced up. "Yes, it created a sensation. You see, as you suspected, Heflin is quite sure that his tame Russians murdered Carpenter. They certainly nearly murdered him."

"There is a difference," pointed out Charles. "In one case you have Carpenter sleeping peaceably in his office; and in the other case you have a spy in disguise burglariously nosing into their private and no doubt seditious papers. You can't say because they wanted to exterminate the spy they must have been guilty of exterminating Carpenter."

"Well, Heflin has the most touching faith in you that I have ever seen in a news editor. But it can't last. You must explain why you know the Russians to be harmless brigands. And you must also tell Manciple just how you came to investigate that cell. So far, Lee Kum Tong, whom I now regard as a very suspicious character, has been repelling all attempts to pump him."

Charles smiled. "I'll tell you everything, as the maiden said. Fetch Manciple and Heflin."

After Grovermuller had telephoned them, he was silent for a moment. When he spoke it was in an entirely different tone.

"Venables, I don't at all like this fabulously mysterious air of yours. I've supported you up to the present, but I don't propose to go much further." He swung round in his chair and looked keenly at the languid figure of his subordinate. He saw, or thought he saw, a faintly sinister detachment beneath the air of studied ease. He didn't like it. "I'll be perfectly frank. I don't believe you're really the slightest bit interested in finding Carpenter's murderer. I won't put it so high as to say that you are shielding anyone. I won't even insist that you are deliberately confusing the trails. But I've a strong feeling you're holding a watching brief for someone; and that your silences and equivocations are inspired."

Charles answered him seriously. "The preoccupation of a good detective should be the discovery of the truth. I admit that. You suggest I've some other interest in mind. Partly you're right. I swear that I am doing all I can to discover what happened to Carpenter on the night of his murder. I don't yet know who killed him. I hardly venture to guess. But I'll find out.

"Yet I must qualify that." He looked broodingly at the carpet. "This isn't my sole preoccupation. I've got another interest; a justifiable one, which I think you would approve of if I could tell you it. I *am* playing a hand for someone else."

"I thought so," said Grovermuller. "Let me tell you that when a young man plays Providence, he plays hell. There's something sinister in the air. I'm not such a fool that I can't tell what your release means. I don't like that sort of thing. I'm an English Liberal by breeding, and I hold to English conceptions of justice. If I get on the track of the influence that is hamstringing Manciple and his investigations – an influence which is shielding you – I'll go for it, tooth and nail. As an editor of a first rank national paper, I conceive it my duty to do so."

Venables shrugged his shoulders. "We must leave it like that, sir. In a short time I shall, I think, be able to tell you more. Meanwhile – well, thank you for the warning! Do I carry on with my duties here, as before?"

"Of course," answered Grovermuller sharply. "What I have been saying to you I have been saying as between man and man, not editor and subordinate."

Heflin and Manciple had been discussing trivialities, with a certain wariness, when Grovermuller rang up Manciple. They came in together, and Manciple refused to notice Charles.

To an American policeman it would no doubt seem all very natural, thought Charles, but Manciple looks as if the world had tumbled about his ears.

Grovermuller gave each of them a cigar and a comfortable chair. He metaphorically patted them into quiescence before he stopped discussing the weather and started on to business.

"You know already, Inspector, that Mr. Heflin, underneath his seemingly stolid exterior," began Grovermuller, "is as romantic as any of us. He was investigating the affairs of what is, I now understand, Shock Cell No. 63B when he was abducted and, as we all know, was saved by the good offices of the police, prompted by Mr. Venables."

"I know that. I don't know, but I suspect, that Mr. Heflin has not been completely frank with me."

Heflin coloured. "Well, I haven't. In this respect. It was true that, as I told you, I have been trying to find what Communism was planning in this country. But over and above that I suspected a revolutionary motive inspired Carpenter's death. I was on the track of that. I firmly believe that it was because they knew this that they attempted to make away with me."

"Indeed," snapped Manciple, "and why did you not disclose this? Mr. Grovermuller, I cannot believe you approved of this!"

"I did," said the Editor calmly. "When you arrested Mr. Venables, he left me a message to restrain Heflin from putting his theory – for it is only a theory – to the police. I showed it to him and we have restrained him."

There was sullen rage in the eyes of the detective as he turned them on Venables, who was studying his fingernails with an air of detachment. "This is outrageous!" he said. "Need I remind educated men that it is the duty of the citizen to help the law against the lawbreaker? Do you realize the attitude you three have taken up; not in this case only, but generally? Be frank with me. If there is any personal bias in this, I am prepared to throw up the case tomorrow rather than let the Yard down. But this cannot go on."

Manciple relapsed into silence and glared up at Grovermuller.

Grovermuller leaned back in his chair. "I think you're completely justified, Inspector. I expected something stronger.

Venables, I think it is up to you to defend yourself and us."

"Yes, of course." Charles turned to Manciple. "You are complaining of my conduct generally, but we are here to discuss a specific case. Let's stick to that for the moment." Manciple nodded. "Mr. Grovermuller will confirm that the message was not to be acted upon till I had been charged. Once I had been charged, that is, once you were certain I was the murderer, your investigations were ended. What interest could it be to you that Heflin had certain colourable suspicions about some Russians?"

The Inspector gave a species of snort. "Very logical. But do you suggest that was the real reason for your message?"

"Oh no. I'm coming to that. As it happens I have first-hand information about this Cell which makes Heflin's mere suspicions superfluous. But what was the use of putting it forward while I was in custody? Would it have been taken seriously? Above all, and with all modesty, could I be sure the information would be rightly interpreted as long as I was *hors de combat?*"

The detective's agreement was grudging. "Give us your information. That's the test."

"Certainly. I collected it from my office on the way up, where I had left it in anticipation, I must confess, of my arrest. It was very nice of you to overlook it when you searched my room. But I flatter myself the hiding place was ingenious."

"You have all the resource of a professional criminal," admitted Manciple, extending his hands for the document.

"Will you read it out?" asked Venables. "Kindly note that it is a carbon copy of a letter addressed by Rogin to his superior in Russia. It is dated, and the copy has been initialled."

Heflin laughed. "So that's why I couldn't find anything compromising? You had been there before—"

"Listen to this," interrupted Manciple, with his first trace of excitement. "After a preamble about the diligence of his Cell,

Rogin says:

"'The greatest blow in the history of the U.S.S.R. has been struck at the counter-revolutionary movement. The Great Enemy in England has been eliminated.

"'Full details will be given by Comrade Rogin on his return to Russia. Meanwhile it may be stated that the liquidation was performed by Comrade Ferenov at 12.45 a.m., using the private way into C.'s suite. No trace was left of the operation; and the police in no way suspect the activities of this Cell or the influence of the movement. The effect in this country has been profound. The counter-revolutionary movement has been deprived of its spearhead. It is in the process of collapse...'"

Manciple looked up with startled eyes. "Mr. Venables," he said gravely, "you have not treated us fairly. Why did you not show us this before?"

Charles leaned over and secured the paper. "I thought this would amuse you. But of course you don't take it seriously?" With a quick movement he folded it and placed it in his pocket.

"I'll have that, if you please, Mr. Venables," said Manciple warningly.

Charles grinned. "No – if you did you might act on it." He swept the astonished three with a cheerful smile. "I'll hang on to it. It really doesn't signify much. And now I must be off."

Manciple gave a strangled groan. "This is too much. I'll go straight to the Commissioner and see what can be done. He's just playing with us. Whether that letter is genuine or faked, which I shouldn't put beyond him, he's obstructing us in either event."

Charles was nowhere to be found. Pacing wildly the green and cool recesses of Kensington Gardens, he was at grips with a problem which seemed, on the face of it, starkly impossible.

"Am I going mad?" he asked a squirrel, who regarded him

soulfully, interrupted in the act of saving up a nut for a rainy day. "How can one have several sets of clues, pointing in different directions?"

The squirrel gave the earth above the nut a final pat, and rolled off like a mechanical toy. "They forget where they've hidden them when the winter comes," he reflected vaguely. "One has, of course, to allow for the squirrel element in human beings. We all perform some clearly purposive act of preparation, and then never take advantage of it. Is that the explanation?"

Defeated and beaten, he crawled into his bed and slept the sleep of physical exhaustion and mental irritation – a heavy sleep riddled with unending dreams. He awoke still tired, and turned up at the *Mercury* office with a ferocious scowl that blasted the questioner in his tracks. Even Miranda hesitated when she came into his room and found him, his chair tilted back, regarding with melancholy hate the carcass of a fowl, whose post-mortem the poultry expert had obviously procrastinated until it was too late.

"I know what you are going to ask me. I don't know." Charles jumped up savagely. "Bysshe is capable of any act of folly. Have the police been questioning you?"

"No. I've told everyone he's gone on holiday. We've got away with it so far. But sooner or later they're bound to find out."

"Of course." Charles looked at her sullenly, "Do you know where he is?"

"No. I haven't the slightest idea. There's not been a word from him. I'm afraid – and there's that awful feeling of helplessness." Her air of gay assurance, so habitual, was gone. She looked tired and worried. "Charles, is there anything that can be done?"

"Very little, if he really did do it. Everything, if he didn't."

Miranda shuddered. "I feel like one of those people in Greek Tragedy, harried by the Furies for some unconscious crime.

Horrors and humiliations seem to follow one another; and all the time it seems to me that *I* am the cause."

"For God's sake, pull yourself together, Miranda," he said abruptly. "It's the first time since I've ever known you that you've talked like a tragedy queen. If you do that once again, you'll have to go away on holiday, where if you can't help, at least you won't be a nuisance."

"Sorry." She took a cigarette from a case and lit it with trembling fingers. "Probably all I need is a drink. Let's get back to our last sensible conversation. What can I do, and what are you doing?"

"You must go on doing nothing. In other words, carry on just as if nothing has happened. As for me," he reflected, "I can't do the impossible. I am doing my damnedest, that's all."

"Oh, I know. Of course we are all doing that. But what are you *really* doing? Are you just rushing round making a useful noise, or do you *know* something?" Charles turned a shade whiter. "You want to know the truth? I'm doing the same as the police are; trying to find if Bysshe is guilty or not. I've got to be certain of that before I can help him."

Miranda, her eyes on his face, thought for a moment. "I see," she said at last. "I suppose that settles it." There was a trace of scorn in her voice. "I had never thought of that. Of course this is only a case from the notebook of Charles Venables, Investigator, isn't it?"

"Don't be deliberately unfair, Miranda!"

"Very well," she said coldly, "I will agree that you have some personal interest in the case. Perhaps the following fact will increase it. If Bysshe doesn't get out of this trouble, I shall never see you again."

"You don't realize what you are saying," he said shortly.

"I realize perfectly. Also I mean it; as you probably know me well enough to realize."

Charles looked at the bright, clear eyes and the cleanly-modelled cheekbones over which the skin now seemed tightly drawn. Miranda stared at him defiantly, a faint flush in her cheeks.

"I see," he said slowly. "You evidently don't give me credit for any abstract beliefs in justice and the law. A woman can forgive a man anything but morality." He spoke quietly, as if musing to himself. "Perhaps they're right. As soon as one hears of oneself talking about right and wrong, one overhears what sounds terribly like a prig. Well, of course I've no option. I'll fight for Bysshe, tooth and nail!"

With all the soothing generosity of a woman who has attained her object, Miranda took his hand. "Charles, you don't know what it means to me. I know you can do it."

He smiled ruefully. "Siren! Well, this will probably be the last case in the notebook of Charles Venables, Criminal Investigator, but it will be a lurid one. As for you, my girl, remember the lady and the gloves. She threw them among the lions, you remember, and challenged the knight to jump in and fetch them. He got them, and slapped her in the face with them before handing them back."

Miranda, her chin cupped on her hand, sighed. "If it were only my gloves..."

Left alone, Charles scribbled idly on the blotting-paper in front of him with an air of profound dejection. He was engaged in this aimless occupation when the phone bell rang.

"You, sir!" he answered in surprise. "I am afraid I haven't thanked you for what you did for me – oh, you want to explain? – I take it that means you feel the situation is now completely in hand? – May I congratulate you? – I shall be round in a few minutes."

Charles hung up his receiver. Wearily he rose to his feet and put on his hat and coat.

— II —

With that sudden reversal of opinion which is an engaging trait of democracy, England had turned pacifist almost overnight. The process is known as reaction, vacillation, or the swing of the pendulum, according to political circumstances. The true inner history of that change-over is still to be written in the memoirs of indiscreet greatness shelved in its prime of power.

So far as it affects the story of Carpenter's death, that historic story need only be briefly recorded. It would be fair to say that the real origin of the desire for war was that Plenty which in the latter thirties threatened to kill civilization of a surfeit. Wave upon wave of surplus commodities beggared nations and distracted statesmen.

In a world groaning from these diseases of its economic organism, suddenly emerged Russia. Russia, too, flung her abounding overplus upon a capitalistic world, behind the secure walls of her Twelve Year Plan. Stalin and his like had given place to rulers gentler in political methods, but though the G.P.U. was dead, Russia's international trading was as ruthless. Not only grain (though that was bitter enough), but motor cars and mangles, pickaxes and pants, flowed from the enormous factories of Siberia and the Ukraine.

Carpenter's campaign, therefore, found fuel and kindling ready at hand. When the belly pinches, one looks for an idol to pelt. Here was one.

The Premier, in those days, showed that there is something to be said for the art of politics – in a democracy. Deeply a pacifist at heart, this was no time to show it. Had he turned in his tracks and faced the mob, he would have gone down, never to rise again. Instead, keeping always in front, he yet contrived to retard the rush insensibly, pressing back on his leaders, who, in their turn, restrained the ardours of the main pack. At last he brought it to a standstill and, still pressing steadily, got it on the run in the opposite direction.

Even so, it was doubtful if he would have succeeded but for his brilliant policy. The idea came to him, like most of his ideas, when he was sitting in a hot bath. He rarely read from one year's end to another, except the Bible (for quotations in speeches to his Scottish constituents), but he happened then to be reading the women's page of the *Mercury*, where a psychologist was discussing the value of "Substitution" in dealing with naughty children.

Hurriedly flinging on a dressing-gown, he descended and dictated a memorandum outlining his famous policy. This was nothing less than a "bloodless war" with Russia. Instead of fighting her on a battlefield, we were to engage her economically, with complete amity and friendship. Every week the comparative trade returns were to be broadcast, every week Government would plan fresh ways of assisting the British trader to sell more to Russia than we were buying from her.

The success of the idea was instantaneous. Fundamentally it was our economic conscience that was outraged by Russia, and this appeased it. Also it had all the sporting element of a game. Put over by the brilliantly persuasive advocacy of Affiliated Periodicals, with the *Mercury* as banner-bearer, the scheme went across "big." First the Anglo-Russian Treaty governing diplomatic relations and guaranteeing frontiers went through, then a series of trade treaties of unprecedented scope. The national rejoicing when visible exports to Russia were larger than visible imports, although the latter figure had trebled, is a matter of history.

One circumstance of that affair bearing directly on the Carpenter murder has, however, never been set down. Perhaps when the Deputy Commissioner writes his memoirs. But so far he has been admirably discreet.

Sanger, Prime Minister of England, his iron-grey hair liberally silvered and his features more careworn than ever, sat at his desk in Downing Street with an expression of almost childish shame on his face.

Manciple, Charles, and the Deputy Commissioner had ploughed their way through the November slush of '39 from Scotland Yard. The Prime Minister himself met them in the hall and ushered them into a sitting room.

"I have an apology to make, a deep apology," began the Premier, the odd concern deepening on his face. "I have put the fate of a nation before the bringing of a criminal to justice. I have deliberately hampered your investigations into Lord Carpenter's murder."

Manciple and his immediate chief exchanged a quick look. A faint apprehension clouded Manciple's eyes. Had the strain of the last few days been too much for the old man?

The Premier studied his nails for a moment. Then he spoke with difficulty. "On the evening of Lord Carpenter's death I had, as you know, an interview with him. I endeavoured to reason with him – even to threaten him. It was useless."

The Premier again looked at his auditors. "So much you know," he said more clearly. "Now I come to the recital of facts of which the police have been unaware. I paid a second visit that night to Carpenter, coming through the private entrance, of whose existence I knew. I told my private secretary before I went that I was determined by whatever means to end Carpenter's campaign." The Premier, living again the scene, lowered his voice. "Many ideas were in my mind at the time. The offer of a bribe in the form of the highest honour in my gift; the threat of prosecution for sedition, by invoking a long-forgotten statute the Attorney-General had discovered.

"None of these was necessary. Carpenter, when I entered his room and switched on the light, was beyond the reach of argument or force. He had been foully murdered."

An involuntary exclamation came from Manciple's lips, but he made no comment. The Premier continued.

"The danger of my position struck me forcibly. Although I felt – I confess it frankly – all the loathing for Carpenter one might feel for a snake of dangerous venom, it would have been against my principles to choose a violent means of ending his existence. To do so would have been to enact the ancient fallacy that is the cause of every war. But I realized that suspicion would inevitably fall on me. Here was Carpenter murdered – for even to me the absence of a weapon from the wound made murder certain. Here was I – having previously declared my readiness to stop at nothing to end Carpenter's campaign. Resignation, an inquiry, suspicion, criticism, an unpleasant scandal though my innocence would be proved ultimately, it would be too late. My administration – the only administration capable of preserving peace – would be weakened – might even fall.

"I shall never regret the decision I made – a decision to conceal everything. I rang up my oldest friend, Sir Colin Vansteen, and told him my story. Although he supported me, he insisted that in common justice the police must know of the murder as soon as possible, before the trail was cold. It was his idea to invent a fictitious telephone call. Not only would it serve the purpose of allowing him to inform the police, but it would give him an excuse for keeping in close contact with the case and holding a watching brief for me."

The Premier ended. A gesture of his hand invited comment.

Manciple spoke. "I'm sure I needn't say this has seriously hampered our investigations. You've laid enough false trails, sir, to confuse much abler wits than mine."

"I fully realize that. I am afraid the worst is not quite told. Just as I was leaving, Mr. Venables, as I ultimately found was his name, came into the room." A faint smile flickered on Sanger's face. "He congratulated me on a very neat job and asked me why on earth I had loitered on the spot after doing it. There was nothing I could do except take him into my confidence. He agreed, I am grateful to say, entirely with my point of view. He very methodically tidied after me, even wiping my fingerprints off the handle of the telephone receiver."

"And like a blithering idiot, leaving my own fingerprints on the knife while pottering round," interjected Charles.

"Rather thin!" commented Manciple, looking at Charles with critical eyes. "It seems to me, now I know the facts, far more likely that you put your prints there to confuse a hard-working officer of the law. They were so beautifully clear and distinct, and carefully placed over one of the only two spots of blood on the upper half of the blade."

A cheerful smile was Charles's only answer.

"When you arrested Mr. Venables," continued the Premier, "owing to his promise to me, he refused to speak. I felt I could not allow him to be penalized. I consulted with my colleagues, and ordered his release."

The Premier was silent. The Deputy Commissioner drew a deep breath. "This is the most amazing story I have ever heard," he said. "I can still barely credit that you, sir, of all people, and Sir Colin, too, conspired together to conceal vital facts—"

The Premier raised his hand for silence. His voice was sonorous with that golden clarity that convinced and charmed as long as the ear was in its spell. "Mr. Commissioner, Sir Colin and I are old friends – and old men. Our careers are behind us – we have warmed both hands before the fire of life and now are ready to depart. Yet still – call it sentiment if you will – we share a hope and a creed that has been in full measure the mainspring of our lives. Providence has seen fit to trust me with the destiny of this nation – so far as man's fumbling and uncertain gestures can affect a destiny that draws its power from the stream of history. When one realizes that, to think what is wise and prudent seems an empty thing. In the last crisis we should meet before we left the stage of life, we acted as we thought right, nor reflected whether our actions were dignified or personally creditable."

The charm of the man, acknowledged by millions, was compelling. Even Manciple's stolid face reflected for a moment the emotional idealism which had brought Sanger leadership and office.

"Well, well, you must pardon me," said the Premier suddenly in the silence that followed, and his rare smile lit his care-worn face. "I am talking like a statesman instead of a human being, as my friend the realistic Chancellor of the Exchequer sometimes reminds me. Now, as you will see, I have a very special interest in this case, and I want you, if you will, Inspector, to update me on developments."

A Young Lady
is in Love

"SO THAT'S THE POSITION at the moment," concluded Manciple.

The Premier, who had asked for news of the progress of the case as an act of politeness, came out of his coma with a start. Never a good listener, he had drifted worlds away while Manciple conscientiously made clear every detail of his investigations.

"Excellent," murmured the Premier, blinking his heavy-lidded eyes. "Excellent."

Manciple, who had emphasized his complete bewilderment, bridled, scenting irony.

Venables smoothed the troubled waters. "I honestly don't see how anyone could get further than the Inspector has done."

"Exactly," boomed the Premier, taking the point. "Don't despair. Light comes when the night is at its darkest. Your work has been excellent – excellent."

"Thank you, sir," Manciple said simply. "But if I may say so, Mr. Venables' attitude still puzzles me. Now I know the true story, I quite see why he acted as he did over the fingerprint and his arrest. But this Russian business! Why is Mr. Venables keeping back an incriminating document? For now we know the truth, it seems on the face of it, more incriminating than ever!"

"Yes, Mr. Venables," said Sanger with a trace of severity, wondering vaguely what the "Russian business" was about. Please be perfectly frank with Inspector Manciple now."

Charles drew the document out of his pocket. "I'll read it out again," he said, "and you must see what you make of it."

The Premier bent forward. In Charles's cool tones the extraordinary confession fell starkly on their ears. At the end Charles looked up.

"This is the second time you have heard it, Manciple. What do you make of it?" The Inspector grunted. "If it's true, it's final."

"You, sir?" he asked the Deputy Commissioner.

"I agree with the Inspector." He looked at Sanger shrewdly. "But the Premier might have something to say. An awkward business coming on top of our sudden friendship for Russia."

Sanger smiled faintly. "Don't jump to conclusions. I shall never disturb the even functioning of the law again. Now, Venables, was this the document you had in mind when you said you wanted to burgle an East End café, and would I arrange for the police to look the other way?"

Charles grinned cheerfully.

Sanger shot an apologetic look at the Deputy Commissioner. "I went over your head there, too. Dear, dear, I'm afraid you have a very low opinion of me." He turned suddenly on Charles. "And why, Mr. Venables, having found this important document, to obtain which I suborned the law, did you not bring it to me at once?"

"I reserve my defence, sir," said Charles calmly.

"Indeed," growled the Premier. "Supposing I tell you what your defence was? With the modesty that seems to be a conspicuous feature of your make-up, you decided on your own initiative that the document might be embarrassing. You decided that what the eye does not see the heart does not grieve over. You supposed, in fact, that I could not be trusted with this precious discovery of yours."

"You are not putting my defence in the best light," Charles reminded him.

"Perhaps not. That is the light I look at it in. Well, strange as it may seem, I am perfectly capable of dealing with the situation." With a triumphant smile he rang the bell on his desk. "Confidential file R93," he said to the quiet-footed secretary who answered it. The Premier chuckled to himself while the file was brought.

"Now," he said, "here is a letter received from the Russian Commissar for Foreign Affairs. Stripped of its verbiage, it states that they have received a communication from one of their Cells in London, which fills them with horror and astonishment. They completely repudiate the action for which their approval is invoked and will give us every support in bringing the criminals to justice. They then enclose a copy of the document which Mr. Venables has been secreting for the last few days."

Sanger's face beamed with a child-like joy as he closed the file. "I hope this will be a lesson to you not to do other people's thinking for them."

"Pardon the suggestion," said Manciple, "but wouldn't it be possible for the Russians to put these people up to killing Carpenter, and then throw them to the lions to prevent the murder ever coming home to them?"

The Premier's face froze suddenly and his eyes became inscrutable. "I am a statesman, not a police detective," Sanger reminded him.

There was silence for a moment. It was the Premier who spoke at last. "See Rogin in prison tomorrow," he said to Manciple, "and charge him with the murder of Lord Carpenter. I wash my hands of this affair. No more interruptions from now on!"

"I said I would reserve my defence," interrupted Charles suddenly. "Now I will give it. I don't think the Russian crowd are any more guilty of the murder than I am. I don't think this document will do anything but confuse all our minds, and that's why I have been reluctant to produce it till the last possible moment."

"Now, now, you are asking us to swallow a lot," protested Manciple.

"I don't think so," answered Charles. "It all seems to me very natural. Carpenter is murdered. The murderer cannot be found. The murder of Carpenter removes Russia's greatest enemy in this country. How natural for a Communist group of agitators, led by a young man almost insane with ambition – I'll answer for that definition of Rogin – to try and claim the credit for it! You see their superior authorities believed them and so if there had been any credit going Rogin would have got it. They could hardly be expected to see that all the credit they would get would be a kick in the pants?"

"It is plausible," admitted Manciple after a moment's thought, "but less plausible than the theory of their guilt."

"I'm not asking you to take my word for it," Charles pointed out. "I'm only warning you so that you don't commit yourself by charging them. Tell them this document has come into your hands, and ask for their explanation. If they tell the truth, it will be the same explanation as mine, and quite probably, as soon as they are in real danger, they will all find perfectly good alibis."

The Deputy Commissioner nodded. "That seems fair," he admitted.

The Premier reserved the archest look of which his heavy North Country face was capable as he bade "Goodbye" to Charles. "You are a very dangerous young man," he said, "as well as a very acute one – I shall always thank my stars that I met you, and no one else, on that night."

The three walked along Downing Street for a short period, during which nothing was said. At last Manciple spoke. "So that's how the country is governed," he said at last, in a voice devoid of bitterness or approval.

— II —

"I was wondering when you would speak to me," Miss Hubbard said coolly. "I expected you to do it long before."

Charles was taken aback, not by the remark, obvious enough, or even the tone, though that was a little surprising, but the type of person who made it.

Ever since the beginning of the case, he had mentally pigeon-holed Miss Hubbard of the Advertising Department, Carpenter's new Delilah, as "a tow-headed little chit," something fair and kittenish. For this reason he had left any cross-examination in the air until he had more time. After all, nothing was less likely than that a brainless young beggar-maid should have interfered with the serious affairs of Cophetua.

Nothing seemed less likely − till he met the beggar-maid. Tow-headed was perhaps correct, although a coiffeur would have called her a chromium blonde. But "little chit" − no, this was something different! There was character in every line of Miss Hubbard's slim young body − in the firm resolute chin, the straight nose, and the crisp whorls of her shell pink ears. Charles paid willing homage to her beauty, but when he met her bright blue eyes, he revised his interpretation of the relation between Carpenter and Miss Hubbard. No defenceless maiden, pounced upon by a brutal employer, had eyes with quite that hard and merciless glitter. Carpenter had been dexterously hunted and scientifically trapped, if Charles knew anything of character.

Miss Hubbard, smiling sweetly, read his surprise in his eyes, and the faintly sardonic curl in her lips signalled that *she* knew *he* knew.

"Well," said Miss Hubbard, helping herself to a cigarette, "what does the big brutal detective want to ask the maiden all forlorn?"

Several lines of attack passed through Charles's mind. "I suppose you didn't love Carpenter?" he said, choosing direct action.

"How dare you!" said Miss Hubbard, her cheeks flushing. "Do you *have* to be a cad to be a detective?" She stubbed her cigarette angrily on the table.

Wordlessly Charles passed the matches. Miss Hubbard flung the box violently on the floor. There was a dead silence for a minute, at the end of which Charles remarked coolly, "A woman of your intelligence must find it boring to have to act like a woman without it."

The girl rose, walked to the window, and then gently hummed the tune of a popular song. "I do occasionally," she admitted at the end. "At the same time I get a great deal of amusement out of doing it well."

"No doubt. But is it necessary now? I already realize that I shall be able to get nothing out of you that you do not wish me to know. Why not be frank about the rest?"

"Unanswerable," admitted Miss Hubbard. "Then here's the truth. I didn't, of course, love Carpenter. At the same time I liked and admired him. Frankly, however, it was his wealth and power that appealed to me most."

"And what appealed to him in you?" asked Charles gravely.

"I gathered it was my foolishness and innocence. Shall we call it lack of experience?" said Miss Hubbard demurely. "It refreshed him to have to deal with someone who thought of nothing but clothes and candies and kisses."

"Did Carpenter ever seem afraid of anyone when you knew him?"

"If you mean afraid of physical violence, no. I never knew anyone more serenely self-confident."

"When did you last see him?"

"Twelve hours before his murder."

"Never again?"

She shook her head solemnly. "No, never again."

Charles was silent for a moment. Then he looked her straight in the eye. "I suppose you know that suspicion points to someone very fond of you?" He saw her lips slowly whiten.

"No, I didn't," she said. "Is it true?"

He nodded.

"But I don't understand it. I thought he was quite cleared. What was it?"

Charles looked at her anxiously. "Can't you guess?"

"Is it – the bonds?"

Something in his eyes made her realize that she had illuminated him unexpectedly. She paused, and tried to read his face.

"The bonds," he repeated slowly. "So you are in love with Jerningham."

She strove to regain her footing. "Why not? Why do you say it like that?"

"Why not, indeed. He is just the type."

Her eyes flashed with genuine anger. "Frank is damned decent – too decent. So you think he's soft!"

"I don't think he's soft. But perhaps he clings a little." Charles made a gesture in the air. "You may have a little difficulty in removing him."

"That woman! Why, she's forty-five if she's a day."

"The one fatal mistake for a clever young lady, or man for

that matter, is to underrate one's opponent. Lady Carpenter is a handsome woman with tremendous character."

"You know her?" said Miss Hubbard with a note of eagerness. "What is she really like?"

Charles gave a brief description.

She considered for a moment with half-closed eyes. "Yes – I was afraid it was like that. She has wealth and position, I haven't – but I'm young. She's handsome and impressive – but I'm young." She looked at Charles defiantly. "So far we're equal. But she dominates him, and I can give him the impression he dominates me." She smiled resourcefully. "No man likes to feel like a gigolo."

"I think you'll get your man," said Charles reflectively. "Do you really want him when you've got him?"

She laughed with infinite self-confidence. "It's the first time in my life I really wanted anything," she confessed. "Now tell me – is he really safe?"

"Quite safe," said Charles gravely. "He's acted very foolishly, and might have got into serious trouble, but everything's all right now."

Satisfied, her restless mind turned to another problem. "Whom had you in mind when you said someone who is very fond of you?"

Charles hesitated before he answered. "Your father," he said at last.

Miss Hubbard burst into laughter. "My father – that old stick. What a priceless idea! Did you picture him taking paternal vengeance on the debaucher of his innocent offspring? My poor man, speak to Father, and ask him what he thinks of me! Why, he believes I went to the dogs long ago, and if it weren't for Mother, he wouldn't have me in the house! It's much more likely that he warned Carpenter against me." She thought a moment, and then asked with a trace of wariness, "Had you any evidence against him?"

Charles smiled. "None – now."

They parted with ironic expressions of mutual respect. But at the door Miss Hubbard hesitated as if a thought had struck her. "Did you really suspect my father?" she asked, "or did you guess about Jerningham?"

"My dear young lady," protested Charles vaguely, "I am incapable of duplicity."

— III —

"I was right about my Russians," said Charles. "They all went queer when they found the police knew everything, and managed to produce perfectly good alibis, much to Manciple's disgust. They are being shipped back to Russia, where the authorities propose to imprison them, *pour encourager les autres*, no doubt. Comrade Perkins, however, has proved his British citizenship and is being dealt with here for his part in the assault on Heflin."

"And what does all this mean?" asked Miranda.

"Oh, it means everything is much simpler than it was."

Miranda slammed the lid on her portable typewriter. "Simple!" she exclaimed ironically.

"Everybody is gradually being eliminated," explained Charles. "The fewer the suspects the greater the simplicity. Except," added he, "in the present case, when you have none left."

"Thanks," said Miranda in a decisive tone. "You do this persiflage admirably. Now will you start and tell me the truth. For instance, what do the police think?"

"As thus. One Viscount Carpenter is done to death between 12.30 and 1 a.m. He was last seen alive by his wife at 12.30 a.m. He was first seen dead by the Prime Minister at 1 a.m."

"What's that?" exclaimed Miranda. "Did you say the Prime Minister?"

"Er, yes," answered Charles guiltily, and with fictitious brightness. "I don't think I mentioned that before. He called in on the corpse at 1 a.m. I was the next visitor at 1.15 a.m. approx."

"No doubt you did mention it," said Miranda ironically, "but it must have slipped my memory. It explains your rather mysterious goings-on, which I may say, young man, I have carefully noted, even if I have not mentioned them."

"Yes, you now perceive the motive. Shady but not ignoble. Do you mind my not having told you?"

"Not a bit!" answered Miranda hastily – perhaps too hastily.

"Good. Now the police admit the possibility of the 12.30 a.m. part being wrong. Lady Carpenter may after all have done the deed herself. They can only say it is unlikely, having regard to all the circumstances. So, Manciple tells me, he is betting on that blank half an hour."

"Has he told you the truth?"

"Yes," said Charles. "He's been completely frank with me. I can't seem to put his back up now, like I used to."

"Do you try?" asked Miranda quickly.

"Yes," confessed Charles.

"I see," she said with scorn. "Masculine logic! You are spying on him, yet because you feel ashamed of it, you want to make him sufficiently antagonistic not to tell you anything worthwhile."

"It doesn't sound very noble put like that," he admitted miserably.

"'Be bloody, bold and resolute.' You're on my side? Then for the Lord's sake make a job of it!"

Charles surveyed the roof tops of Fleet Street unhappily with his monocle. "Your word is law, Lady Macbeth!"

"Then prove it by coming to the point you've been avoiding so brilliantly for the last quarter of an hour. What do the police know about that blank half an hour?"

Charles turned slowly. "You have probably guessed," he said wearily.

Her lips whitened as she stared at him. "Bysshe?"

He nodded. "I'm afraid so. Bysshe was seen coming from the Chief's suite, looking white and shaken. And it had gone twelve-thirty some time then – and it wasn't yet one o'clock!"

Miranda slowly got a grip on herself. "I see," she said slowly. "But is there no one else? Haven't you even a possibility on your list?"

"I have. I would have called him a probability. Until your brother ran away."

"Oh, don't you understand he's capable of doing anything – anything, however mad? It's our father's temperament – who gave us our mad names and mad ways of thinking – but it's double-distilled in him. You can't judge him by ordinary standards. He's quite capable of doing it merely to puzzle the police, out of sheer devilment."

Charles was silent. Miranda turned away with a gesture of despair. "You're quite right. There's no need to answer me. Directly I've said it I realize how weak it sounds. It's only what I try to make myself believe."

"Did you know he'd written to Grovermuller?"

"No!"

"A mad letter – a fatal letter," said Charles quietly. "And Grovermuller has shown it to the police."

"Then if they find him–"

He nodded. "I should think that tomorrow morning a warrant for his arrest will be taken out."

— IV —

Inspector Manciple delivered himself of a pronouncement. He was not much given to them, and P.C. Arbuthnot harkened to it and treasured it up as if he had travelled toilsomely to obtain it from the frenzied lips of the Delphic Pythoness.

"Nothing," said Manciple, "is simpler than a murder case – in essence. If there are complications, they are not the murderer's. They are the result of sheer bad luck."

"Yes, sir," agreed the hatchet-faced young detective. He memorized the words and the tone. He would use them himself later, discoursing on crime in the billiard-room of his rifle club.

"The really intelligent murderer," went on Manciple, "belongs only to detective novels, which I rarely read. Nobody fakes alibis in a murder. Those are utilized entirely by the professional safe-breaker. Your murderer goes off the boil some day, and nips in and cuts Thomas's throat when nobody is aroused, or else he drops a screw of weed-killer into Laura's soup while Laura is picking up her napkin. Strip any murder case of its essentials, and you get something simple like that. The trouble – our trouble – occurs when somebody else has been heard quarrelling with Thomas a minute or two before, or when Laura has been heard to swear that she'll make away with herself one of these days, that she will."

"I see what you mean, sir. The Chief's wife seeing him, and Mr. Venables' fingerprint, and the rest."

"Sheer bad luck," repeated Manciple. "Bysshe Jameson nipped in when no one was around and stabbed Carpenter. That's all there is in it."

"What about the motive, sir?" asked Arbuthnot, not in any spirit of criticism, but to give his superior the cue for further explanation.

"Potty, of course. Not Broadmoor potty, but what you and I would regard as potty. Vegetarianism and nudism and such like. You're always getting political assassinations, aren't you? Well, Jameson is just the type that always does that sort of assassination. Generally a student or youngster of some sort."

"I heard, sir," said his junior diffidently, "that his sister and Carpenter were a bit thick, so to speak. Don't you think he might have felt–"

"What you mean," said Manciple kindly, "is that in his position, you might have gone round and bashed Carpenter's face in – so why mightn't he have done the same a bit more drastically?"

"Just what I mean," agreed Arbuthnot triumphantly.

"Which shows," retorted Manciple with sudden acidity, "that you're still a bloody young fool. You start giving your own motives to a murderer, and you'll get into a fine tangle. You've heard about Jameson; you've read about him in the depositions; you've seen him. Don't you know a man of that way of thinking believes a woman's as much right to choose her friends as a man? A fine fool you'd look when he went into the witness box, and everyone would see that the motive you'd put forward couldn't affect him in the slightest! Don't be so old-fashioned, Arbuthnot," he ended severely.

"Not," added Manciple slowly, "that there may not be something of the Jocasta complex in it after all."

Arbuthnot nodded solemnly. He, too, had read Freud and Jung at the instance of his Chief, and he had never quite got over being recommended, as a textbook, the kind of thing he always understood the police were supposed to seize. Life was very puzzling for a young detective.

He contented himself by examining once more the damning piece of evidence which a search of Jameson's rooms had revealed. There was a shirt and a coat pitifully thrust into a corner, and carefully washed. Needless to say the blood was still traceable. The coat, the landlady was almost sure, belonged to the suit he was wearing on the day of the murder.

"A light grey it was," Mrs. Twemlow explained, "and if that is the only light grey he has, why that would be the suit because I remember thinking how well it reely suited him. That was on the Monday, and him not having had a grey suit before, leastways as I'd noticed, I said joking like when he came down..."

Manciple abruptly dammed the tide. "Have you any suspicion where he is at the present moment?"

"How do you mean suspicion?" asked Mrs. Twemlow indignantly, flipping back a wandering lock of hair from her nose with a vicious bang.

"Did he give you any hint before he went? Did you see any letters going to a foreign address a little time before he went?"

"Do you think I spy on my young gentlemen's comings and goings?"

"Did he tell you how long he would be away?"

"He gave me a month's money, and said if he were not back in three weeks, or if I didn't hear from him in that time, to let the rooms and send his stuff to his sister's. Poor gentleman, if he'd known police would have come busting in and turning my rooms topsy-turvy!" exclaimed Mrs. Twemlow.

"Thank you, Mrs. Twemlow," said Manciple firmly, "we shan't need any further help now."

"He seems to have been burning something in here," interjected Arbuthnot, as she left the room reluctantly.

Manciple joined him on his knees before the fireplace.

"What a fool," exclaimed the Inspector gleefully. "He simply set fire to this, and because it blazed and looked like a heap of ashes he thought he had destroyed it. Carefully now, Arbuthnot. Turn your head on one side, or you may breathe on it. There we are. Shove it in this cigar box of his. It looks like the remains of a notebook."

Manciple carefully prised apart two scorched leaves. "My God!" he exclaimed.

The Accused
is Unhelpful

"You've seen the letter to Mr. Grovermuller from Jameson?" said the Deputy Commissioner to his Chief interrogatively.

"I have. He said, if I remember rightly, that he couldn't stand it any longer and was going away for good. I don't know what right Grovermuller had to hold up the letter," growled the Chief, "but anyway it's not very decisive. A good defending counsel could make it mean nothing except that he was overworked."

The Deputy Commissioner produced a cigar box with a triumphant smile. "This will hang him all right, sir," he said. "It's a diary which he didn't succeed in burning. I've copied out relevant fragments with our reconstruction of obliterated words. Here's an entry two days before the murder."

Pinned on a board were the enlarged photo prints of the damning pages, with a typewritten transcript beside them.

"*Surely this is really evil.*" read the Deputy Commissioner slowly, "*to press perseveringly and with a clear head towards the ruin and physical destruction of hundreds of thousands of men. I was at one of C.'s interminable conferences today. When he got on to his policy he was a different man. His face became an implacable mask. He no longer discussed the matter with any show of reason. He treated it as an inspired faith treats its central religious dogmas.*

"*Sometimes I can believe in devils and imagine Carpenter possessed by one. I can almost see the piteous look of the real man in Carpenter's eyes, begging to be set free.*"

The level tones paused. "H'm, this is reasonable enough," said the Commissioner. "What's the next entry?"

"*To be or not to be, that is the question. Do ends justify means? The means. These must not be too cunningly contrived to save myself. This would turn an execution into a vulgar murder. Yet one is entitled to a sporting chance...*"

The Deputy Commissioner raised his head from the board. "I see there is no more until we come to the date of the murder; and then there is one entry – *Now or never.*"

"And after?" asked Manciple.

"For two days nothing but a quotation – *I could bound myself in a nutshell and count myself king of infinite space, were it not that I have bad dreams.* Poor devil! Here is another a little later. *I seem to have completely lost the faculty of sleep!* His 'just cause' doesn't seem to have been much comfort to him. And here we are once more, finally. *Amazing! They've arrested Venables. By some extraordinary coincidence he seems hopelessly involved, and won't say anything. Of course the explanation's obvious – he guesses. Can't allow that of course. This is my cue to fly dramatically. A letter to Grovermuller would finally do the trick.*"

The Commissioner idly traced a circle on his blotting pad. "I'm glad you've got this cleared up," he said at last. "I don't think I've ever known a more cast-iron case. Of course it's going to be a feverish trial – this odd creature with the temperament of a young Russian Nihilist of the nineties. I suppose an international 'wanted' message has gone out?"

—   —

A youth with pale face and black hair which glinted purple in the sun, sat on a terrace overlooking Lake Geneva. Beneath the icy fire of a late autumn sky the lake lay like a jewel of gaudy brilliance and doubtful taste among the austere mountains round Geneva.

The young man sipped an aperitif and looked forlornly at the mountains. The day, all things considered, was reasonably warm, but he looked blue with cold and was palpably shivering. He was alone except for a tired-looking Chinese delegate – for Geneva no longer basked in the glories of the twenties. The League was now merely a clearing-house for pacts and covenants already ratified, and delegacy to the League was a sinecure whereby a tactless and tiresome diplomat was shelved.

Deep in thought, the young man started at a touch on his shoulder. Two figures, one of them unmistakably English, were behind his chair. His companion was as unmistakably Swiss. He looked at the Englishman interrogatively.

"Yes," said the other in painful French, "this is the man, my friend."

Bysshe Jameson rose wearily to his feet. "So you've found me. Well, I'm not sorry."

The lake, the lake of Rousseau, symbol of the freedom of centuries, guarded by impregnable mountains, attracted for a moment his gaze. He straightened himself. "Now lettest thou thy servant depart in peace," he said with a wry smile. "The Anglo-Russian Treaty was deposited here today."

"Anything you say," he was told, "may be used in evidence against you."

— III —

Grovermuller drummed thoughtfully on the top of his desk.

"You remember that soon after some unknown admirer tried to throttle me you gave me a warning?"

Charles nodded. "I named someone I suspected," he admitted.

"You also indicated certain precautions," Grovermuller reminded him. "I took these and it is quite true that no one has attacked me since. At the same time, they make me feel foolish, for they depend on your guess as to the suspect being accurate."

Charles nodded. "They do. And of course you think the police have the right man?"

"They have a certain case."

"There is no such thing surely, in criminal investigation?" suggested Venables.

"Well, I'm retaining Freeth-Jones for Bysshe, and we're prepared to spend any money to get him off. As far as I'm concerned I regard him as a benefactor to the human race. All the same I'll lay you one hundred to one in pounds he doesn't get off."

Charles smiled wryly. "You want me to risk a pound on it? Do you know I've already been forced to risk what I most value today on a verdict of 'Not Guilty.'"

Grovermuller looked at him anxiously. "Then I'm afraid you are the poorer. I've been going over the case with Oakley. The young man has acted like a lunatic. Do you know he left a diary in which he virtually confesses to murdering Carpenter? He tried to burn it, he washed some blood off a coat after the murder, he flees the country, and he writes a mad letter to me. What can Oakley do?"

Charles felt that cold and gurgling dejection with which a full-sailed vessel of hope founders.

What could he do? What would Miranda do? His love sharpened his perception. He had seen today a look in her eyes which showed she was on the verge of one of those spiritual crises possible only to women whose temperament is strong, but so is their will. Such characters do not grow like a plant, but are convulsed overnight when the sticking-point is passed. Already Miranda was regarding the world – and him – like someone transported to a different planet, like someone staring at different creations through the glass of an aquarium. Her words to him – that if Bysshe were hanged she would never see him again – were not a threat, it was a simple statement of fact. She might see him with her eyes, but the mind would have changed.

Grovermuller read Charles's struggle in his expression. He put it down to the bitterness of young vanity wounded by reality.

"Cheer up," he urged. "One's career, whatever the field, is littered with blunders. We rise on stepping-stones of them to higher things. While I am quoting, remember that he who never makes mistakes never makes anything."

"Tell me, sir," answered Charles absently, "supposing you were up against an impossible task, would you still make the motions of attempting to undertake it? Mrs. Partington, for instance, and her attempt to brush back the Atlantic with a broom. If you were in her position, would you sit down and let the flood swill into your house? Or would you up and have a shot with the vacuum?"

"I see." Grovermuller paused for a moment. "I should let it rip." Then his eyes twinkled. "That happens to be my temperament, however. I owe my success, as no doubt the reporters' room has told you in a less complimentary way, to my skill in bowing to superior forces. But I have nothing but respect and admiration for the man who takes up the broom."

Charles jumped to his feet. "That settles it. Like Mrs.

Partington, I won't give in. I'll assume my original theory holds good until assumptions are useless. Therefore, sir, I advise you to go on with the precautions I suggested when you were attacked."

Grovermuller smiled "You can't expect me to breast the Atlantic. I must disregard your warning."

Charles smiled. "My duty has been done! With all respect, I should love to come in here tomorrow and find you with your neck wrung. It would be the one concrete proof my theory needs."

— IV —

Haggard, and with straggling hair from which the dye had washed in streaks, Bysshe stubbornly regarded Venables.

"I don't want to make a defence."

Oakley drew in his breath with a hiss, and looked despairingly at Venables. He turned to Bysshe, and his casual tones were coldly curious. "Do you mean you really *want* to be hanged by the neck until dead?"

"My God!" Bysshe buried his face in his hands and his shoulders twitched dreadfully. Then jerkingly and spasmodically he paced the room. At last he stopped before Oakley with a venomous smile. "The lawyer with the wisdom of experience deals with the difficult client. You're quite right. I'm a physical coward. I can't stand the gaff." Pale and shaking, he dropped into a chair.

"Much more sensible, Mr. Jameson. Now let us look at this case from my angle." Oakley, his purpose achieved, spoke soothingly. "There are two sides to every question. That is the nature of truth. It is our duty to the State and my duty to you to present one side of this question as convincingly as we can. Let us first examine the other side."

Jameson raised his head. With visible effort he had mastered a nervous quiver of his knees. Now, with face rigid but controlled, he looked at Venables. "It's strong enough, I suppose," he said bitterly.

The solicitor dipped into his case and produced some papers. "Let us probe the foundations of the prosecution's case. First there is the matter of motive. The suggestion will be that the motive was a desire to secure the termination of Carpenter's militaristic policy. Needless to say, we will be able to attack this strongly. We shall point out the absurdity – the unprecedented nature – of such a fantastic motive."

Oakley's voice was tinged with satisfaction. "I think Freeth-Jones can awaken a good deal of doubt in a commonsense English jury about such a fantastic motive."

"No doubt," said Bysshe with sardonic inflection. "Fantastic, isn't it? Will the Crown really ask twelve worthy citizens to believe a man would exterminate Carpenter just because his continued existence would cause a war?" His laugh made the solicitor look at him anxiously. Then he turned again to his notes with a trace of uneasiness.

"Another foundation of their case is opportunity. All that they can prove is that you cannot produce an alibi for the time in question, and that you were seen in a place near Carpenter's room at a time consistent with your having come from it after 12.30 p.m. and before one. Here again we can be aggressive. No one can be found guilty because they cannot prove what they were doing at the time a crime was committed or because it can be shown that their known movements were consistent with having done it."

"I'm glad to hear it. I can always say I was on the way to another room."

"I don't quite follow you," said the solicitor slowly. "If you were on your way anywhere, it will naturally help us if we can say so." Oakley's voice grew grave. "We will now pass on to the serious points in the case." He paused, and the upholstered arms of Jameson's chair creaked in his grip.

"First, your running away. I needn't point out the inadvisability of that action now. I think, however, we can call evidence to prove that Manciple already showed he suspected you. You lost your head and bolted, and your letter to Grovermuller, foolish as it seemed now, was natural in the circumstances."

Oakley burrowed among his papers with a preoccupied air. "Mr. Jameson," he said diffidently, "can you give us any explanations as to why it was necessary to wash some bloodstains from a shirt and coat before you went?"

Jameson looked at the ground; "They found that, did they?" he said, his voice trembling. He hesitated. "I cut my face some time ago when shaving, and the blood dripped over my coat and shirt. I lost my head when I thought Manciple suspected me, and when I came across the coat and shirt it suddenly struck me how bad they looked."

"I see." Oakley's voice was professionally non-committal. He spoke evenly. "You would, of course, shave before you put your coat on, but it was apparently bad enough to go on bleeding after you had dressed. Do you remember where the cut was? The point of the chin? The point of the chin." Oakley emphasized the words as he wrote them down.

Somebody else who doesn't believe in breasting the Atlantic, thought Charles. He believes Jameson did it and is endeavouring to affect the usual compromise between his legal conscience and the necessity of coaching the prisoner in a reasonable defence.

Oakley finished writing. "Now, Mr. Jameson, we come to the most serious thing, the diary—"

"The diary! But there's nothing in it! My God, the times

I've wanted to put what I felt in that diary. But I never did it. Never!"

"I am afraid they have recovered the greater part of the diary from the ashes," said the lawyer, his eyes averted in mere pity. "They have found the entries for four days before and after the day of the murder."

Jameson got up. The nervous trembling had broken out again and his eyes were dark circled in a face drained of colour. Just as in the rigour of death a family likeness will assert itself with strange and touching distinctness, Charles saw in the white mask of Bysshe's misery the features of Miranda. Bysshe moaned. "Oh, what's the use of all this endless talking? Why prolong the agony?" He leaned his head on his arms, and Oakley and Charles, confused by embarrassment, searched vainly for the comforting phrase.

"Mr. Jameson, a diary is not a confession. The prosecution cannot read a direct confession into the entries they have preserved." Oakley was choosing his words with care. "It is exactly the sort of diary that a man would write who had attempted to nerve himself to a criminal action, had failed to do so, and yet was stricken with a terror of being suspected. This may or may not have happened with you. You must tell us. But there is nothing illegal in being tempted to commit a crime. It is necessary to prove that one has succumbed."

Jameson said nothing. He stared at Oakley with stricken eyes, and hardly seemed to notice what was being said. Oakley, with a glance at Venables, gave him time to compose himself. "You must not lose heart. Things are by no means so black as they look." He rose to go. "I shall be coming back tomorrow with Freeth-Jones."

"You see how it is, Venables," Oakley said later. "The only line of defence with a dog's chance depends on his own testimony.

182

Yet how dare we put him in the box. You heard me in effect outline our case. Go on investigating, but investigate with one object – to find evidence to corroborate our explanation."

"You think I'm a fool to go on nosing round for another murderer?"

The lawyer looked uncomfortable. "It is so easy to cloud the issue. And there is so little time." He patted Venables' shoulder. "I'm sure you can find the kind of evidence I want. Remember that diary. It is the forefront of the prosecution's attack."

— V —

"Given the circumstances, how Bysshe can be saved."

Having given this heading to a blank sheet of paper, Charles thought for some time without writing any more. Half an hour later, however, he had accumulated the following in subscription:

1. He can be proved innocent. If he is innocent, either
(a) He suffers from a complete or partial delusion that he is guilty or
(b) Appearances against him are so black that he has given up hope.
In the case of (b) the blackness of appearances may be
(i) Accidental.
(ii) Malicious. (Find the enemy?)
(iii) Both
2. Alternatively, let us assume he killed Carpenter. He can still be saved either
(a) If he were so provoked the jury can be persuaded to regard it as manslaughter.
(i) In that case we shall have to find out if idealism was the motive. But the only other conceivable motive is, of course, Miranda. Rotten for her if I follow it up. (You know damn well you won't.)

Or (ii) We shall have to make the most of the fact that the weapon was not brought, but seized from the wall. (Unfortunately he would have known it was there, anyway.) However, this, with other evidence, would go to prove self-defence. (You know you can't get away with that.)

(b) Or he may have intended to wound Carpenter, thus incapacitating him, without killing him. (Anyway, that makes it constructive murder. Query: what is the usual penalty for this? Answer: penal servitude for life.) Bysshe's remorse would help this line of defence and he could be put in the box, but how the devil could you prove it?

Or, and finally (c) he may have done it unknowingly. Somnambulism, for instance, or temporary insanity. (Note, look up epilepsy in Lockhart's, and have a word with Dr. Attlee.)

Charles studied this logical masterpiece for a few minutes. Then he began to pace endlessly up and down the narrow room; and so Miranda found him.

He handed her the sheet in silence, and she studied it for a moment. Then without a word she took up a pencil and struck it violently across the paper.

Charles took up the paper. She had crossed out the clauses under the heading: "HE IS INNOCENT"

"Bysshe has confessed to me," said Miranda wearily. Her eyes were hard with suffering. "Oh, Charles, it's unbearable, he's in such agony."

The memory of the scene with Bysshe overwhelmed her, and Charles reconstructed it from broken sentences, which spoke as if she were recalling the unreasonableness of a nightmare.

As Bysshe had steadily given himself away, with actions that showed he lived and ate and slept with guilt, Miranda's soul had frozen. She realized that in her heart she had up to now refused to believe him guilty of plunging a knife into Carpenter. Now, with every word, he drove that belief into her inmost convictions.

"It's not fair," he burst out with the first trace of passion. "I did it for the best. I didn't do it for money or revenge. Why should the guilt stick and corrode, so that I can't wash it as I washed off–" He broke off suddenly, his eyes glaring, as his keen intuition sensed her shrinking. "Damn you," he screamed, "you're worse than any of them, you little prude. I suppose you hate me for having done in your lover." And then, to add the final horror to a scene which made Miranda's flesh crawl all over in recollection, he had burst into tears, and abjectly implored her pardon.

"What hope is there?" Charles repeated her question. "There's always hope."

"I see," said Miranda slowly. "Only a miracle can save him."

A Landlady is Helpful

CHARLES WAS HORRIFIED AT the change which had come over Jameson in the course of a few days. In that space of time Jameson had lost his grip on reality. A conviction that he was doomed had combined with some vast sense of guilt to mould his mood to a weak and abject fatalism. The details of his defence, in which he should have taken a close and lively interest, were apparently of no concern to him. Freeth-Jones, K.C., had confided to Oakley that it was the blackest case he had ever handled, not so much because of the evidence, but because of the attitude of the accused. It is true that he placed himself now unreservedly in Oakley's hands, but he seemed unable to concentrate on any point that was put to him. Immersed in his own forebodings, he emerged only occasionally to give information which he forgot or contradicted almost as soon as it had left his mouth.

"The diary is the vital point, Jameson," Charles had pressed him for the fourth time. "Did you or did you not keep a diary?"

"I kept a diary," said Jameson sullenly. "Everyone knows it. What's the good of denying it?"

"Very well, then. Did you make the entries you are supposed to have made?"

Jameson slowly turned his head and looked at Charles with lacklustre eyes. "No, I didn't write what they said I did."

Charles endeavoured to keep the incredulity out of his eyes.

"Good, that's something gained. You are certain you didn't write the words the police accuse you of writing."

"Of course I didn't. I know quite well what I wrote. But what does it matter? The police are certain I did it, and they are determined to make sure of getting me. Why fight them?"

"You think, then, that the police faked those extracts from the diary?"

Wearily Bysshe Jameson emerged from his mood of abstraction. "Who else could have done it? Who else could have wanted to do it?"

Charles thought for a moment. Fantastic as the idea was, why should he have invented it? Coupled with the protestations of innocence, the suggestion would have been incredible. But it came out of complete indifference to any possibility of escape from the verdict which impended. Nor did he advance the suggestion as if he wished it to be believed.

"Now pull yourself together, Bysshe," he said. "Your suggestion that the diary was faked by the police is absurd. But if some enemy 'planted' it for them, and we can prove it, it is a gift to the defence. Why, the whole case might turn on it."

A faint gleam of interest appeared for the first time through Bysshe's dejection. "Is it really important?" he asked.

"Good God, man, it's vital! Let's begin at the beginning. Who knew you kept a diary?"

He thought for a moment. "Almost everyone I can think of at the office," he admitted at last. "You see it wasn't a self-revelatory kind of diary, but more a record of interesting people and events. I often used to enter it up at the office when I had an interesting assignment, and sometimes I read out the entry to contrast it with the report I had actually written. I had a vague idea it might have historical value some day. I am not at all the sort of person," went on Bysshe with still greater signs of animation, "who must pour out his soul in a diary. I pride myself on being a man of action!"

"I shouldn't rub in the conception of a man of action into the jury," commented Charles dryly. "It's a pity so many people knew about it. Where was it kept?"

"Obvious sort of place – left hand top drawer of the desk in my sitting room, but I generally carried it about with me in my dispatch case."

"Now think over the people you came into contact with at the office. Has any one of them got a grudge against you?"

Bysshe was silent for a moment. "It sounds vain, but I can't think of anyone who dislikes me. Actually though, it's due to my insignificance. A reporter is not in sufficient authority to make enemies unless he tries to."

"You've made an enemy somehow. Think it over and let me know. Meanwhile I have at least some information to go upon."

Bysshe looked up as Charles rose to go. "Do you think there really is something in what I've said? What are you going to do?"

"Follow it up," said Charles as cheerfully as possible. "There are several possible lines of investigation opened by what you tell me. I've got to follow them. I can't find out the truth of the diary business by intuition."

"No, of course not. You must investigate." The fugitive brightness went from his eyes and with his elbows on the narrow deal table, he relapsed again into lassitude.

"But really, you know. I'm afraid it's useless. I've been a damned fool. Now I'm paying for it..."

The dying tone in his voice, the weariness of his figure, drooping despondently on the hard bench and filling the bare room with the atmosphere of despair returned to Charles again and again during the next few days, with the persistence of the climax of a tragedy, present long after the theatre of its action is left.

— II —

"Give me blood," said Mrs. Twemlow, buttering a thick slice of bread. "Give me action; and give me love. Say what you like, none of them ever comes up to Edgar Wallace, not for real thrillers."

Thus had Charles discovered that Mrs. Twemlow was an avid reader of detective stories. It followed that the dramatic arrest of her lodger, Jameson, had filled her with complete confidence that he would be proved innocent. She had watched the investigations of the police with contempt. They were like that. She awaited with complacency the arrival of the foolish-looking private detective who would find the truth.

Charles arrived. She thought the monocle was carrying it rather too far, but here obviously was the man to clear up this baffling mystery. It was eleven o'clock in the morning, but as if by magic Mrs. Twemlow produced a cup of good hot strong tea.

"Now, Mr. Venables, you sit down there with this and make yourself at home and tell me who really did it."

Charles took the thick brown liquid and the major portion of a loaf spread with butter with a pale smile. Then he looked at her sternly. "How do you know we are not being overheard?"

"Good gracious, I never thought of that," she answered, her jaw dropping. "Fancy, and me knowing how easy it is to be eavesdropped on."

With a dexterity that showed first-hand knowledge of her subject, Mrs. Twemlow opened the door and then looked carefully out of the window.

"There, that's all right," she said with a sigh of relief.

Charles shook his head reproachfully.

"Supposing they have installed a dictograph in this room," he said coldly. "They may be sitting next door hearing every word I say."

Her eyes rounded. "There, it shows how little one really thinks of," she whispered. "Shall we write to each other?"

"No," said Charles hurriedly. "As it happens I looked carefully on the walls outside for signs of wiring before I came in." He leaned forward and attempted to reproduce, as far as he could remember, the confidential undertone adopted by the detective in the last mystery play he had seen.

"It's like this, Mrs. Twemlow. The police found in Mr. Jameson's sitting room a diary. In that diary he is supposed to have made a full confession. Now we have reason to believe that this diary was a forgery, planted there by the true murderer on purpose to implicate Mr. Jameson."

"There, I knew it was like that," exclaimed Mrs. Twemlow triumphantly. "Only the other day it was, I said to Mrs. Peabody – 'Mark my words, Mrs. Peabody, that poor Mr. Jameson was the victim of a dastardly plot, like I've read of hundreds of times,' although the old cat being jealous, didn't believe me, and said as how I might think her queer but she preferred quiet gentlemanly lodgers to victims of plots – which she's got a nerve to say, Mr. Venables, seeing as how that Johnson man on the second floor back was fined £5 for being D. & D. on Boat Race night. I saw a piece in the paper about it for all she tried to tell me it wasn't him. But that's her all over – neighbouring in out of people's houses as sweet as you please and then scratching them behind your back."

"You needn't worry about her," said Charles with assurance. "We've had our eyes on Mrs. Peabody for some time, you may be surprised to hear."

Mrs. Twemlow was almost inarticulate with delight.

"No, I'm afraid I daren't give you any further details, Mrs. Twemlow," he said firmly. "Now to get back to Mr. Jameson. We must find out when that diary was placed there."

A moment elapsed while the full implications of this dawned upon her. "Good gracious me, then that murderer must have been in my house and my not knowing it!"

"Exactly. You should be a detective yourself, Mrs. Twemlow. Now do you remember any stranger calling here who could have gone to Mr. Jameson's room?"

She wrestled with her memory in silence. "I can't think of a soul," she said at last.

"Hasn't anyone been about taking the rooms?"

"No. They're not to let yet – Mr. Jameson gave me a month's money, and nobody sets foot in those rooms until that month is up."

"No friend of his has called?"

"No one at all except that one messenger from the *Mercury*."

Charles felt that stir of divination which is the flair of the criminal investigator. "What did he come for?"

"Oh, he came from the Editor with a note to say that he had come to collect some of Mr. Jameson's things to send away to him at an address they had got."

"Did you leave him alone in the room?"

"Yes. I'm not the inquisitive kind, as I've always said. Why, only the other day–" Illumination silenced her in the middle of a sentence. She stared at Charles wide-eyed. "Was that the murderer?" she whispered.

Charles nodded. "Can you describe what he was like?"

"Well, I didn't notice him particularly," admitted Mrs. Twemlow, screwing up her eyes in an agony of recollection. "Bearded fellow he was with dark glasses. I expect I should recognize him again."

Charles smiled. "Without the beard and glasses?"

"Ow, of course, that was a disguise!" exclaimed Mrs. Twemlow. "There now, I never thought I should see a disguised person. And in my own house! Of course he would look different without all that stuff on his face. But he had a funny sort of voice. I reckon I should know it again."

"Was his voice at all like this?" squeaked Charles.

"Well I never, but it was too... Do you know who it is then?" she said excitedly.

He shook his head. "No," he said with resignation. "Disguised persons always talk like that."

He pressed her but could get no coherent description. Middle height, he summarized at last. Probably middle-aged or elderly unless he was clever enough to disguise his tread. But then she noticed his hands seemed wrinkled when he did up the parcel, so he probably was old. Means of identification – none.

"Did you notice those ashes in the grate which the police found?" he asked, trying another tack.

"No, I didn't," she admitted. "I don't want you to think I'm neglectful. No one keeps a cleaner house than I do – there isn't a room, let or unlet, but what you could eat off the floor, as I've often told poor Mr. Jameson. But those ashes as I learned from that policeman were all tucked neatly behind the orningmental painted fan that my niece gave me the Christmas before last – every bit of it her own work except the figures which, of course, the teacher helped in."

Charles reflected. "The messenger may have left some fingerprints. I'd like to go over Jameson's sitting room and see what I can find."

The peak of Mrs. Twemlow's thrilling day was reached when she watched Charles at work with the insufflator and his pocket camera. "There, the times I've read about fingerprints and never realized that was how they found them. I wish I could use one of those puffing things. I'd soon frighten that thieving slut of a maid, trying to tell me the cat takes the butter." This grievance occupied the time while Charles photographed a mixed batch of fingerprints on the handles of the desk drawers, the bars of the grate and the 'orningmental' fan. "Probably all police, but worth trying." He would take along his batch of films to the ex-police detective, now in business on his own, whom he made use of for routine jobs of this kind. He could develop, separate, and classify them that evening.

"There, Mr. Venables, if you haven't left every drop of your tea and your nice bread and butter. You eat it up and let me pour you out a cup from the pot. Nice and strong it'll be now."

"I am sorry, Mrs. Twemlow," said Charles solemnly, but once I've started on a job I never eat, drink or sleep until I've seen it through."

— III —

"A bad business this, Mr. Venables," said Hubbard with conventional concern. "Has the lad any chance?"

The librarian gazed up at Charles like a moulting adjutant stork. His skin, pasty from protracted sedentary work was now moulded with hollows and seemed to cling to the bones without any interposition of flesh. His eyes were the only bright thing in his dusty face. Out of the senile wreck of his body they glittered with intellectual life. Again and again, during the last five years, one member of the staff had said to the other, "Surely old Hubbard is getting past it." But an encounter with the librarian made them revise their ideas. The brain still had its memories as neatly sorted as ever, and was still as nimble in handling them.

"Your evidence was pretty damning, you know, Hubbard,"

Charles reminded him. The librarian reflected for a moment. "It was. I regret sometimes not having kept quiet. After all, Carpenter was an evil man engaged in evil work. Yet had I the right to hold back my evidence from the law? What finally decided me was, I think, cowardice. I had no wish to be an accessory after the fact."

"I think most people would take the same point of view," answered Charles. "The point is that I'm helping Oakley with Jameson's defence, and I'd like to get your story from you at first hand. So far, we've only seen the police depositions."

"My story is simple enough. I went up to the top floor but one to Mr. Angell's office to see him about a reference book he had asked for. I found him out and was a little surprised, as he does not leave as a rule until 12.30. I looked at my watch and found it was later than I thought. It was past 12.30 – nearly 12.40 in fact. I went back to the lift and was about to press the button when the lift passed me going down. In it I saw Mr. Jameson, and it was impossible not to notice that he looked profoundly troubled."

"The lift passed you going down," repeated Charles. "The point is, of course, that the only floor above that containing Angell's room is in the roof, and has no rooms in it but the Chief's."

Hubbard nodded.

Charles looked at him closely, on the verge of a decision. Hubbard's face, reptilian, or rather bird-like in its cold sagacity, was not that of a man to whom to make an appeal to the heart. Yet if it did not show sympathy it showed overwhelmingly that intellectual curiosity which can become almost passionate. With no good reason, even against the interests of its possessor, it may put him to the expenditure of time and trouble. Charles decided to rely upon it for the aid he hoped to get from Hubbard.

"Look here, Hubbard," he said. "I'm going to take you into the confidence of the defence. For good reasons we are working on the hypothesis that Mr. Jameson is the victim of a plot. He has been 'framed' as the Americans say. It is more than likely that the murderer has faked some of the most important evidence for the prosecution."

The librarian looked genuinely astonished. "Good heavens! Is such a thing possible? Who do you suspect of such an outrageous act? Besides, how did they manage to deceive the police?"

"It was not difficult in the circumstances," Charles hesitated. The fingerprints were conclusive, but to go on to make the accusation he had in mind was fraught with risk. Well, he must take it, and trust to his reading of the librarian's character. "You realize what a difference this makes to the case. As we see it, Jameson happened to be incriminated to a certain extent by evidence which was fairly well known to the murderer. He took advantage of this to help the incriminating evidence out by fresh additions. They were brilliantly done, and there is every likelihood of an innocent man going to the gallows. Whatever you may think about the murder of Carpenter, the murder of Jameson, as in effect it would be, is indefensible."

"It is horrible," agreed Hubbard. "I cannot, frankly, conceive any man setting about to do such a thing in cold blood."

"It's a powerful incentive to save one's skin," Charles replied. "What is more, we have a definite and well-grounded suspicion of the real murderer. We may suspect him wrongly. If so, we shall never even be able to name him in public, and there is no harm done. But I'm going to go a little farther, because I want your help. I'm going to tell you the name we suspect in confidence. However much it shocks and startles you, may I ask you to promise never to give any indication that you suspect him, either directly or by implication."

The librarian's eyes glittered with interest and curiosity. "Certainly I promise that," he said. "And now you mention it I will say that I found it difficult to believe Jameson was a murderer. I can imagine him quarrelling with Carpenter and striking him down, but stabbing him in cold blood – that I found difficult to believe."

"You may find this more difficult to believe," said Charles deliberately. "Carpenter was stabbed by Grovermuller."

"Good God, Venables, Grovermuller, of all men!" The librarian looked at him with dismay on his bleached face. "Surely not!"

"It's no good appealing to one's prejudices. Admittedly they tell us that Grovermuller is impossible. But look at it clearly and logically, making for the moment only one assumption, that Jameson is not the murderer. Then Grovermuller stands out at once as the next likely candidate. First of all, Grovermuller was completely inimical to Carpenter's policy. It is true he bottled up his dislike, but that would only make it the more dangerous. Directly Carpenter was dead he showed his real feelings. Carpenter's policy was completely reversed."

"Yes, that is so, but surely that is hardly sufficient motive?"

Secondly, he benefited more greatly than anyone in this office as the result of Carpenter's death. He is now Managing Director and virtually controller of Affiliated Periodicals. His salary is now almost double, and in addition he was left a big block of shares by Carpenter. Knowing Felix Carpenter as he did, he would be able to foresee with certainty that this would happen when Carpenter died."

"Yes, that hangs together as a plausible motive."

"Thirdly, his movements during the interval in which the crime is now known to have been committed are not vouched for by anyone else."

"But surely that is not conclusive?" protested Hubbard. "I have no alibi either."

"Fourthly, I am certain the mysterious attack upon him was

a complete fake, designed to distract suspicion. I was the first to see him, and I have always been of the opinion that it was not genuine. The coma he was in was much more the coma of a narcotic than the unconsciousness resulting from strangulation. The marks on his throat were so faint that I suspected at once that they were self-inflicted. Now, no innocent man would try to distract suspicion from himself."

The librarian looked astonished "If that is so, of course, it is final. It is impossible to give any other explanation of Grovermuller's conduct." His bird-like eyes were still for a moment as he reflected. "This diary," he said, "which the police think so important. You believe it was faked. How could Grovermuller have got it into the hands of the police convincingly?"

"Oh, that was done brilliantly. A messenger called on Jameson's landlady representing that he was from the *Mercury*, and had come to collect some of Jameson's belongings. He even showed a note written on *Mercury* note-heading, which he was careful to take away with him. He was left alone in the room for some time, and it was in this room that the police found the charred remains of the diary. Grovermuller could, of course, count on the police searching his room directly they suspected him at all. Remember that the only reason the police ever suspected him was because Grovermuller showed them a mysterious letter he claimed to have received from Jameson. Probably it was a genuine letter, because it can be read in a perfectly innocent sense as well as a guilty one. Grovermuller saw the possibility of reading it in a guilty sense, and this perhaps gave him the idea of faking the diary. Naturally the messenger from the *Mercury* was disguised, but the landlady's description agrees nearly enough with how Grovermuller would look in disguise."

"This is all staggering." The librarian gnawed his pen-holder thoughtfully. "These facts of yours as you arrange them seem to carry a strange air of conviction. Yet against that I cannot picture Grovermuller, gentle, wise, and a little shy, as a murderer – a murderer for self-interest." He was silent for a moment, and then he shot a keen glance at Charles. "You say I can help you, Venables. Why are you telling me all this?"

"At last, I come to the point! Here it is. Ever since the beginning of this case I have been convinced that the cuttings which disappeared from Carpenter's desk and reappeared in the file, have some vital connection with the murder. No explanation has been given why those cuttings should have walked a hundred yards or so. Nobody knows anything about them. Here is something intimately associated with the dead man – almost the last things he studied. He dies; they have vanished. I want you to study those cuttings again, and try to find why or how they could have affected Grovermuller so that he was unwilling to leave them on the Chief's desk. You are probably the one man in Fleet Street of whom I can feel with certainty – if there is a connection it will be found."

The librarian rubbed his chin thoughtfully. "Surely if they give anything away he would have destroyed them?"

Charles smiled. "No, you see he knew you. Unless your reputation is overrated, your filing system would soon show if they were missing."

"Yes." The librarian beamed with childish pride. "It is fool-proof. See that card index with those red tabs sticking up? They all represent cuttings which are being used to write up stories. As soon as they are returned, the tab will fall back. They are arranged in lines, you will see. The line on the left indicates the cuttings that were borrowed on Monday. If any still remain sticking up in the line on Thursday, I shall want to know the reason why."

"Exactly. You see it was only reasonable for Grovermuller to have the cuttings put back somehow or other. Will you therefore look up these cuttings and see if you can trace any possible association. One very definite possibility comes to my mind. Doubtless it will occur to you, but I don't want to mention it in case it starts you on your search with a prejudice."

There was the gleam of the enthusiast in Hubbard's eyes as his eyes ranged the serried files. "It's a task after my own heart you've set me, Venables. If there is any connection between Grovermuller and those cuttings, I will trace it."

— IV —

"Tomorrow," said Miranda, looking out of her window with expressionless eyes, "the trial begins."

"Oh, I know," said Charles, "and I've done nothing, nothing at all."

She smiled bitterly. "Well, at least you've not held out any useless hopes. No one could have been more pessimistic than you have been."

"Face facts, Miranda," he protested. "What sort of hope have I? How can I help him when he refuses to help himself? What can I do? Only what I have been doing: ferreting out discrepancies in the prosecution; trying to create little doubts and difficulties that may make the jury uncertain."

Lost in thought, she did not hear his justification. "To be hanged by the neck until dead," she repeated thoughtfully. "Isn't it extraordinary, I feel more deeply for him, I feel more desperately anxious to get him off, as if he were some poor trapped thing, now, than if I knew for certain he were innocent. Do you understand that?"

"I don't understand you," he said humbly. "I don't understand the bargain you have made, why my life's happiness should depend on the verdict which tomorrow's trial will decide."

"Bargain! Happiness!" she exclaimed fiercely, the animation bringing back her old warm beauty. "Have I made a bargain? Am I responsible for your happiness?" The tears rolled down her cheeks and she turned her head violently away. "Or for my own either," she added. "If this terrible thing happens, do you think I have any feelings left in the world except a blind instinct to creep into some hole and forget, forget how to feel, and love, and pity?"

The evening gathered in the darkening sky. A flight of starlings flew stealthily westward from their gathering place on St. Paul's. Lights shone from the windows in the aged buildings of the Temple near by. Behind one of them Freeth-Jones hastily scanned the brief of Rex v. Jameson for the last time.

A Trial Begins

THE REASON WHY A woman was crushed underfoot (and two men were treated for bites on the ankle) when the Jameson case came on at the Old Bailey was due to the celebrity of the victim. There was none of the usual eager curiosity, "Did he – or didn't he?" The summary of the police court evidence had been enough to convince every newspaper reader that the verdict could safely be delivered without further trial. Every member of the jury was wholeheartedly prejudiced before he took the oath, but all felt satisfaction in the fact that the immemorial ritual of the law would take its tortuous course with decency and dignity, affording an interesting psychological spectacle and a topic of conversation for the dreary pauses which infest suburban up-trains and City tea-shops.

It is possible that if the case had not been tried before Angevin, J., it might have taken a slightly different course, and been a less interesting precedent in our judicial annals. But in that case it would have been very much less exciting for the spectators.

Mr. Justice Angevin's judgements are rarely upset. There has never been any suggestion of prejudice in the numerous cases over which he has presided. The only criticism that has ever been made of him was summed up by Sir Hector Abrahams, K.C. – "A brilliant lawyer and a bloody fool." Abrahams had just lost a case he would almost have been prepared to guarantee, so perhaps he overstated the case. All that this criticism really amounted to was that Mr. Justice Angevin was not able to keep his court in order if it really got out of hand. Abrahams tells with malicious delight the story of Angevin's trial of a woman criminal who, in the usual way, had been asked if she had anything to say before sentence was passed on her. This gives the criminal an opportunity to plead pathetically for mercy, or thank the judge for his anticipated leniency. The woman had said in a loud clear voice, "All I want to say, is that you're a – – little – –." Amid the ensuing titter, Abrahams swears, Angevin was heard to say pathetically, "I'm not! Really I'm not!"

All this, besides being in contempt of court (because Abrahams whispered it to his junior in court during a case which was getting uproarious), was quite probably untrue. But it was certainly recognized that when two leading K.C.'s were engaged in an Angevin case, the most unlimited vituperative combats might take place, with Mr. Justice Angevin interposing like an unpopular referee, and getting knocks from both sides.

Sir Benjamin Elder, K.C., the Attorney-General, was leading for the Crown because, as he explained to his junior, Mr. Arthur Harness, Carpenter's celebrity made the trial a full-dress affair. There were also other factors which made it imperative to appear. A glance at the list of witnesses for the prosecution made this perfectly clear to Mr. Harness. Sir Benjamin, however, had resolved to leave a great deal of the real work to Harness – a promising young fellow, he couldn't go far wrong, and it would help to make his name. However, it was precisely the type of case that suited Sir Benjamin. His renowned air of courtesy, of deference almost, his use of the subtle question as wounding as a knife but propounded like a compliment, these had their fullest and most damning effect in cases where any commonsense view was bound from the start to possess a prejudice of the accused's guilt. In such cases brow-beating a prisoner already sufficiently bruised in the grip of fate may awake sympathy in the mind of the jury. Sir Benjamin's "one gentleman to another" manner forestalled all sentiments of pity. He asked for their verdict as if it was a kindness to the accused.

In spite of the strength of the prosecution's case, Sir Benjamin did not make the obvious mistake of underestimating Freeth-Jones. No prosecuting counsel could afford to now. Granted that Freeth-Jones's talents were histrionic rather than forensic, granted that his knowledge of the law was possibly less than that of many a barrister newly called, granted any of the derogatory generalizations which had collected round his name to dispose of them only one witness need be called: his amazing record of successful verdicts.

Freeth-Jones excelled in three branches of the criminal lawyer's art. His eloquence was of a kind that at the time of the Jameson case was unmatched by any other leader. None of them even attempted that blend of plangent sincerity with the soaring sweep of noble rhetoric. His eloquence was reinforced by cross-examination which unnerved even that most difficult of propositions, the obstinately forgetful witness. Faced by that tall presence, those black beetling eyebrows, and that voice which seemed to make the ledge of the box vibrate beneath the witness's hand, the cherished hopes of the prosecution wavered and fatally hesitated or, slightly dazed, stumbled into traps whose subtlety was evident a step too late. Freeth-Jones's third asset, and one for which he was given least credit, was an amazing skill in constructing, almost out of thin air, theories which would fit the facts put forward by the prosecution and yet exculpate the accused. It has already been a matter of comment at the Criminal Bar that the stars in their courses fought for these fantastic theories. But in the main this was the result of brilliant cross-examination coupled with a deep understanding of the mind of an expert witness.

At ten o'clock Mr. Justice Angevin bowed. His eye caught that of Sir Benjamin − a nice polite man who accepted the ruling of the court without any nonsense. His eye then rested on Freeth-Jones with a mild trepidation. He had never had a really bad scene with him, but sooner or later he knew it would happen. Angevin remembered with horror the terrible episode between Birkenhead and a judge when the young junior, as he then was, had brow-beaten his lordship in open court. Angevin knew he would be quite incapable of dealing with such a scene. Then he frowned on Harness. At any rate these young juniors realized who a judge was. Finally his eye rested on the prisoner. Poor fellow! The case looked black! Well, there was no knowing with a jury.

Sir Benjamin opened with a speech which set the key for the prosecution from the start. "Here," he said in his clear calm voice, after dealing briefly with the circumstances that led up to the fatal night, "we have a murder which, in its main outlines, is as simple as such a complex crime can ever be. Here we have the motive, the opportunity and the material clue, each plain and unassailable, each vouched for by witnesses of character and integrity. Not only will the Crown give you these." Sir Benjamin paused for a moment while two jurymen (who were watching a baby being bundled rapidly out of the court by a red-faced mother) returned with a guilty start to attention. His eyes locked with theirs as he took up the thread impressively. "We shall give you more. We shall produce the record written by his own hand, of mingled satisfaction and remorse with which the prisoner contemplated his dreadful deed." He enunciated the adjective judicially, and as if anxious to clear himself of any suspicion of eloquence, hastened to qualify it. "I call it dreadful, gentlemen of the jury, not with any thoughtless repetition of a hackneyed phrase, but because the taking of a fellow-creature's life, in whatever circumstances, is a deed which fills the mind with terror and dread, and when we cease so to regard it, then are we indeed reduced to the level of the beasts that perish, that perish and none questions how or why."

The faintest flicker of a smile illuminated Sir Benjamin's lips as he gave, in his cool clear tones, this recognizable imitation of Freeth-Jones's best style. He relapsed again to dryness. "Finally, as if this superfœtation of evidence were not enough, we have the prisoner's precipitate flight and his attempt – and he little knew it was only an attempt – to destroy our incriminating record of his inmost thoughts."

So much for the jury. Sir Benjamin caught Mr. Justice Angevin's eye dexterously and got down to facts. "It will be the Crown's object during the next few days to establish beyond all reasonable doubt that Bysshe Jameson had a clear-cut motive for the murder; that he was seen leaving the scene of the murder in an agitated state; that blood was found on the garments he was wearing at the time; and that he expressed both verbally, and in writing which forms one of the exhibits, the remorse which affected him when he realized the terrible thing he had done. You may even feel that we are carrying this too far, that we are pressing the obvious, that we are weighing this man down with proof and certainty until perhaps you feel, as a kind of reaction, a certain pity for him." Sir Benjamin, his eyes fixed on the foreman of the jury, speculated as to whether he was a big enough fool to believe this. He decided he was. "No," he said gravely, "you must not think that is our object. Your task is a difficult one. Our object is to make it an easy one. We want to enable you to give, with no doubt, no qualms in your mind, the verdict to which I know your commonsense will lead you." Sir Benjamin invariably followed a reference to the common sense of the jury with a dig at opposing counsel. "In the course of this case my learned friend and brilliant ornament of the Bar will put to you many alternative possibilities and make many ingenious explanations of the damning facts. I merely ask you always to bear in mind the simple outline of the Crown's case against Bysshe Jameson. He had the motive; he had the means; he was stained with the blood of his victim; he committed to paper the remorse that ate him up; he fled in terror and disguise. Make a mental note of these facts – they are simple, concrete, and, I submit, utterly incapable of any but the one construction."

Being composed of twelve humans, the jury's attention strayed frequently during Sir Benjamin's calm marshalling of the facts, but it strayed always to one point, the prisoner. Pale as chalk, with heavy circles under his eyes and dark red hair brushed wildly back, he looked like a man pursued by devils. Impossible, reflected twelve sensible men, to believe they were merely devils of apprehension. They felt almost embarrassed to see how his eyes kept returning, with horrid fascination, to the knife which was the most prominent exhibit. His sister, watching him with a sick fear, saw also the furtive and embarrassed glances of the jury at his blatant misery. Close-lipped and bird-like, the judge, aloof in his ermine, rested his eyes for a minute critically on the prisoner. It was pity she read in them, but an impersonal, unhelpful pity. And Freeth-Jones, black and gaunt, was bent forward listening in his seat, without lifting his glare from the point on the floor two feet in front of him at which he gazed.

The first witnesses called by the Crown prepared, as it were, the general setting of the crime. They described the editorial conference, at which Carpenter's policy was outlined so unmistakably. Jameson's outburst was duly recorded, and when Grovermuller described in his clipped, precise tones the theatrical reference by the dead peer to the dagger on the wall, there was a perceptible hush in the body of the court.

Under Sir Benjamin's careful questioning, Grovermuller recounted at length Carpenter's policy. This led to the first sortie by Freeth-Jones. The following questions had been put by Sir Benjamin.

"Did the accused express his opinion on Carpenter's policy on other occasions?" – "Often."

"What was it?" – "He thought it a wicked policy. (After a pause) He said it should be stopped."

"Now think carefully. Did he ever suggest any remedy to you?" – "He suggested that Carpenter should be lynched."

"Those were his actual words?" – (Pause) "Yes."

Freeth-Jones rose to cross-examine with slaughter in his eye. The witness regarded him coolly.

"Would you say that Mr. Jameson was addicted to denunciatory statements of this kind – I mean of all sorts of characters and individuals?" – "He was certainly prone to sweeping generalizations of this nature."

"In your hearing has he suggested, for instance, making away with butchers, the leader of the Tory party, and the Archbishop of Canterbury?" – "Yes, and others."

"You did not take these threats seriously? You did not urge their objects to apply for police protection?" – "No" (with a smile).

"This is no smiling matter, Mr. Grovermuller. A man's life turns on it. If you must smile, smile at the fact that these threats are being seriously put forward as proof of this murder–"

Sir Benjamin bobbed up with an acid smile. "I am anxious to give my learned friend every facility in his cross-examination, but he appears to be launching into his opening speech."

Dear me, thought Mr. Justice Angevin unhappily, they've

started already. He gave Sir Benjamin and Freeth-Jones an impartial frown. "Learned counsel for the defence will be good enough to reserve his comments till later."

Freeth-Jones gave his gown a ferocious twitch. "Very well, my lord. Let me put a final question on this point. Did you ever consider Mr. Jameson's threats as anything but the forcible turn of speech natural to an enthusiastic young man speaking on subjects near to his heart?" – "Emphatically never."

"Thank you. Now, Mr. Grovermuller, what was your own opinion of Lord Carpenter's policy?" – "I was against it."

"Against it?" (assumed surprise) "But you were the Editor?" – "Yes."

"Excuse me if I show ignorance regarding the practice of your profession, but is it usual for an editor to sponsor a policy in which he disbelieves?"

Grovermuller tugged at his short moustache. "About as common," he answered quietly, "as for a barrister to defend a client he believes guilty." (Laughter)

Freeth-Jones glared at Mr. Justice Angevin indignantly. "My lord, will you indicate to the witness that he is in the box to give evidence and not to exercise his undoubted gifts of humour?"

The judge pursed his lips. "You must endeavour to refrain from attempting to score off counsel, Mr. Grovermuller. Counsel no doubt will exercise the same restraint."

Freeth-Jones drew himself up dramatically. "Do I understand from your lordship's observation that he disapproves of my cross-examination?"

"As always, it is extremely competent," replied Mr. Justice Angevin hastily, "but witness's reply was justifiable."

Freeth-Jones glared defiantly round the court and made another set at his witness. "Now, Mr. Grovermuller," he said, with exaggerated politeness, "would it be correct for me to say

that you had the greatest loathing for Lord Carpenter's policy?"
– "Hardly loathing. I considered the policy would result in
consequences damaging to this country."

"I see. There is a subtle distinction. Dare I ask if you *greatly*
disliked this policy?" – "I did."

"But you continued as editor, to assist the contrary policy." – "I
continued to carry out the instructions of my employer."

"Now that Lord Carpenter is dead, all this is changed?" – "The
Mercury's policy is changed, yes."

"It is only because somebody killed Lord Carpenter that you
now have the policy you want?" – "Lord Carpenter's death made
it possible, certainly."

Freeth-Jones was silent for a moment. He looked at the foreman
with such significance that the latter wondered suddenly whether
it was his duty to make some comment. Luckily he refrained.

Freeth-Jones's next question was apparently quite irrelevant.
But it was put very seriously.

"Mr. Grovermuller, would you describe Mr. Jameson as a highly
strung and imaginative young man?" – "Oh, very much so."

Grovermuller was allowed to stand down. The examination
of the sub-editor, the leader-writer, and the art editor were
on similar lines. Sir Benjamin elicited Jameson's nervousness
and his excitability and his open-condemnation of Carpenter.
Freeth-Jones, by skilful cross-examination, endeavoured to bring
out Jameson as a hare-brained youngster whom no one took
seriously, while underlining the fact that several members of the
staff had as much dislike of Carpenter's policy – and therefore as
clear a motive – as Jameson.

So far, therefore, honours were easy. But it was realized
that the prosecution had merely ranged on the objective. The
bombardment was yet to come.

The next witness was Lady Carpenter. Sir Benjamin called her with a certain amount of trepidation. It was necessary to call her to establish the exact time at which Carpenter had last been seen alive. At the same time he foresaw all kinds of unpleasantness when Freeth-Jones cross-examined.

Lady Carpenter testified that she had an interview with her husband on the night mentioned. It had lasted till about half-past twelve. He had then gone back to bed to sleep. Sir Benjamin relinquished his witness to Freeth-Jones with a sigh.

Freeth-Jones rocked gently backwards and forwards on his feet as he looked sternly at the black-clad woman. "Are you aware that the knife, marked exhibit R2, which you see there, caused your husband's death?" – "Yes."

He leaned forward suddenly. "Are you aware that the handle bears your fingerprints?"

As Lady Carpenter nodded, a murmur ran round the Court.

"How do you explain this?" – "I handled it during my conversation with him."

"Come, come, Lady Carpenter. You mean you threatened him with it. I see Sir Benjamin is on his feet, so perhaps I had better tell you that you need not answer this question." – "I prefer to answer it. I did threaten him."

"Seized it from the wall and threatened to stab him dead?"

There was a silence. Lady Carpenter looked coldly at the K.C. "That is so," she said quietly.

"And why did you do that, Lady Carpenter?" – "It was a rather theatrical gesture, you will understand, made in the heat of the moment. I was angry with him for the way in which he was, shall I say, flaunting his love affairs."

"In other words, you were jealous?" – "No, I merely objected to the publicity, which I considered humiliating and unpleasant."

"Now, Lady Carpenter, when you were menacing your husband, in this theatrical gesture of yours, with the weapon with which he was subsequently killed, did he know you were planning to run away with his private secretary that night?"

Sir Benjamin rose wearily. "Really, my lord, I feel forced to ask whether this is a criminal court or a divorce court?"

"I am afraid," said Mr. Justice Angevin, "that I do not see the relevance of this cross-examination, Mr. Freeth-Jones."

"My lord, I hope to show that this witness is hopelessly prejudiced and hopelessly unreliable. The prosecution are putting her forward as the last person to see Lord Carpenter alive. I intend to prove that any evidence of this nature she has given is coloured by her personal interests in the matter."

"Very well," said Mr. Justice Angevin; "as long as your questions bear directly on the credibility of the witness, you may proceed."

"Now, Lady Carpenter?" – "He did not know."

Freeth-Jones leaned forward menacingly and so collected the attention of the jury for his next question.

"Supposing he had known," he began in a voice full of sinister emphasis and vibrant with suggestion. He paused, and as he calculated, the judge interposed.

"The witness is not compelled to follow you in your suppositions, you know."

"Very well, my lord, since I am not allowed to probe further into this strange matter, I will close my cross-examination."

Mr. Justice Angevin speculated as to whether to stigmatize this as an improper observation, and decided not to. With a meaningful glance at the jury, Freeth-Jones sat down. He had not made the mistake of labouring the point, or committed the clumsiness of attempting to accuse Lady Carpenter. A hint, he knew, was more effective and unsettling.

Mr. Jerningham was the next witness. Sir Benjamin contented himself with obtaining his corroboration of Lady Carpenter's story. Freeth-Jones's cross-examination was contemptuously brief.

"Did you see Lord Carpenter alive after Lady Carpenter's interview?" – "No."

"He might have been dead before the alleged interview for all you yourself positively know?" – "Yes."

"After the interview with Lord Carpenter, did Lady Carpenter give you a sum of money in bonds?" – "She did."

"You understood they were given her by Lord Carpenter?" – "Yes."

Lord Carpenter would have been infuriated if he had known what had become of this gift of his?" – "I am sure I cannot say."

Freeth-Jones laughed sardonically. "You don't think he would have tried to recover it, by force if necessary?"

Sir Benjamin, who did not care much what happened to Jerningham, was out of court. Mr. Harness rose. "How can the witness possibly know what Lord Carpenter might or might not think?" he asked. He asked it wearily. Freeth-Jones as usual had achieved the effect he desired. With a wave of his hand, counsel for the defence sat down.

The court stood adjourned. The judge rose. Twelve good men and true ate and slept behind guarded doors.

An Editor Struggles

WHEN NEXT HUBBARD MET Venables there was a gleam of surprise in the eyes that peered out from behind the thick glasses.

"Are you a wizard?" he asked. "The pursuit of those cuttings is proving fruitful beyond all words."

Charles felt all the thrill of an investigator whose trail clears before his eyes.

Hubbard outlined his speculations. "You must realize that in spite of my care, there are certain cuttings missing from the folder, although the folder is replaced. They are not altogether easy to trace. That is to say that it is possible to find their subject, and in what part of the file they were, but as the guard sheets as well as the cuttings have gone, it is not possible to trace when they appeared.

"The question is what are their subjects? In the case of text the subject is indicated by one or two headlines. In the case of photographs the caption is given. This is all we have to trace the missing cuttings."

Hubbard pressed his hand over his greying hair with a quick, bird-like movement. "Let me read out certain text headings, together with one or two illustration captions. I shall make no comment – I leave it to you."

"One missing photograph has the caption, 'A Moscow Reception. Left to Right – So-and-so, So-and-so, and the British publicist, *Eric Grovermuller.*'"

"Here is a headline, 'The Great Experiment in Russia. By *Eric Grovermuller.*' I find another cutting was headed: 'My Visit to Russia. By a Well-Known Journalist.' Another photograph was headed: 'The Soviet Trade Delegation Banquet: *Mr. Grovermuller's* table.'" Hubbard paused. Charles made no comment, and the librarian said slowly: "All these cuttings I can date approximately. They are at least fifteen years old. Mr. Grovermuller has, of course, been with us not quite fourteen years."

Charles swung his monocle thoughtfully. "Now I have found what I wanted I am disappointed. Silly, isn't it? I suppose I expected something more conclusive. And yet how significant it is – signposts to Grovermuller's association and sympathy with Russia, matters we never guessed at the time, and now more significant still, carefully destroyed."

"It is significant, Mr. Venables," the librarian said shrewdly, "but I am still waiting for your real opinion as to how they implicate Grovermuller."

Charles traced an airy circle with his monocle. "Obviously Grovermuller was not afraid of *our* knowing his sympathy with Russia. Otherwise he would not have changed the policy of the paper in the open way he has done. Why, then, destroy the cuttings and put them back in the file in the way he did? There seems to me to be only one possible reason. He was afraid of our knowing that Carpenter knew of his association with Russia.

"What can we deduce from that?" asked Charles of his new-found ally. "Surely that here was the motive of the crime. One can visualize a quarrel, threats to secure his discharge, to turn him again on to Fleet Street, old and a little threadbare, at a time when editors are somewhat of a superfluity."

Charles wrinkled his brows in thought for a moment. "Of course I cannot imagine Grovermuller, with his talent for smoothing things over, allowing this matter of his association with Russia to grow into a serious quarrel. It is easy, after all, to give a reasonable explanation of such a thing. There must be more in it than that. Carpenter must have had definite information from other quarters. He must have sprung the whole thing on Grovermuller suddenly. Perhaps he even told him to get out that night?"

"It is possible," admitted Hubbard. "But how can we prove it? At present, if you will forgive my saying so, you are acting on a wild hypothesis. Admittedly we have just stumbled on a discovery which, by a strange chance, confirms your hypothesis. But I think you'll admit that it rests on a very slender basis of fact."

Charles shrugged his shoulders. "I appreciate that well enough. What would you do in this situation?"

Hubbard smiled. "I am a librarian, not a detective, thank heavens. But I know enough about your profession to suppose that the next thing to do is to search Grovermuller's room and see if you can find any evidence."

"I shall, of course, do that, but I'm not very hopeful. There's not much in the way of evidence one can find."

— II —

"What, may I ask, are you doing?" came the calm level tones.

Charles, with a drawer in Grovermuller's desk half open, wheeled round. Grovermuller was behind him.

Charles turned back again, and shook an envelope and letter free of the miscellaneous bundle in the drawer. "Looking for something," he said coolly. "I am glad to say I have found it."

"Sit down, Venables," said Grovermuller in tones of icy disgust. "I didn't think I'd find you snooping around my personal belongings in that way. What the devil are you looking for?"

Charles raised his eyebrows. "You surely don't expect me to tell you?"

"I not only expect you to tell me, but if you don't, this is the last time you set foot in this building." Grovermuller crimsoned with indignation. "I don't mind your damned incompetence, but when it comes to sneaking into people's rooms and turning over their private letters, your play-acting must stop."

"I hoped," said Charles wearily, "when I first heard your equable voice, we were going to avoid a vulgar row. I appear to be wrong, however." He inserted his monocle and gazed at Grovermuller with a gentle smile. "May I deal with your remarks one by one? First of all you complain of my snooping. May I point out that 'to snoop' is merely an irritable translation of 'to investigate.' My job here is criminal investigation. Hence," he explained reasonably, "you cannot justifiably complain of my snooping. I am the *Mercury's* paid snooper. Next you ask me what I am snooping for? But you, with your usual alertness, have already grasped the fact that my snooping is directed against you. Obviously it will be no longer snooping – I might just as well have done it openly – if I tell you its object. I am sure you must realize that, in your own interests, and to spare your feelings, I cannot possibly tell you. Finally you warn me that this is the last time I set foot in this building. I must point out, however, that under God and the shareholders, the final say in the matter belongs to Lord Carpenter, and I have already taken the precaution of informing him as to what I was about to do, and getting his consent."

Grovermuller unexpectedly burst into a laugh. "This is so outrageous that I find it impossible to be annoyed. My God, what do you think you are likely to find?"

Charles, his head bent, was studying the letter he held in his hand, and he did not at first reply. Then he raised his eyes and looked slowly and steadily at the other. "I have decided to change my mind. Shall I tell you what I expected to find? Listen!

"This is a letter addressed to you." He paused a moment, and said slowly, "It is signed by Carpenter, and it is dated the day of his murder. Do not interrupt me, please. In this brief interesting note he says that information about you has come to his ears that fills him with horror and concern. He says that it looks as if he had come to a parting of the ways, and that you must thrash it out with him after the meeting tonight."

Charles folded up the letter and put it in his pocket. "Instructive, isn't it, remembering that you have no alibi for the time of the murder."

The look in Grovermuller's eye was terrible to see. He paced once up and down the room and then faced Charles.

"Oh, so that's your game, is it? It's well played," he said. "But try it on. Do you think the police will believe your evidence against mine? Don't you know that they've got Jameson where they want him, that they'll keep him there, and that he'll hang before the month is out? You poor fool, you've got the letter, have you? You found it in my desk, did you? Do you think I can't explain it away? Do you think I'll ever need to, with a perfectly good criminal in the dock, and the verdict due in twenty-four hours' time? Do you think that when he's been found guilty the police will be interested in your story?" His lips curled in a smile. "I'm disappointed in you, Venables. I never thought you were a fool."

Charles looked at him thoughtfully. "Do you know, of the many ways I thought you might take this, I never thought you would take it as you have done. Shows how the best of us can miscalculate, doesn't it?"

He hesitated at the door. "There is one point you haven't given me credit for. Some cuttings were missing from the file.

I've spoken to Hubbard about them. It seems they form an interesting link between you – and Russia!"

Grovermuller turned crimson with temper. "So that interfering old dodderer is in it too, is he? By God, that's too much. If I can't get rid of you for the moment, I'll get rid of him. I've told him before I'll sack him, and now out he'll go – before the week's up if I have my way."

Charles left him thoughtfully.

— III —

"I possibly made a mistake in confronting him," said Charles shamefacedly to Hubbard, as he related his interview. "Yet after all, once he found me going through his desk, I was in the most foolish of all positions, of knowing *he* knew what I pretended to keep secret. I thought bluff might succeed where deception had failed. It didn't. And now at any rate I know the strength of his hand. And its strength is due to his strength of mind, a quality I hadn't given him credit for."

The librarian wrinkled his brows. "But do you mean that with all the evidence you have – and now this crowning business of the letter – you can't move against him?"

Charles frowned gloomily. "He's right. He's in an infernally strong position. The police have got their man. In twenty-four hours' time they'll probably have got their verdict. Then the matter's closed. What good will it be then for us to go with our innuendoes of guilt, our documents, and our circumstantial evidence to Scotland Yard? Look at the Oscar Slater case."

"If we could follow up those cuttings..." said the librarian, biting his lip.

"Yes, that is the one thing he is scared about apparently."

Charles related exactly his closing words with Grovermuller.

"I'm afraid it made him furious with you. He's breathing fire and slaughter, but I don't imagine he'll really dare to do anything overt. After all, you're an older employee than he is."

Hubbard turned white. "I wish you hadn't mentioned me, Venables," he said agitatedly. "After all, it's your job, this detective work, and anyway, you've no ties, but it's awkward, damned awkward for me."

Charles shrugged his shoulders. "Well, there it is. You could make your peace with him separately easily enough. He'd be glad to see me isolated. Why not do it?"

"No, Venables." The librarian shook his head. "Now I'm for it, I'll stand by you. After all, I promised to help you. I'll do it. But the point is, what can one do now?"

Charles paced slowly up and down. He turned at last to Hubbard. "We have at the worst twenty-four hours. With a little luck, and Freeth-Jones putting up a good show, we may have forty-eight. Here's a case, I think, for both of us to work our damnedest. What can you suggest?"

They were silent for a moment. Hubbard cracked his knuckles reflectively, while his eyes ranged the crowded shelves. "I've got rather an absurd idea. But I suppose even absurd ideas have some value now. Today is Tuesday, the first Tuesday of the month. Grovermuller is always away on that date – it is accepted as a matter of course. Now we've always joked about what he did on that day. Once or twice one of the staff has chaffed him about it, but he's been furious."

"Yes, I've heard about it," said Charles. "The story goes, you know, that one of our reporters, with an assignment down at the docks, once saw a tattered figure creeping along a street in Limehouse – Vincent's Alley I think it was. The figure hesitated for a moment in the light of a lamp before diving into a doorway. It was Grovermuller!"

"Yes, Bernard saw him," replied the librarian. "He's a sound man and his story's been confirmed. One of the 'chars' here swears she saw him in the East End one of these Tuesday nights."

"Well, we'll take it that it is so, then," answered Charles indifferently. "Is his absence going to help us at all?"

"Doesn't it suggest anything to you?" asked the librarian. "Think. His mysterious visits to the East End; his reluctance that anyone should know; his old connection with Russia."

"By Jove," exclaimed Charles. "A rendezvous with a Russian agent, eh?"

Hubbard nodded. "Exactly. It's a mad idea, perhaps. But why not test it out? He leaves always at six o'clock. It's dark by then. I realize it is probably a wild goose chase, and as time is so short it is foolish to send you on it. I'll go myself."

Charles looked at him anxiously. "It's an expert's job this shadowing, Hubbard. Do you think you can do it?"

The librarian smiled. "I'll probably make a mess of it," he said, "but I'm game to try. I know the general idea, you know. It'll be dark. If Grovermuller expects anyone to follow him it'll be you and not me, and the difference in our statures will mislead him."

Charles nodded. "That's true," he said. "Right, try it on. We can't afford to let any chance slip us."

— IV —

In the shadowy gloom of a street in the East End there was a sudden clatter of feet, jarring the stillness of its evening rest. High above the long blank wall, unpierced, unadorned, which ran along one side of the street, a lamp flickered sullenly. It lit up two figures struggling grimly and silently – except for a steady panting – beside the wall.

A long lean figure streaked from the shadows towards them. The two struggling shapes threw up, as it were, into the light a shining object which winked cheerfully as it turned in the air. It swayed backwards and forwards over them, and the newcomer, bounding forward, grabbed it in both hands. With quick purposeful jerks he attempted to pull it loose. At that moment a police whistle rang out clearly. The rapid and decisive tramp of footsteps sounded down the street. The three figures separated, and revealed themselves to the inquisitive lantern of the law as a grey-haired and precise-looking elderly man in greasy tattered clothing, a dried-up bespectacled man in a mackintosh, and a young man with a cheerful smile and a monocle, balancing a wicked-looking knife in his right hand.

"I say, really, you know, what's all this about?" asked the police constable, one of the new draft from minor public schools imported to "stiffen the Force" under the Verteuil scheme.

The elderly man pointed at the mackintosh-clad one with a shaking finger. "This man set on me with a knife and tried to murder me," he said. "Then this other fellow ran up and tried to help him. You came just in time to save my life."

"My God, officer, he's lying! He tried to murder me. If that young man hadn't arrived when he did, I'd have been dead!"

"By Jove, how odd," answered the policeman. "You can't both be right now, can you?" He turned to the monocled youth. "What do you say – who was murdering whom?"

The other hesitated. "Well, all I could see was the two struggling for the knife. I was late on the scene, you know. But I'm prepared to swear that my friend in the mackintosh is right. In fact, I rather feared this would happen."

The policeman groaned. "Good God, what is all this about? Why did you fear it would happen? Is this old chap a notorious murderer or something?"

The young man grinned. "We believe him to be a murderer – but notorious, hardly. You see the fact is—"

He was rudely interrupted. "Don't listen to him, constable. They're both in this together. They've tried to fasten a murder on me, and now because they've failed, they're trying to kill me in cold blood."

Without replying, the police constable held the knife to the light. "I see there are a couple of initials scratched on the haft," he said slowly. "They look like E.G."

"My initials are E.G.," said the elder man. "But it's not my knife. It is all part of the plot. It would be ridiculous if it were not tragic. Had you not come on the scene I would be dead now, and yet these two assassins have the intolerable impudence to accuse me of murder!"

"This," said the police constable, "is one of the little awkwardnesses they have forgotten to mention in the *Police-Constable's Pocket Book*. You will all come along with me to the station, where I shall have the pleasure of seeing my sergeant sort out the mess."

The three individuals gave their names as Eric Grovermuller, Walter Hubbard and Charles Venables. At the last name, the elderly sergeant pricked up his ears. "Didn't we have some rather peculiar instructions through about you from headquarters a little while ago?"

Charles grinned. "That is so. Probably you have never had instructions like them before."

The sergeant grunted. "I should hope not! Well, you seem to have some very powerful friends, Mr. Venables. Let's hear your version of the incident."

"That's easily given. I saw these two struggling for the knife, and got hold of it myself. That's all I actually saw. But when I tell you that I have good reason to suspect Grovermuller of murder, that Mr. Hubbard here was shadowing him by agreement to find it out, and that because I feared danger to Mr. Hubbard, I was following them both, unknown to either, you will see that I have no hesitation in believing Mr. Hubbard's story."

The sergeant looked astonished. "What an amazing story. And what a pity you didn't see it with your own eyes, Mr. Venables! And what murder is this you suspect him of?"

"The murder of the late Lord Carpenter."

The sergeant was silent for a moment. "I don't like this," he said suddenly, throwing down his pen. "To begin with, this fellow, whoever he is, couldn't have murdered Carpenter. Carpenter's murderer is in the dock at the Old Bailey at this moment, and if you knew what I know of the evidence against you, you'd realize that what I say is true. You're barking up the wrong tree, that's what it is, Mr. Venables. Who is this old fellow, anyway?"

Grovermuller turned red. "I'm the Managing Director of Affiliated Publications, damn you," he shouted.

The sergeant, a broad grin on his face, turned to Charles. "Is he just – mad?" he said.

"No. He's what he says he is," Charles answered coolly.

The sergeant started in alarm. "Good heavens! Why, then, he's your boss!"

"That is so," answered Charles. "He is also Mr. Hubbard's boss. Incidentally, why not ask what the Managing Director of Affiliated Publications is doing in greasy old clothes in the East End."

"I was going to," said the sergeant grimly.

"And I refuse to answer!" shouted Grovermuller violently. "What the devil business of yours is it what clothes I wear or where I am going, eh? My God, what sort of police force is it we've got! Here am I, falsely accused of murder and nearly murdered myself, and all you do is stand round chatting amiably with my assassins, and asking me personal questions."

"You won't do any good by being violent, sir," said the sergeant mildly. "At the same time I admit you're perfectly entitled to refuse to answer my questions."

He thought for a moment. "This is really extremely awkward. Mr. Grovermuller accuses Mr. Hubbard, a respectable employee of his, of attempting to murder him, and thereafter of falsely accusing him of murder. Mr. Hubbard also accuses Mr. Grovermuller, the celebrated head of a famous business organization, of trying to murder him. Mr. Venables, recommended to us from unimpeachable sources, unfortunately saw nothing more than would fit in with either story. At the same time he joins Mr. Hubbard in accusing Mr. Grovermuller of Lord Carpenter's murder. But as I know for a fact that Lord Carpenter's murderer has been found, this latter statement seems if anything to support Mr. Grovermuller's assertion that he is being falsely accused. On the other hand the weapon has his initials on it, but then this again might be consistent with his belief that he is being 'framed.' What, gentlemen, am I to do? Neither appears to have a witness. I can't put you both in the dock on each other's mutual charges of attempt to murder, but I'm damned if I can decide which side to support myself. I could charge you both with brawling, but I imagine that won't content you. I don't care if it doesn't, but the magistrates will expect me to give some explanation of the extraordinary story told by you – three respectable, and in fact well-known people; why, I think one of you gave evidence in the Jameson case today! Yes, of course you did. I thought I remembered your names! Well, I can't give any explanation to the magistrates. Personally I think there's some misunderstanding, and perhaps a little private grudge behind all this, and I suggest you forget all about this visit to the police station and smooth it over between you."

Charles looked at Grovermuller. "It looks like stalemate. Shall we accept the situation – with no concessions, mind you?"

Grovermuller glared at him. "Yes, damn you! But you won't get away with it next time."

When they were gone, the sergeant had a long conversation with the Yard. "And that's how I left it," he ended. "I gave them the impression I didn't believe any of their stories. Meanwhile I'm having the ownership of the knife traced. Will you look after the other end? It will need very careful investigation. Quite. Goodbye."

The sergeant settled himself in his chair. "Observe how a difficult situation of this kind is handled," he said severely to the police constable. "You passed the baby on to me. I in turn have deftly passed it on to the C.I.D. I am now going home to bed."

A Court is Electrified

"THE RIGHT HON. CLAUDE SANGER."

The murmur in the court rose suddenly. There was, there could be, only one Claude Sanger. What was he doing in this unsavoury case as seventh witness for the Crown? Only five days before, with all the laurels of his country's gratitude thick upon him, he had retired from political life with the double excuse of age and ill-health. It was freely whispered that the first creation of a non-Royal dukedom since the Iron Duke would have been exercised in his favour, if he had not refused it. The rumour was an exaggeration; actually a Marquisate only was contemplated, but it indicated the respect and reverence that was felt for the Grand Old Man of Politics. The first three rows of spectators in the Old Bailey consisted of men and women second only in eminence to the gaunt but still imposing silver-haired figure in the witness box.

His old friend Sir Benjamin leaned forward blandly. "Until five days ago you were Prime Minister?" – "Yes."

"You were Prime Minister at the time of Lord Carpenter's death?" – "Yes."

"You were in opposition to his Russian policy?" – "Very decidedly."

"You remonstrated with him on the afternoon of his death?" – "Without effect, unfortunately."

"So you determined to try one last appeal that night?" – "That is so."

"At what time did you enter his suite?" – "It was not quite a quarter to one by the Law Courts clock as I came up Fleet Street."

In a law court as hushed as death, an ex-Prime Minister told the story of how at 1.00 a.m. he had found the body of a murdered man, lying in darkness, blood welling from a wound in the breast. Not without shame, but in calm and level terms, an ex-Prime Minister related his decision to hide his part in the discovery from the police. He told how Sir Colin Vansteen had been drawn into the conspiracy and how "a certain member of the *Mercury's* staff" had also agreed to aid the deception. Never had more sensational unexpected evidence been given in a court of law by an ex-Minister of the Crown.

His cross-examination was short.

"You saw no one when you entered?" – "No."

"Your last interview with Lord Carpenter had been a stormy one?" – "It might be described as that."

"You made no attempt to revive Lord Carpenter or call medical aid on the assumption that there might be a spark of life in him?" – "He was beyond all question dead."

The Premier's evidence was followed by that of Sir Colin Vansteen. Sir Benjamin had decided to elicit all the unfavourable features of this witness's action rather than leave it to Freeth-Jones, and his direct examination was subtly designed to anticipate him.

"At 1.15 a.m. on the night in question, the Premier rang you up and told you of his dilemma?" – "That was the approximate time."

"You unhesitatingly believed his story and agreed to support him." – "I did. I have known him for more than fifty years."

"Did you qualify your support in any way?" – "Yes. I stipulated that the concealment should only be for the period of the national crisis, and that I should consider myself free of my promise should it appear to be obstructing the course of justice."

"And in fact you did not find that your action was obstructing the police?" – "No."

"How did you inform the police of the murder without involving the Premier?" – "I rang them up, and on the spur of the moment, attributed the Premier's telephone message to a fictitious person."

"Subsequently you conducted the post-mortem examination?" – "Yes, on behalf of the Home Office."

"Are you still retained by them?" – "No, I resigned my post five days ago."

"What do you find the cause of death to be?" – "Do you wish me to express this technically or in simple language?"

"As plainly as possible." – "Death was the result of penetration of the heart by a steel blade."

"How soon would death take place?" – "Immediately the aortic ventricle was completely penetrated."

"Did you form the conclusion that the victim was taken unawares?" – "From the state of the brain and the body position I should say he was stabbed while asleep, and never fully recovered consciousness."

"Is the fatal wound consonant with the use of this weapon?" asked Sir Benjamin, holding up exhibit R2. – "Yes, entirely."

"You analysed the blood on this weapon. What conclusion did you form?" – "That it was deposited approximately an hour before I examined it – that is, soon after midnight. The blood shows characteristics similar to those of Lord Carpenter's blood."

Sir Benjamin held up Jameson's shirt and coat. "You analysed the blood stains on these garments? What conclusions did you form?" – "The blood shows characteristics similar to that of the deceased. The staining, I should say, took place within twenty-four hours of Lord Carpenter's death. This, however, is very approximate."

"How did you ascertain that the garments were stained with human blood?"

"The test is a well-known one," answered Sir Colin."The presence of blood can be detected in minute quantities by the quite unique specific pigment of the *haemin*. The nature of the blood is ascertained by a more elaborate test. It depends on the power of living blood to form 'antibodies' when injected with foreign blood. A rabbit is injected with small quantities of human blood until it is immunized by the formation of 'antibodies.' In the immunized blood a small portion of the suspect blood is dropped, and if this also is human blood, a small flocculent precipitate is observed in the microscope. I should explain, however, that the test is equally successful with ape's blood, there being virtually no difference between the blood of apes and men. The test, however, will differentiate the blood of apes and men from that of any other animal."

"It is now possible, I understand, to identify blood groups from a small stain?" – "Yes. The Schick-Zimmerman test, depending on the polarization of ultraviolet light by the blood crystals. It is extremely complex, but remarkably successful."

Sir Colin Vansteen, with the assurance of years of experience, turned slightly to face Freeth-Jones's cross-examination. "When the Premier rang you up, were you much disturbed by what he said?" – "I was."

"Did you ask him to assure you that he had not committed the murder?" – "I did – at once."

"Of course." Freeth-Jones paused for a moment to let this picture of an ex-Premier agitatedly avowing his innocence of a murder sink into the minds of the jury. Then he went on. "Now, Sir Colin, you said that the blood on Mr. Jameson's coat and shirt had the same characteristics as Lord Carpenter's. You mean it belongs to the same group?" – "Yes."

"How many groups are there?" – "Four."

"So that the blood on these garments might equally be that of ten million other people in the British Isles?" – "It might."

"Would you be surprised to hear that Mr. Jameson's blood is in the same group as Lord Carpenter's?" – "Not at all."

"In that case you would be quite unable to say whether the blood was Lord Carpenter's or the prisoner's?" – "Oh quite."

"We have heard your evidence with interest today. There are no more fictions in it by any chance, are there, Sir Colin?"

Sir Colin Vansteen flushed faintly. "I suppose I cannot resent that question. I must say on oath, no."

Sir Colin's place was taken by the *Mercury's* librarian. He described how he saw Bysshe coming down the lift about a quarter to one, and how the only rooms above the floor he was on were the Chief's. With considerable reluctance he admitted under pressure from Mr. Arthur Harness that young Jameson had seemed to him disturbed about something. He had the impression that he was alarmed. The general trend of the evidence was all the more damaging for the reluctance with which it was given, and Freeth-Jones got up to lead a forlorn charge into the enemy's country.

"The lift is what is known as an automatic one?" – "Yes."

"It is operated by the person using the lift?" – "Exactly."

"Would it be fairly easy for a man to press the wrong button and go up instead of down?" – "I have done it once or twice myself."

"Directly you notice this, you can press the right button and come down again?" – "Oh, yes."

"So that although Carpenter's suite is the only one above where you are standing, Jameson need not have come from visiting it when you saw him?" – "Not necessarily."

Freeth-Jones leaned forward with one of his disconcerting swoops. "Why did you not report this to the police at once, Mr. Hubbard?" – "I did not realize that it might be of importance until Mr. Jameson came under suspicion."

"Not important to have seen a person in a state of agitation leaving the scene of the crime at the time the murder was reputed to take place?" – "It didn't occur to me like that."

"Do you think, after all, Mr. Jameson could have looked so agitated?" – "I merely say what I saw in a fleeting impression. The lift was descending fairly rapidly."

"A man flashes past you in a gloomy lift-well, unexpectedly, yet you are prepared, in that fleeting instant of time, to swear that he was in a state of extreme agitation?" – "Not extreme."

"Not extreme? Not even sufficiently agitated for you to report this vital fact to the police?" – "If you put it in that way, no."

"Mr. Hubbard, remembering that you are on oath, knowing as a man of intelligence how difficult it is to be sure of our recollections a day or two later, are you prepared to swear that any expression of discomposure you observed on Mr. Jameson's face could not have been due to his suddenly finding he had pressed the wrong button and was going up instead of down?" – "No, I am not. I am prepared to admit it as possible."

"One more question. Did you, subsequently to the discovery of the murder, flatly refuse to give your fingerprints to the police?" – "I did refuse such an unwarrantable trespass on the liberty of the subject. My views on the infallibility of fingerprints, though controversial, are at any rate well known."

The last witness to be called by the Crown was Detective Inspector Manciple. He described the visit to Jameson's rooms, the finding of the bloodstained garment and of the ashes of the diary in the grate. With stolid assurance he identified exhibit R4, the photographic reconstruction of whose blackened pages was universally acknowledged the most damning item in the case of Rex *v.* Jameson.

Sir Benjamin sat down. There was a glint in Freeth-Jones's eye when he rose to tackle Manciple. It was not the first time the two had come into contact. His first question set the pace from the start and the duel proceeded without the slightest discomposure of either side.

"How many persons have you previously arrested in connection with this case?" – "One, and detained one as a witness."

"There was another person you considered sufficiently implicated to be charged with this crime." – "That is so."

"Are you sure you have the right man this time?" – "I believe that is a question which is decided by the jury."

"Have you made any inquiries as to whether Jameson had any enemies?" – "No."

"Did you find out whether any stranger had been in Mr. Jameson's room between the date he left them and the date you searched there?" – "I did not."

"Would you be surprised to hear that a man, purporting to come from the *Mercury*, but actually an impostor, called on Mr. Jameson's room alone?" – "Possibly it was a representative of the *Gazette*." (Laughter)

"Will you please defer your witticisms till you return to the Yard? A man's life is at stake. You made no attempt to ascertain the fact of such a visit?" – "I did not."

"Did you examine Mr. Jameson's room for fingerprints?" – "I did not."

"Did you inquire at the *Mercury's* office or elsewhere to see whether Mr. Jameson's keeping a diary was well known?" – "I did not."

"Have you made any inquiries except for material tending to incriminate Mr. Jameson?" – "I have made all inquiries that seemed to me proper to establish the truth about this crime."

"Yet the possibility of a substitution by an enemy of this diary had not occurred to you?" – "Frankly, I find it incredible."

"The jury will decide on the credibility of evidence. The function of witness, even police witnesses, is to provide the jury with facts. You never even considered the possibility I have mentioned." – "Not for one moment."

By the time Freeth-Jones had finished with Manciple, the dry bones of the case had stirred for the first time. Who was the mysterious enemy that had been introduced with such an assured air? Had the defence really evidence for his existence? Was it another fantastic theory of Freeth-Jones's? And would it, like his others, prove plausible, even likely, by the end of the case? Even the Attorney-General's skilful re-examination could not dissipate the doubt that had begun to gather round the diary. At present no bigger than a man's hand, it might eventually fill the sky.

At any rate, Freeth-Jones gave it no time to get smaller. In an eloquent opening speech he promised to show that the prosecution was an empty shell. It was based on harmless coincidences twisted to support grave conclusions. They had heard of the long arm of coincidence? But perhaps they might think in this case it was too long? He would prove to them that it had been deliberately stretched. The prosecution had been cleverly deceived. They had been helped to find what they wanted to find. But the jury, approaching the case with an open mind, would see through the deception.

Immediately after he had opened his case he called as witness for the defence Mrs. Twemlow. She gave a graphic story of her mysterious visitor. Mr. Arthur Harness's cross-examination only induced her to add to his sinister reality while somewhat confusing his general appearance. The small seed of doubt in the minds of the jury sprouted.

Meanwhile Freeth-Jones was studying a message from Venables, which ran as follows:

"DEAR FREETH-JONES, – This will be brought by Dr. Szerky, of whom I told you. He is absolutely full out for us, and will kick the prosecution in the pants. Let him rip. He's got all the doings with him.

Please, please, please delay the case all you can. I am on the track of something. If I send you a wire 'Adjourn' ask for an adjournment, and say that vital evidence is forthcoming. I won't send the wire unless I have real evidence. Back me up; I won't let you down."

Freeth-Jones studied this wild note for some time, and then spoke to Dr. Szerky. He placed great faith in Venables. He had met him at a time when Charles had saved a friend of his from the Razzini gang and the depths of narcotic-sodden degradation. Well, the story is sufficiently well known now. One may admit that it was Freeth-Jones's wife who owed her salvation to Venables...

The great advocate was smiling broadly when he came into court again, while his junior, Tommy Roebuck, was examining the members of the *Mercury* staff, who testified unanimously that no messenger was dispatched to Jameson's room at the time of the visit of the bearded stranger. Watching counsel whispered to each other as Freeth-Jones surveyed the court triumphantly. Evidently the case was looking up.

Even when permission had been obtained for the defence to call Dr. Szerky, the name meant nothing to them. A grimy and unprepossessing Jew stepped into the witness box.

An expert witness. Rapidly Freeth-Jones ran over his qualifications. Yes, he was consulting graphologist to the Royal Bank of Wales, the Spanish New National Bank, yes, also to the Condor Insurance Company. Yes, the largest American banks and insurance companies retained his services. Yes, the Governor of the Bank of England had, he agreed, written a preface to his last book describing him as the most brilliant graphologist of modern times. He coughed deprecatingly. He had been fortunate enough to be of service to the Bank on one or two occasions.

The scene was now set for the sensation. Deliberately Freeth-Jones produced the charred pages of the diary, and the photostat copies.

"You have seen authenticated specimens of the writing of Mr. Jameson, obtained from the 'copy' files of the *Mercury?*" – "I have."

"You have inspected these photostat copies of the diary found by the police?" – "Yes, very carefully."

"Do you incline to the view that the diary was written by the prisoner?"

Dr. Szerky cleared his throat. There was a silence in court. "On the contrary," he said, loudly and clearly. "I do not think a word of it was written by him."

This unequivocal pronouncement made by the expert whose credentials had been so convincingly established, created a stir of whispered comment. White wigs bobbed, and the judge's pen spluttered industriously.

Szerky's explanation was in the main beyond the grasp of the layman. With the aid of photographic enlargements he endeavoured to illustrate the difference in pressure and letter formation between the two scripts. One, he declared, was a flowing natural hand. The other was a forgery, executed by someone with obvious knowledge of graphology, but without the executive skill necessary for a really convincing forgery.

Mr. Arthur Harness meanwhile was making protesting noises. Sir Benjamin was on his legs in another court. It was quite unprecedented for expert evidence to be suddenly produced like this. He did not object to that – naturally they were anxious to give the defence all reasonable scope, but they must be allowed to call further expert evidence later. Moreover, after they had called it, they must be allowed to continue the cross-examination of Dr. Szerky.

Pacified by the consent of Mr. Justice Angevin, Mr. Arthur Harness wrestled competently with Dr. Szerky.

"Your various retainers as consultant demand only the verification of signatures?" – "That is so."

"A man's signature – the one group of letters he writes over and over again – tends to become much more stylized and formal than his ordinary writing." – "Yes, I agree."

"So that your work for these retainers has been entirely concerned with a special kind of writing, distinct from the ordinary calligraphy of a manuscript?" – "My work as a paid consultant has certainly been concentrated on that field."

"In this case there is no question of the verification of a signature?" – "No."

This was a stout effort at short notice, but it was easily demolished.

Freeth-Jones rose wearily. "Have you published several well-known books dealing with the distinctive characters of ordinary handwriting?" – "Yes."

"Was it these that originally made your name?" – "So I am told."

"Is one still a police text book?" – "I understand so."

By the time the lunch hour was over the Crown's two expert witnesses had been brought from the Yard. They expressed their belief that the diary was written by Jameson in a state of agitation. They appreciated the differences pointed out by Dr. Szerky, but they considered these explicable by the different circumstances and the use of a different pen. It was not a very convincing display. Cross-examined, the first admitted that in his last book he had described Szerky as "the master of us all." Yes, the second witness admitted, it was true that he had been trained by Szerky. The Crown wisely refrained from having any more to do with Szerky.

But Freeth-Jones had lost his look of triumph. As he afterwards admitted, he was faced with the greatest problem of his career. Out of a black case against his client, he had conjured up that whisper of doubt which in previous trials he had turned into a releasing spell. All, in fact, that now remained to give him a reasonable hope of success was for the accused to maintain his innocence, deny ever having written the diary, pour ridicule on the motive which the prosecution alleged, explain the bloodstained garments, explain his flight and letter to Grovermuller, and generally give a convincing performance, helped by Freeth-Jones's skilful prompting, of a harmless young fool who had lost his head. This done with skill by a pleasant-faced and educated young man, would put the coping stone on the defence. That would, Freeth-Jones considered, give his client a fifty-fifty chance. On the other hand, for the last ten years, no accused in a murder trial who had not given evidence in his own behalf had been acquitted except where he had been proved insane.

Yet Freeth-Jones, in spite of this, decided not to put Jameson in the box.

He knew that for the rest of his life, if Jameson were condemned, it would be held against him by his brother barristers. But equally inevitably, to place him in the box would be to hang him.

It was bad enough for Jameson to look, as he looked now, as if all the remorse of hell was gnawing his breast. It was bad enough for him to plead hysterically, during the lunch interval, that he should be spared the ordeal of giving evidence. It was worse for him to demand the next moment that he might be put into the box and "end the farce by telling the whole truth." He would deny that the diary was not written by him with the persistency of monomania, but on everything else he would evade and contradict himself, and finally ask piteously – What did it matter? He could not escape.

The advocate caught for the last time his eyes, haunted by more than the apprehension of doom. "I shan't put him in," he said with finality. Judge, jury, and prosecuting counsel stared as he rose and intimated that the case for the defence was closed.

Sir Benjamin's closing speech was typical. It was aridly devoid of flowers of speech, but its logical simplicity was barbed. It stuck in the minds of the envenomed jury with unescapable fact.

The bodily presence of the prisoner at the scene of the murder had been proved; and the motive had been made clear. This was the foundation of the Crown's case. On top of this the bloodstained garment, the prisoner's agitation and subsequent flight, and the diary. It was true that the expert evidence conflicted on one point. But never in all the cases in which he had participated had he discovered two experts called by opposing sides whose evidence did not conflict. The jury would no doubt remember the classification by an eminent judge, of the varieties of Not-Truth into lies, damned lies, and expert evidence.

The jury would also know how to treat what he might term, in mystery story vein, the Episode of the Sinister Stranger. This creation, as he ventured to call him, of his learned friend's brilliant imagination was indeed about as credible as a mystery story. Unfortunately the jury were there as judges of the fact. And the facts were much more humdrum. It was true no one would come forward and admit they called on Mrs. Twemlow. But since if they did so the defence would at once fasten the label of murderer on them, this was not surprising. Even he would hesitate to come forward after he had been metamorphosed into something so rich and strange as the lurid creature Mrs. Twemlow had not very consistently painted.

No item of this remarkable story had been confirmed by the prisoner, nor had he denied writing the diary. The significance of this fact the jury would fully appreciate. And so on.

Freeth-Jones's reply occupied four hours. He traced movingly and convincingly the character of the prisoner – enthusiastic, nervous, highly-strung. His panic was as natural to him as his enthusiasm. One followed the other. Both were guarantees of his innocence. Now, faced by all the dreadful might and fearful pomp of English justice, he was still more appalled. Suddenly overwhelmed by this terrible thing, accused of so loathsome and impossible a crime, he was almost prostrate. The jury could see for themselves. His sister feared for his reason. Only unremitting medical attendance made possible his appearance in court today. The jury would see why he had been spared the ordeal of the witness box, where he could do no more than assert his innocence, as he had already done in his plea, and his ignorance of every detail of the unjustifiable fabric of circumstantial evidence with which the prosecution had endeavoured to enmesh him. The political motive alleged by the Crown was ludicrous. Could the circumstantial evidence, superficially plausible, be mere coincidence? Most certainly it could. It appeared that another person had been involved sufficiently for circumstantial evidence to warrant his arrest. If it could be coincidence in the one case, it could equally be so in the case of his client. What was the foundation stone, the one tangible evidence of the prosecution? Was it the bloodstained garment? No. Their own witness stated that the blood on it might as well be the prisoner's as Carpenter's. Was it the knife? No. There were fingerprints on the knife – but not his client's. Oh no – fingerprints of people they were told were innocent! Was it the presence of his client at the scene of the crime? No, no attempt had been made to prove that. They had only proved that his client was using a lift he had every right to use, frequently used, and which gave access to every portion of the whole *Mercury* building. What, then, was the one sheet anchor of the prosecution? An alleged confession, a thing always regarded with suspicion in English law – but in this case it stank to high heaven. For it was a faked confession. What a testimony to his client's innocence! Who troubled to fake evidence against the guilty?

His learned friend had let fall a jocular remark. If he had understood it aright, he was in complete agreement with it, for he understood that Sir Benjamin had stated that the evidence of the Crown's expert witnesses was a degree worse than damned lies. No doubt they had already formed the same conclusion. Sir Benjamin had been equally witty about what Sir Benjamin had described – and again he welcomed the description – as the Episode of the Sinister Stranger. But even the prosecution had not denied his existence, and failing any reasonable explanation of his visit by the prosecution, he remained a sinister figure, a flesh and blood person in a beard, who had visited Mr. Jameson's room with a faked excuse and a forged letter, and after whose visit the police had discovered a diary which the world's most brilliant graphologist had declared was forged. They must not be led astray by baffling and unusual coincidences. It was not, thank heaven, a crime to be touched by the long arm of coincidence. The weak nature of the case which – even giving these coincidences their full value – the prosecution had put forward was suspicious enough. But beside it stood the figure of the Sinister Stranger, compelling their attention, pointing with unwilling finger to the explanation of the coincidences.

Freeth-Jones ended with one of his famous perorations. The position of a juryman was an unenviable one. Truth dwelt in a well, evidence was bewildering, human beings were fallible. Yet here they were, assembled solemnly together, to settle the fate of a human life, quench it like a candle flame that has lit its little world with light and laughter but

> *"If I quench thee, thou flaming minister,*
> *I can again thy former light restore.*
> *Should I repent me, but once put out thy light,*
> *Thou cunning'st pattern of excelling nature,*
> *I know not where is that Promethean heat,*
> *That can thy light relume."*

What a terrible decision! How dreadful to condemn a human being, on evidence specious enough, but admitting doubt, and to be haunted by that doubt all the days of one's life! Well, the English law, the ripe accretion of a thousand years, rich with human kindness, had allowed for that. If they had any doubt they were at liberty – nay it was their bounden sacred duty as jurymen, to acquit the accused.

The Crown's reply was as emotionless as possible. Sir Benjamin pointed out the importance of each of the clues the defence had treated so lightly. Once again he mocked the Sinister Stranger who, it seemed, not only faked the diary, but now apparently unwillingly instructed the jury. This, however, was properly his lordship's task. And inexorably, coldly, and for half an hour, Sir

Benjamin rubbed in Jameson's refusal to go into the box.

Mr. Justice Angevin began his summing-up with an inward feeling of relief that no scene had marred the even tenor of his case. Well, no one could deny his ability to sum up, and now he began.

It had for Miranda, listening intently, the cold inevitability of doom.

One by one he related the salient facts as told by the witnesses, as interpreted by prosecution and defence. In the light of the conflict of evidence, although graphology was not an exact science, they must not let the diary influence them too greatly in considering their verdict. Perhaps they might, for a start, put both the diary and the individual who had been described as the Sinister Stranger out of their mind for a little. Was the Crown's case proved apart from this? They had reduced the time during which the murder took place to a short space of time and had produced evidence presumptive of the accused's presence in the suite during that time.

So it reached its close, a model summing-up, nor did Mr. Justice Angevin fail to caution the jury, as had so many of Freeth-Jones's judges, that his peroration must not mislead them. The doubt which was needed for an acquittal was a reasonable doubt, and he elaborated the difference between reasonable doubt and scruples.

The jury, it is regrettable to say, had already made up their minds. The man was guilty. His behaviour alone had shown that. The extracts from the diary had proved it. As for graphology, well that was too much for them to swallow. They might as well believe palmistry!

Miranda watched the jury with agonized attention. They were agreeing on something in the box. The foreman was collecting opinions, heads were being nodded. They were going to give their verdict without leaving the box! She knew too well what that verdict would be. Her heart seemed to liquefy inside her.

Whether the jury were going to commit such an unprecedented action was, however, never decided. For suddenly both Mr. Justice Angevin and the jury became aware of a disturbing element, a protesting voice, the stir of movement, the upright figure of Freeth-Jones, with a white paper fluttering in his hand, taking the most impudent decision of his career.

"My lord, I beg that you will stop the case. Vital evidence, evidence that will completely acquit my client, has come to hand!"

A Wife Betrays

"WHAT HAS THE WISDOM of the East to say on the problem of an irresistible force meeting an immovable object?" asked Charles of Lee Kum Tong.

"It says," answered Lee, "that scholars do not look for the phoenix's nest."

"I see. You mean you believe there is no such thing." He threw himself disconsolately into Lee's chair. "Well, I haven't looked for the phoenix's nest, but I've trodden on the darn thing. At this moment Bysshe Jameson is standing his trial for murder. The police have a perfect case. Jameson gives almost every evidence of guilt. Yet as I live I am certain that another man did it, and every move I make I stumble upon confirmation after confirmation of it."

"Oh-ho, I wonder if I know your suspect?" exclaimed Lee, dropping for a moment his expression of bland imperturbability. "I know something of medicine. What about a plain case of megalomania; epileptic history somewhere, I should imagine; I've always been afraid of trouble from that quarter."

Charles started. "Well, I'm damned. After days of hard work, quantities of thought and five distinct cases of sheer luck, I've arrived just at the place you've been at for the last week."

Lee raised the palms of his hands deprecatingly. "The fool treads on the white fox by accident in the evening; the hunter has been trailing him since the dawn. I know nothing against our friend except his obvious constitutional weakness."

"Well, I know more," said Charles, and told him.

Lee nodded. "I am convinced by the irresistible force. Can we not budge the irremovable object? What have we against Jameson? An apparent sensation of guilt, you will say? But do not myriads of the wild and unlearned give themselves up to the police after a murder alleging their guilt, in spite of the evident impossibility of this? And even say it was possible, why should Jameson be right? And *even supposing he was right—*"

"Good God" said Charles, "supposing he was right. Do you realize what you are saying? Mercurial heavens, I see it all now. Or am I goofy?" Desperately Charles plunged his head in his hands. "Lee, you may think you were only burbling, but you have spoken words of wisdom worthy to be wrapped in peach blossom and proffered to the thirteen-toed Dragon of the Milky Way. They will make you a Mandarin of the Ruby Button for this, Lee. I'll see to it—" Babbling wildly, Charles hunted for a telephone directory. He started to mutter incoherent threats. "I'll get the truth out of the old bounder if I have to flog him with his stethoscope..."

— II —

Sir Colin's voice was pained. "My dear Mr. Venables, what are you suggesting? Not, I hope, that my death certificate was fraudulent?"

"Come off it," said Charles rudely. "We were both in the original ramp together. So don't, please, suddenly become professional. What I wanted to know is very simple. Have you deposed the truth, the whole truth, and nothing but the truth concerning the death of Lord Carpenter?"

"I have told the truth, the whole truth, and nothing but the truth concerning the death of Lord Carpenter," said Sir Colin coldly.

"You said *that* as if you were equivocating," commented Charles thoughtfully. "Ah, I've got it, concerning the death of Lord Carpenter. But have you mentioned every unusual feature in the body of Lord Carpenter as revealed by your autopsy? Something, perhaps," insinuated Charles, "that had no relation at all to his death, that you think didn't really concern the police at all?"

Sir Colin rubbed his chin helplessly. "You've cornered me. There was an unusual feature – most unusual. But how did you guess it? Oh, I suppose the Premier told you."

"The Premier!" Charles smiled seraphically. "Ha-ha, *that* explains it now! How perfectly it fits in. Of course the Premier would account for it. The obvious conclusion! Yet how deliriously wrong!" For a moment the young man seemed unable to continue.

"Will you kindly explain," said Sir Colin with a trace of irritation. "You have shown yourself sensible to my friend's best interests in the past. I should expect you to do so now. I take it you have some object in raking up a matter which I should have thought, in view of Sanger's tremendous services to the nation, had much better be dropped."

"I am sensible to all you have so eloquently pointed out, but as Gilbert remarks, it has nothing to do with the case, tra la. But your private mystery has got a great deal to do with the murder, it has in fact had terrible consequences, which you will realize in a moment."

"I am afraid you do not take me with you. I have formed the opinion that my little reservation has in no way perplexed the police in the performance of their duties."

"Perplexed the police! My dear Sir Colin, it has perplexed

Charles Venables!! Now listen. Am I correct in saying that when you came to perform the autopsy you found the following – if you will pardon a layman's terms."

Sir Colin listened with growing interest to Charles's concise suggestions. "I could almost believe you performed the autopsy yourself!" he said at last. "But how can this have affected the issue?"

Charles wagged his head reproachfully. "Prejudice, Sir Colin, prejudice! The last thing one should expect in a professional witness! You formed a conclusion, and of course everything seemed to bear it out. But as it happened, the explanation of this peculiarity is very different to what your prejudice supposed."

Except for an occasional snort of amazement, Sir Colin listened without comment to Charles's explanation. "You are right," he said at the end, "I have been ridiculous. I can never forgive myself. Yet how can you establish the truth of what you have told me? It seems to me that you are up against an amazingly astute man."

"I realize it," Charles answered soberly. "So far, he has just slipped out of my grip at every turn. And time is so infernally short. But I still have a card or two to play."

— III —

Charles had a long interview with Grovermuller. It began stormily, but the man was fundamentally able to see reason. After all, even one's worst enemy is accessible to the logic of facts. When Charles left him he had extracted the promise he wanted.

His next interview was with Mrs. Jerningham *née* Hubbard.

He waited till the after-luncheon cigarette. "Frightfully sorry I was not able to come to the wedding, but I was desperately busy – or perhaps I was in prison. I forget now, but I know there was some reason. So you got your man! Well, I feel rather sorry for the Dowager Lady Carpenter. You know I felt she hadn't a chance from the start."

Mrs Jerningham smiled sweetly. "You do say such extraordinary things, Mr. Venables. I don't know what you mean. You could have knocked me over with a feather when Mr. Jerningham proposed to me – I was that surprised. I never guessed for a moment that he thought of me like that."

"You do it beautifully," commented Charles admiringly. "And it still doesn't bore you?"

"Not a bit! I am quite a success in Surbiton. We have a dear little house there. My husband feels so pleased he married something sweet and simple-minded."

"Poor fellow. I hope he never finds out."

She shrugged her shoulders. "I shall be a fool if he does. The art of managing them is not to let them know." She paused. "We can, of course, go on discussing this subject endlessly. That is not, however, what you asked to see me for. The trip up from Surbiton was very pleasant and this little place we are lunching at all very proper for a suburban bride. I admire your discretion. But supposing we are frank?"

Charles sighed. "How mercenary you make me feel. My object in taking you here was no more than to enjoy your company, of which that lucky man, Jerningham, has so cruelly deprived us."

"I see, and that's why, after not even turning up at the wedding, I get a perfectly frantic phone call from you this morning, saying I must lunch with you, today, and it must be today."

"All very natural," he answered lightly. "But now we are here, there is a matter that may as well be discussed." He tapped the ash from his cigarette and hesitated, then he spoke meaningly. "You will be relieved to hear that it is not a dominant hereditary taint. Any little Jerninghams will be quite all right."

She paled suddenly. Her hand trembled as she raised a cigarette to her lips. "What *are* you talking about?"

"I see you understand me. I suppose it's much worse at home than it is here."

"Terrible," she said in a low voice. "I knew someone would see it sooner or later."

"Well, it's not an easy thing I am going to ask you to do, but you must help us."

She smiled. "No. Quite definitely, no. Why should I? Do you think I want the scandal and publicity – now of all times?"

Charles looked at her keenly. "Would it mean nothing to you if I reminded you that an innocent man's life is at stake?"

"Of course, there is the sentimental aspect. But might I point out that it doesn't come very well to the ears of a loving and dutiful daughter."

Charles sighed, "That's what I thought, so I didn't advance it very seriously. Let me remind you of something else. This is only the beginning; more will follow. Hadn't it better be stopped while there is time?"

She smiled. "I should think he's been scared badly enough not to do it again. Besides, I don't think he will need to. I am sure he wouldn't do it unless it was absolutely necessary. I agree with you in principle of course, but I must think of myself. The scandal would be terrible; we should all be dragged through the mire. Why, we would have to move from Surbiton." She shrugged her shoulders in mock dismay.

"I fear you will have to move from Surbiton anyway. Grovermuller and I have decided, oddly enough, that if Jameson is found guilty your husband will be dismissed from the Company's employ. You see we have reason enough over the bonds business – reason enough to refuse him a character reference as well. But

Grovermuller just hates to do it. And I have persuaded him to keep Jerningham on – oddly enough – only if Jameson gets off."

Her lips curled in contempt. "You are a cad, aren't you?"

"Well, you are a bit of a bounder yourself. So we understand one another. And I can assure you this case means a lot to me. Not professionally, but personally as well."

She nodded. "Oh, of course, the sister. Extraordinary how we intelligent people always fall for our mental inferiors. Now we two ought to be made for one another."

She looked at him coolly, her cigarette drooping from her beautifully shaped mouth. "But I suppose you dislike me as much as I dislike you."

"My very dear lady," protested Charles.

"I see. I should have said 'more than I dislike you,'" she amended quickly. "Well, you've got the better of me this time. My vulnerable point. So Jameson must get off, must he?" She thought a moment. "I can't do anything myself, you know, but I can give you the necessary hint." She stubbed her cigarette reflectively on her plate. "I should pay a domestic visit. My brains, I should explain, did *not* come down the distaff side." She gathered up her bag. "Now I suppose you will say 'you must dash.' Goodbye."

Charles hurried out. He looked at his watch disconsolately as a taxi bore him lumberingly northward. "Two hours wasted! Still I don't see how I could have got the facts any quicker! I said it wasn't hereditary, but I think it must be contagious. She gives me the cold shivers."

— IV —

42 Lilac Avenue was a small terrace house with a bright green door, a neat garden, and red plush curtains. The fat woman

who opened the door to Venables appeared to belong to that type who, either by nature or training, have the ability to keep their homes scrupulously neat but, as a kind of reaction, exhibit the other extreme in their persons. She brushed the wandering strands of fair hair out of her eyes with one hand, while with the other she perfunctorily straightened some vague entanglement on her bosom. Yes, this was Mrs. Hubbard.

"I'm from the *Mercury*," said Charles, looking at her coldly.

Her large blue eyes rolled. "Oh, dear," she said, "has anything happened?"

"I think, if you don't mind, we'll discuss that inside."

Charles was conducted in dead silence into a sitting room, adorned mainly with portraits of Hubbard, with and without whiskers, as a Territorial, in his hood as Master of Arts of a Midland University, as a member of a cricketing team... The furniture matched the house. Charles observed the corner of a tray and the foot of a glass masked by the billowing folds of drapery from a sofa. He deliberately sat down above it. Yes, there was a distinct odour of the juniper berry which, combined with alcohol, has done so much to solace feminine hearts.

Charles remained silent for a moment. The silence was broken by a quite sudden sob, which rather lost its pathos by becoming entangled with a hiccup in mid-career. Mrs. Hubbard produced a greyish handkerchief and applied it to her nose with a perfunctory sniff. She then smiled pallidly at Charles.

"You gave me a turn, coming so sudden like."

Of course, reflected Charles, he would have married "beneath him." They always do. I suppose they want to be sure of having someone who will look up to them, anyway.

"I saw your daughter, today," he said suddenly in a bright conversational tone. "Terrible for her to know about her father."

The blowsy woman flushed with indignation. "Terrible to her.

A lot she cares. She's as hard as nails – harder than her father – for all her soft, simpering looks. Never a word of sympathy have I had from that girl, mister – I didn't catch your name. Even as a little mite she was like that – hard, why you wouldn't credit it. Come and found me crying in the early days, many's the time and oft, and do you think she's said a kind word and put her arm round her mummy's neck like any normal child would? No, just bite her lip she would, the pert little miss, and tell me to stop as bold as brass. Do you think she cares that I've been driven crazy with worry? Not a bit. She's got her man, and off she goes, as pleased as punch, leaving her pore mother all alone." This time the dirty handkerchief found something genuine to wipe away. The next moment Mrs. Hubbard was staring craftily at him.

"But there, I am rambling on! Such a chatterbox – you must excuse me – many's the time and oft my husband's told me so." She achieved a titter. "What did you ask me now? I don't reely remember."

"What time did your husband come home on the night Lord Carpenter was killed?"

"I don't remember. Fancy you asking me that."

"What clothes was he wearing when he came back?"

A flicker of fear showed itself in her eyes. "I don't remember," she answered sullenly.

"Did he tell you what he'd done?"

"I don't remember," she answered again. Then her temper flared up. "I don't know what you mean!" she shouted. "Who are you, and what are you doing here? What right has a little whippersnapper like you to come round tormenting and badgering me? You say you're from the *Mercury*, but what do you want? Who sent you? Don't fiddle with that bit of glass – you'll drive me crazy."

Charles smiled nastily. "So he warned you someone would come,

252

did he, and he told you to say nothing but 'I don't remember'? Hasn't much opinion of your intelligence, has he?"

"Well, I never set up to be one for brains, did I? What call is there for him to despise me? Always sneering at me, Irene and him, in a nasty underhand way you can't get back at. Many's the time and oft I've told him, where's your book-learning got you to, anyway? My pore father, for all he had no education and kept a shop in the Old Kent Road, he had more money put aside for a treat if he wanted it than we ever had and no need to stint and scrape to look as if we were better than we were. Oh, what would pore father say if he could see me now?" She subsided into great gusty sobs.

He warned her, so that she must have found out something, reflected Charles. What the devil could it have been? He wouldn't have confided in her – not in his wildest moments.

"I know what you have gone through, Mrs. Hubbard," he said kindly. "I've come here to help you. Do you realize the position you are in? Remember, *they always turn against the people they love!*"

A shudder ran over the fat woman's back. She looked at him with the fascinated eyes of the rabbit that sees the stoat within springing distance. "I know. That's what I'm afraid of. I daren't meet his eyes." She looked round wildly. "I daren't turn my back on him! I always wait till he's asleep before I dare go to sleep. And then I don't know whether he's shamming or not."

"There you are, you see! And so it'll go on. And then one day you'll turn your back on him; one day he'll be shamming sleep. And that will be the end. Much better to tell the truth and end it."

"Oh, dear! I feel so bad. I think I'll have something to drink. Just under your foot, young man." She gulped down a liberal glass and wiped her eyes. "I'll tell you," she said decisively, "if it's with my last dying breath! He came back that night with a little parcel under his arm. 'Why,' I said to him, 'you've come back in your nice office coat.' 'Yes,' he says shortly, 'spilt some ink on my other coat. I've brought it back in the parcel.' 'There,' I says, 'a nice coat that was too, let me get it off for you.' 'No,' he snaps back at me, 'I'll get it off. You'll only make a mess of it, go back to bed.' Well, when he went into another room, I says to myself, well, I'll surprise him, and show I'm not such a fool. I'll get some of that ink-remover I used to use for baby's clothes when she went to school, and take it off and surprise him. Then I opened the parcel, and there was blood on the coat. Just at that moment he comes in."

She stopped, and looked at Charles. She was reliving again the terror of that scene. "I says, 'Why it's blood! You've hurt yourself!' His face went as black as night, and he roared and carried on. Then he went all quiet like, and said he had been annoyed at me opening the parcel when he told me not to. He said someone had cut their selves at the office and bled on it, but he hadn't said so to me for fear it would turn me up. But then the next day the papers were full of the murder."

She gave a moan. "And then I knew – Gawd help me I knew – and he saw that I knew. Hit me, he did, so that I carried the bruise for days, and raved and carried on as if he would never stop. I thought my last hour had come. Told me never to unlock my lips if I wanted to keep alive." She looked at him, her face puckered, her eyes red-ringed and moist, with the blonde strands of hair clinging to them still. "Well, now I've told you, and I feel better. It's been awful, just awful. Every time the doorbell rings – jump goes my heart."

"What happened to the coat? Have you still got it?"

"Yes, it's put away in the cupboard," she said listlessly. "But of course I washed it – scrubbed it and scoured it with soap and soda so that there's not a trace to be seen."

Charles smiled. "A trace of *haemin* equivalent to one part in 1,870,000 can be detected by the Toscanini reaction. Does that mean anything to you? Possibly not. But because of it all your scrubbing and scouring is no good."

As Charles packed up the coat in its parcel, the inevitability of the gesture seemed to fill her with fresh apprehension. Charles endeavoured to soothe her, without much success. He paid a visit to Hubbard's library before he went, and left her lying on the sofa, sobbing softly, with the tide steadily receding in the bottle of gin beside her. He stopped at a telegraph office on the way back to Fleet Street.

— V —

"I've something here that will interest you," said Charles to Hubbard casually. He produced a parcel and shook out of it with elaborate indifference, a coat. Hubbard's eyes narrowed and his lips compressed as he watched it, but otherwise he never moved a muscle of his face.

"Pity you didn't add a little elementary biology to your graphological accomplishments," he said, putting down a couple of books beside the coat. "Szerky on the *Elements of Calligraphy* and Button's police text book on the *Technique of Criminal Forgery*. They appear to be well-thumbed. If you had only added to them some elementary manual on forensic medicine you would have seen that by plunging the coat in a very dilute solution of hydrochloric acid after its wash, the Toscanini reaction would have been neutralized. Anyway, it's always better to burn them, even if it is awkward to explain what you have done with them."

"I don't know what you are talking about," said Hubbard, his lips curling. "But in order that the conversation will not languish, may I say, quite at random, that a couple of books on graphology and a trace of who knows whose blood won't carry you far in whatever object you have in mind."

Charles nodded. "True. But there's the visit to Mrs. Twemlow – fingerprints all over the room – very careless that. Then there's the faked entry in the diary. I see you have a respect for Szerky. Well, he recognizes your self-trained touch in the entries, and he is bursting to say so. So far, of course, he's not been asked. Then there's your sad lack of an alibi. And your refusal to give fingerprints. And of course, apart from Carpenter's murder, there's your attempts on Grovermuller. Another forged letter, I suppose, that one from Carpenter! What a pity I didn't catch you in the act of knifing Grovermuller. Just my luck!"

"On the contrary. I took care that when I did attack him, it was in such a place that no one could see me without showing themselves."

"Well, we'll pass over the Grovermuller affair – including even the faked cuttings. But finally we come to the most damning thing of all, your wife's evidence."

Hubbard laughed coldly. "Don't try and bluff me! Do you think I don't know the law? Of course that won't be admitted in evidence."

"Not in evidence, no, but there's nothing to prevent the police hearing it. And having heard it, you can be sure they'll have sufficient encouragement to nose round and get enough evidence to hang you apart from that."

Hubbard eyed him balefully from behind thick spectacles. "As I said before, Venables, I'm not the man to be bluffed. I'll speak to you straightly. It's four o'clock now. Before half-past five Jameson – as you know and I know – will be a condemned man. Do you think the police will be too keen on the story of an hysterical woman, a story that upsets their weeks of careful work? Do you think you can make use of this today at the trial? Do you think you can put up witnesses to say and prove that they know nothing about Jameson, but they can prove that Hubbard did it? Come, you must know enough about legal procedure to realize that no judge would permit that line of defence. I'll be fair with you, Venables. You're a clever little devil and you've got me in a nasty corner − I'll admit it. But I've got an even chance and it'll take more than an even chance of danger to run like a fool, confessing my sins to the police, and imploring them to give me the opportunity of atonement. What in hell are you smiling at?"

Charles told him.

A Judge Is Angry

MR. JUSTICE ANGEVIN LOOKED at Freeth-Jones as at some mad thing.

The telegram he was waving in his hand was from Charles Venables. It read: "Adjourn. Arriving in two hours' time." On this only, Freeth-Jones, with quite inexcusable impetuosity, had risked his action.

"Mr. Freeth-Jones," said Mr. Justice Angevin, "you have closed your case. The jury are about to deliver a verdict. Will you kindly sit down."

"But my lord," protested the counsel, "this is vital evidence, evidence that will acquit my client beyond all peradventure."

"You have had ample time to prepare your case," said Mr. Justice Angevin coldly. "You are aware that if any fresh evidence of importance arises subsequent to the case, the Court of Appeal can order a re-trial."

At this moment, the judge received a flank attack. It was unfortunate that the foreman of the jury, Peterson, was an ardent amateur politician and one of those middle-aged sticklers for the rights of the subject, generally misconceived, which have caused so much trouble in our rough island story. It is men such as Peterson, dour and acid-mouthed, who are foremost in enforcing rights of way, claiming ancient lights, and attempting to put into practice such ridiculous tenets as, "An Englishman's home is his castle."

Peterson rose to his feet.

"All I can say, my lord, is that if Mr. Freeth-Jones has fresh evidence, we want to hear it."

"Mr. Foreman, I decide whether evidence is admissible or not."

"Well, we decide on the verdict, and you won't get one till we hear what Mr. Freeth-Jones has to say."

"I have a good mind to commit you for contempt of court," said the judge angrily. "I shall adjourn for two hours to give the jury and learned counsel time to come to their senses."

"I trust we shall all be in a calmer frame of mind by then," replied the K.C.

Mr. Justice Angevin's voice trembled with indignation. "Your observation is most impertinent."

"And his was most improper," soliloquized Freeth-Jones loudly.

The judge rose to his feet.

"The Court is adjourned for two hours," he said. "I will be prepared to hear you in chambers, Mr. Jones." He rose. Mr. Freeth-Jones bowed gravely. Mr. Justice Angevin bowed gravely. The scene ended.

Now Mr. Freeth-Jones was in difficulties. His correct procedure was to see the judge in chambers, explain the nature of the evidence he wished to call, and come to some amicable arrangement. Unfortunately there was just one drawback. He himself had not the vaguest idea of the evidence he would be calling. And if he showed Angevin the telegram from Venables as his sole justification for the scene he had created in court, he was aware that even his magnificent bluff would be unable to carry it off.

Ten minutes before the two hours were up, Charles arrived.

They were crowded minutes, minutes during which Freeth-Jones's brain worked at lightning speed.

His best friends were unable to deny that the great advocate liked publicity. His enemies said he revelled in it. And when he had heard Charles's story he determined that the case must be played out to the finish in open court.

It would, he knew, be the one topic of discussion in every home for nine days. It would mark the peak of his career as a criminal lawyer. He arrived in court half a minute late to find Mr. Justice Angevin sitting bolt upright with two red spots on his cheeks.

"Mr. Freeth-Jones, I have a good mind not to hear you. However," he added hastily, seeing Peterson get grimly to his feet, "I had better hear your apology."

"I am deeply sorry I was not able to see you in chambers, my lord. I have spent a crowded time endeavouring to sift and marshal the new evidence, to ascertain that I was really justified in making such an unusual application. My lord, I feel I am fully justified. I again ask you to allow the re-opening of the case."

"It is impossible. There is no precedent."

"May I humbly suggest that precedents are made by judges, not judges by precedents."

"You may. But it will not necessarily alter my mind. The case must proceed."

"Not while I'm on the jury," Mr. Peterson was heard to remark ominously. "I've never heard of such red tape."

Very wisely, Mr. Justice Angevin decided to be a little deaf. Mr. Freeth-Jones and Sir Benjamin whispered for ten minutes.

Sir Benjamin rose. "The Crown is anxious to give the defence every facility, and I think, with all due respect, that it is possible to find a way out of the difficulty. There is a precedent for witnesses already called to be called again, at the request of the jury, to clear up certain points. I understand from my learned friend that this is what he is mainly anxious for. He requires to call only one fresh witness – the prisoner himself. Unusual though this is, at such a stage of a trial, I feel that the wide latitude shown by the law to accused persons in capital charges – I submit this with all due deference to your lordship – would justify the Crown in supporting such an application and yourself in granting it. I feel, however, that I must warn your lordship that I gather, from what little my learned friend tells me, that issues of law as well as of fact – grave issues, and unprecedented issues – will be raised. In that case the Crown will feel compelled to ask for a further adjournment."

"I regret to see you supporting such an irregular application, Sir Benjamin," said Mr. Justice Angevin huffily. His temper had now subsided, and he felt quite unable to oppose the two K.C.'s any further. On their own heads be it. "I shall grant it, but whether I grant an adjournment depends entirely on the view I form of the evidence Mr. Freeth-Jones considers so vital."

Meanwhile Charles Venables had been talking to Bysshe Jameson. Miranda saw with incredulous surprise how her brother's eyes lit and his shoulders squared.

Nobody noticed Mr. "Tommy" Roebuck. Yet he betrayed the greatest agitation. For his leader had given him only half an hour to get down to the roots of one of the most amazing points of law ever raised in a murder trial.

Bysshe Jameson stepped into the dock. Freeth-Jones met his eyes reassuringly, and with a smile. "Mr Jameson, will you please tell the court in your own words exactly what happened at 12.30 a.m. to 1.00 a.m. on the night of Lord Carpenter's death?"

Bysshe Jameson looked round the crowded court. Freeth-Jones had sat down, and was in earnest conversation with Sir Colin Vansteen.

For the first time he caught Miranda's eye. He smiled. "Soon after 12.30 on the night in question," he said clearly, "I stepped into the lift that gives access to the Chief's rooms. This was the result of a resolution I had formed over a period of days. The office was lit, but the Board Room was in darkness. However, I knew it well, and a faint light came in from the open window. I was in a state of great excitement. I pulled over my hands a pair of gloves I carried in my pocket, and took down a Florentine dagger which I knew to be on the wall."

Bysshe Jameson halted for a moment. There was a complete and utter silence in the court. His face was now white and strained, and it could be seen that his hands clasped the ledge of the witness box tightly. When he spoke again it was hurriedly, and in gasps.

"I took down the dagger and gently opened the door of the bedroom. Here also there was a little light, and I could see the Chief. When I had felt sure he was not awake I went up to him," – again he paused and looked, wild-eyed, round the court – "and stabbed him through the heart!"

A murmur in court rose suddenly to a cry. Mr. Justice Angevin's voice rose loudly and shrilly above it, demanding silence. "This is outrageous!" he said, white-faced. "Mr. Freeth-Jones, you are a disgrace to your profession. I shall report you to the Bar Council. How dare you conduct a case in this manner. Such an action as you have committed is unheard of in the annals of our law. I can only hope you have taken leave of your senses."

Suavely, Freeth-Jones raised a hand. "My action is unusual, but then the case is unusual. If your lordship will permit my client to finish his evidence-in-chief, he will, perhaps, later see the exonerating effect of my client's evidence."

Sir Benjamin also rose to his feet. "Astonishing as it may seem, my lord, I believe Mr, Freeth-Jones is conducting his defence with admirable correctness."

"This trial appears to be a farce with counsel for the prosecution and the defence as chief actors," said Mr. Justice Angevin. "Proceed. I shall make no attempt to protect witnesses in future."

"And then–" said Freeth-Jones mildly.

"Then I went back and replaced the dagger. Horrified with what I had done, I ran from the room."

"At what time exactly did you enter the room?"

"My thoughts were in a turmoil throughout. I had only the vaguest sense of what was happening. It was probably after 12.30 – perhaps nearer one when I entered. It must have gone one before I came to myself."

"Did you examine the dagger closely before picking it up?" – "No, it was much too dark. I felt for it more than picked it up."

"Which way was the blade pointing on the wall?" – "I do not remember, but the supports are so arranged that it can only hang up in one position."

"Did you see anyone on your way up or back to your room?" – "No, I did not."

"Do you think anyone saw you on either occasion?" – "I am positive they did not."

"Did you make any record of this in a diary?" – "None at all."

"Why did you run away?" – "I thought the police had found me out."

"How did your coat become bloodstained?"

Jameson shuddered. "In pulling out the knife I had to steady the body with my other arm against his breast. It was covered with blood when I got back to my room."

"Thank you. That is all."

"No questions," waved Sir Benjamin airily.

Jameson got down.

The next witness was Hubbard. Freeth-Jones's first question

was startling.

"You have already given evidence that you saw the prisoner on the night of Lord Carpenter's murder. Have you anything to add?"

The wizened librarian looked slyly round the court. "Yes, this much. It was entirely fictitious."

"You mean you never saw Mr. Jameson?" – "That is so. The story was an invention of my own."

"I see. Will you now favour us, in your own words, with a true account of what happened on this night?"

"On the evening of the day in question I decided that I hated Lord Carpenter more than any man on earth." He raised a protesting hand. "You must accept this fact as explaining everything. I am a man of tremendous willpower below the surface. I resolve – and it is done.

"I resolved to murder–"

"The witness is not forced to incriminate himself," interrupted Mr. Justice Angevin wearily.

The librarian drew himself up haughtily. "My lord, will you kindly not interrupt me? As I was saying, I resolved to murder Carpenter. Soon after half-past twelve – but I am not sure of the exact time – when I was certain that no one would dream of disturbing him – I went up the stairs that wind round the lift well and lead to his suite. The office was lit, but the Board Room was in darkness. There was sufficient light for me to see the dagger on the wall to which Carpenter had so theatrically called attention on the day of his murder. I had taken the elementary precaution of putting on gloves before coming upstairs. I seized the hilt, barely visible in the darkness, and then boldly opened the door of Lord Carpenter's room, the dagger held behind my back. A reflected glow from an advertisement sign outside enabled me to make out his body. I plunged the dagger into his heart. I quickly removed it and walked slowly and deliberately out, closing the door after me. I put the dagger back where it had been before and made my way back as I had come. I saw no one either coming or going and I am quite certain no one saw me.

"My coat had blood on it, and I spent some time in changing it, and in going over the scene in my mind to decide whether I had made any slip. It was gone one o'clock by the time I dismissed the matter from my mind.

"I had one unpleasant moment when Inspector Manciple declared he had found a fingerprint. Could I, by some strange mental aberration, have handled it with my gloves off at some time? I lost my head and refused to give my fingerprints. I made up for my rashness, however, by my subsequent presence of mind. Jameson left the country for a reason I was unable to find out. I knew he was one of the people who were unable to produce alibis. I knew he kept a diary. I went to his rooms in disguise and secured the manuscript. With no slight knowledge of graphology – Dr. Szerky, I was flattered to see, recognized a skilled hand – I had forged an incriminating series of entries and I artistically deposited these in the grate (after charring them) behind a particularly vile painted fan. It was only with the greatest restraint that I refrained from burning this also.

"I then returned to the office and apparently with great reluctance told Inspector Manciple that I had seen Jameson coming from the scene of the crime. Everything went to perfection. In fact I should not be here now, in the act of confession – always somewhat humiliating for an intellectual mind – unless the astute Mr. Venables had got on my track. I must confess, however, that I also made the fatal mistake of letting a woman into my secret."

He was silent. Once again the court was filled with noise, with excited talking. Unmindful of the judge's irate rebuke, full-bottomed and short wigs bobbed excitedly in the well of the court. Mr. Freeth-Jones rose. "Thank you, Mr Hubbard, for an exceedingly well-told narrative," he said, not without a trace of contempt.

"No questions," said Sir Benjamin.

With a self-satisfied smile, Hubbard returned to his bench. The occupants on either side shrank noticeably from contact with him. He appeared unperturbed.

When Sir Colin Vansteen's name was called, and his silver mane appeared in the box, there was silence. It was broken by a Cockney voice, speedily hushed into silence—

"Garn, 'ere's another gorn an' done the old man in."

"Sir Colin Vansteen?" said Mr. Freeth-Jones precisely, you gave certain evidence as to the cause of Lord Carpenter's death yesterday. Was that evidence correct?"

The pathologists eyes twinkled. "It was perfectly correct as far as it went."

"As far as it went. In the light of subsequent events, perhaps you have something to add?"

He nodded. "I have. In addition to the wound, previously described, which caused Lord Carpenter's death, I found another, very similar, and obviously caused by the same instrument, but inflicted after death."

"*After death!*" The advocate glanced significantly round and then addressed his witness again. "Are you certain of that?"

"Beyond any manner of doubt. I made it my business to ascertain that. The second wound I have mentioned was through the heart, penetrating this time the aortic auricle. There was no bleeding from it, however. It was perfectly well-defined.

"In other words, it was made through a heart of coagulated blood. Such a heart is the heart of a dead person – dead beyond all possibility of revival."

"Consider, Sir Colin — for it is a matter of vital importance — are you certain no other hypothesis could account for the wound being in the state in which you found it?"

Sir Colin shook his head with finality. "It is absolutely impossible. The second wound was made when Lord Carpenter was already dead."

"You will realize that had the police been aware of this it would have materially altered their attitude? No doubt you would like to give some explanation of your concealment."

"I should. I regret to say that I jumped to an entirely false conclusion. When the Premier rang me up in such a state of agitation, I suspected that he had actually had the intention of murdering Carpenter. I did not blame him, of course. I accepted his assurance that he was not guilty of Carpenter's murder.

"When I made the post-mortem, it seemed to me obvious that Sanger had actually stabbed Carpenter, and then found he was stabbing a corpse. In pursuance of our agreement, I therefore said nothing about the second wound. I imagined I knew the truth; and — in my folly — that the truth would not help the police.

"After that first night the matter was never discussed between us. I assumed he knew I knew, and I respected his reluctance to discuss a subject so painful to him.

"When he revealed in the witness box his presence at the scene of the crime, and still made no reference to his murderous intention, I still respected what I thought was still his wish. It was understandable enough that, full of years and honour, the acknowledged saviour of his country, he should wish to go down to Lethe with no brand of Cain on his forehead. I understood his reluctance to say in public to the world what he had only confessed by innuendo — as I thought — to me his trusted friend.

"Only now do I see what a different — and what a fantastic construction — must be placed on this second wound. Only now do I see how ludicrously I have wronged my old friend." Sir Colin Vansteen gazed coldly and defiantly around the room. "No doubt the world will censure my conduct. I do not care. I regret nothing in this case – neither my concealment of material facts, nor my confusing of the ends of justice. I did what seemed – and still seems – in the best interests of this country. But I do regret, deeply and hopelessly, my misjudgement of my oldest friend."

"No questions," said Mr. Arthur Harness, rolling negligently to his feet.

The final Crown witness to be recalled was Detective Inspector Manciple.

"Did you check Mr. Hubbard's movements for the time of the murder?" – "I did."

"What did you find?" – "They were entirely unconfirmed from half-past twelve to one."

"Would it have been possible to get from the library to Carpenter's suite during that time without being seen?" – "Yes, that would have been quite easy."

"No questions," breathed Mr. Arthur Harness, barely rising to his feet.

The final defence witness to be called was Dr. Szerky. There was a faint smile on his face.

"You have examined certain authenticated specimens of Mr. Hubbard's writing?" – "I have."

"And what was your conclusion?" – "That the forged diary to which reference has previously been made was forged by Mr. Hubbard."

Mr. Arthur Harness wearily shook his head, while the two full-bottomed wigs were in earnest conclave. Then Sir Benjamin rose.

"My lord, I am now going to ask you to adjourn until the Crown has had leisure to investigate this new evidence which has been so unexpectedly put in."

Mr. Justice Angevin gazed round the court. He noticed a triumphant gleam in Mr. Peterson's eye. Foolish fellow! He noticed a pretty girl talking, with flushed cheeks and excited eyes, to a tall fellow with a monocle. Neither was taking any notice of him.

It was a difficult world, reflected the judge, but at least he had presided at the most sensational criminal trial held in this country.

"The case is adjourned for forty-eight hours," he said.

— II —

Once again an expectant mob filled the Old Bailey. Sir Benjamin's tall, distinguished figure, erect in the well of the court, obtained silence. It was observable that before his place on the long table, and also before Freeth-Jones's was an immense pile of law books. Mr. Justice Angevin, too, betrayed traces of having spent a sleepless night the day before.

"The Crown," said Sir Benjamin, "does not, after investigation, wish to examine any of the witnesses whose evidence was given at the close of the last proceedings. I wish, however, to offer certain observations on the legal aspect of the case, while in no way disputing the facts established two days ago. I rather suppose from appearances that my learned friend wishes to do the same."

The discussion which followed – with a vacant jury box, not without protests from Peterson – has its important place in legal text books. It is not, however, necessary to give it here. But when it was finished, the jury again took their places for instructions from the judge.

"This case," said Mr. Justice Angevin, "is unique. It is likely to remain so. There is a maxim to the effect that hard cases make bad law. Its purport is not to criticize the law, but to indicate that it must be applied regardless of special cases, even cases where its applications may appear oppressive or inhuman. For the experience of civilization has shown us that only in laws rigidly and strictly applied is there justice and certainty.

"In this case also, we must apply the English common law to special circumstances, wresting neither one nor the other, but interpreting both according to the immemorial traditions of English justice. In this case, however, such application will not seem to you oppressive or inhuman. On the contrary, it may seem to you unduly lenient.

"In this strange and disturbing trial you have, in fact, had presented to you two cases – one prior to my summing up, the other subsequent to it. The evidence of the first was adequately presented to you in that summing-up. But we now know it to be false. In a murder trial it is no unusual thing, so fallible is human nature, to be given false evidence. But it is unusual to find it out so completely and utterly as we have in this case.

"Dismiss, therefore, from your minds everything in the earlier part of the case save the fact that Lord Carpenter was killed by a wound in the heart between 12.30 and 1 a.m. on that eventful night. Turn now to the evidence given later. It tells us more in less time than any evidence given in any proceedings that have ever come under my knowledge or have, so far as I know, been reported in the annals of this courthouse.

"What does this evidence establish? It establishes that the prisoner and one of the witnesses, Hubbard, at the material time, entered Carpenter's room and plunged a dagger into his recumbent form. It was understandable for them to use the same weapon which the victim himself had indicated. It was explicable for both carefully to replace it. It was lucky – for them

– that neither met each other or any other living soul on their murderous errand. It was odd, yet believable enough, that both assumed Carpenter was sleeping, and saw nothing to disillusion them. It was wholly natural for them to work in the dark and so veil the details of their dark deeds from themselves and from others. It is strange, yet not surprising, knowing the vagueness of the human mind at moments of emotional stress, that neither is certain of the exact time he entered or left the victim's room.

"Given, in fact, the initial coincidence of two men wishing to murder one in one night, the rest is far from being as miraculous as it sounds at first.

"Sir Colin Vansteen's part in these tangled issues deserves a special censure. He grossly betrayed his professional honour and failed in his duty as a doctor, a citizen, and a paid servant of the Crown. He attempted to play Providence, with the result that the truth of this strange crime might have been hid from human eyes for ever, and known only to the all-seeing eye whose dispositions he so rashly endeavoured to anticipate. But, opprobrious as is his action morally, humanly speaking his explanation is credible. We must accept his story, and leave his castigation to his brother doctors and his conscience.

"The subsequent conduct of Jameson and Hubbard is such as might be expected from the characters of the men, their consciousness of guilt, and their ignorance of each other's actions. Jameson acted like the weak young fool that he is. We may call him a dangerous fool; we may recognize that he is a peril to the community; but we may admit that his conduct was not altogether base; that the dreadful fire of remorse which has raged so evidently has left some finer spark behind. But what shall we say of Hubbard – who confesses proudly his murderous intentions, who narrates boldly his vilely cunning attempts to fix the guilt on a – to him – supposedly innocent party? Can you regard him as human? Can we – doubtless, gentlemen of the jury, this will have occurred to you all – can we indeed regard him as sane?

"Nonetheless we must, I think, accept him as capable of giving acceptable testimony. It is evidence which no one would wish to invent. And accepting it, we come to the conclusion that either Hubbard or Jameson murdered Lord Carpenter and no one – not even they – knows which.

"You may feel dissatisfied with this, gentlemen. You may feel that a closer investigation should establish the guilt of one or the other. You may feel that one, in his heart of hearts, must know his knife was plunged into a living man. But we must take facts as we find them. We are not here to range at large over the possibilities of this case, but to judge evidence of witnesses and the arguments proffered by learned counsel, and after judging them, to decide which verdict they seem to you to demand. Evidence to the effect that neither knows which inflicted the fatal wound has been given us. It has not been challenged by the prosecution, in spite of the time permitted for investigation. I may remind you that we are here to judge between suggestions offered by the prosecution and alternatives offered or denials proffered by the defence. But when the prosecution accept the defence's statement of the case, then, gentlemen, it is not for you to doff your judicial function, and set up alternatives of your own.

"It is therefore established that either Jameson or Hubbard murdered Carpenter and the other stabbed his corpse. No jot or tittle of evidence has been offered us to point in the direction of one or the other. Even were we permitted to leave our judicial function, no possible evidence occurs to me that might suggest which inflicted the first wound. The chances are equal. Toss a penny in the air. It may fall heads down. It may fall tails down.

Such are the chances that either of these two was guilty of that first and fatal stab.

"What was the other man guilty of? With murderous intent he mutilated a corpse. It is possible to suggest certain offences of which he was guilty. But he was not guilty of murder, either as principal or accessory, and it is with murder Jameson is charged.

"Gentlemen of the jury! Your duty is to deliver a verdict in the case of a charge of murder preferred against Jameson. You are not concerned with Hubbard, who is merely a witness. It is easy to suppose that he is liable in certain respects both in the civil and criminal courts. But in this case he is merely a witness.

"Nor is there any suggestion of collusion between Hubbard and Jameson. The prosecution has not suggested it, and it will not suggest itself to you. All the facts point the other way, to the complete ignorance, each of the other's intentions and acts. Had there been collusion, then on the facts as stated both would be in peril of being found guilty on the capital charge. But here is no shadow of collusion.

"Therefore Jameson is either guilty of murder or of stabbing a corpse. The chances are precisely balanced.

"The question of 'reasonable doubt' has already been discussed. I produce a penny from my pocket and place it on the desk. You cannot see it. I have covered it with my hand. Have you a reasonable doubt that heads are uppermost? Most certainly you have.

"It is my duty to instruct you as to the law of England in this respect. Bysshe Jameson is charged with the wilful murder of Lord Carpenter. On the evidence as stated so much doubt exists as to whether he did indeed murder Lord Carpenter, that I direct you to return a verdict of 'Not Guilty'."

After a short conference Mr. Peterson arose and gave the

verdict of them all as "Not Guilty, with the strongest censure of the accused, Mr. Hubbard, and Sir Colin Vansteen."

On being informed that this verdict was inadmissible, Mr. Peterson conferred again, and gave as their unanimous verdict – "Not Guilty, with a grave stain on his character."

At the third attempt Mr. Peterson, not without protest, gave a simple verdict of "Not Guilty," and the prisoner was discharged.

A Truth is Revealed

"A HAPPY FAMILY PARTY," observed Charles gravely. In Grovermuller's comfortable chairs, Detective Inspector Manciple and Hubbard sat facing him. Grovermuller leaned back at his desk with a shadow of a smile wrinkling the corners of his eyes.

Manciple looked at Charles stolidly. "I haven't congratulated you. Finest piece of work I've seen. Combination of inspiration and hard work."

"In other words, luck," answered Charles. "You see we each started with a prejudice, you that Jameson was guilty, I that he wasn't. Between us we found the truth. If you hadn't proved so incontestably that Jameson was guilty, and if I hadn't been so violently set on proving the reverse, I should never have stumbled on the truth."

Hubbard broke into the conversation. "Have you seen this morning's papers? By Jove, I'm the most famous man in England today. It is really amusing to read the leaders. You see they daren't say anything rude about me – beyond what the judge says – for fear of the law of libel!" He laughed suddenly. "I had two hundred letters this morning, including twenty-one proposals of marriage and two offers to go on the stage. And still pouring in! I have been asked to write my life for the *Sunday Newsletter.*"

Manciple, Venables and Grovermuller exchanged a glance. It

was Manciple who cut him short.

"Very interesting," he said coldly. "But we are waiting to hear Venables' story..."

Charles settled himself into his chair and thoughtfully clipped a cigar. "My story is simple enough. Right from the outset my suspicions fell on Hubbard. The story of my investigations is merely that of a continuous attempt to bring it home to him, long periods of wavering, and latterly, an incessant struggle to find a hypothesis which would reconcile his guilt with the extraordinary weight of the evidence against Jameson, and his behaviour. His behaviour was the most puzzling. Even as early as the day we refused our fingerprints to you, Manciple, I guessed by Miss Jameson's action that she feared her brother was involved, and wished to shield him.

"I must admit therefore, that at the start my suspicion of Hubbard wavered. It was a suspicion founded on one inexplicable fact. Why did the cuttings that Lord Carpenter was studying the night he died disappear? There were various possibilities. The first requirement was to trace the cuttings. I took the distressingly obvious course of looking for them in the cuttings file. There they were, quite happily nestling in their proper places. And yet no one would own to having put them back.

"This for me, disposed of the likelihood of the subject of the cuttings connecting in any way with the crime. For obviously they would not have been put back; they would have been destroyed. In spite of my ingenuous inquiries at a later date, I took the precaution of discovering the system on which the cuttings file worked, and ascertaining that none of them was in fact missing.

"I always believe in working in an investigation along obvious lines. Who would be the obvious person to replace them? The person who took them out – Hubbard. Yet he had not

276

acknowledged doing so. Therefore he must have some reason for not wishing it to be known. What could that reason be? It springs at once to the mind. Because whoever took the cuttings from the desk, must have taken them at or near the time of the murder.

"So far so good. But what *reason* could there have been for Hubbard to put them back. Let us follow the obvious line. Because it was his duty as custodian to keep them in order. Merely a natural instinct for tidiness. But we have already assumed that to take them he must have been to Carpenter's room at or near the time of the murder. Yet he never revealed this important fact. Therefore he could not wish it known. Therefore his reason for being there was a guilty reason.

"Suppose this was so. Suppose even that he was the murderer. What are we to say of a man with such a passion for tidiness that on the way from a murder he tidily collected some scattered cuttings and filed them? Obviously such a man is hardly sane.

"I watched Hubbard closely. I won't bore you with the jargon of the alienist, but it was easily possible to trace all the clinical symptoms of the characteristic megalomaniac. The library revolved round Hubbard, the *Mercury* revolved round the library, the world revolved round the *Mercury*. Leading his stunted and starved existence in that dusty haunt, day in and day out, crazed with the pangs of frustrated ambition, racked with the psychoses of an inferiority complex, endlessly perfecting his cramped and involuted routine, it is difficult to say whether his madness produced his environment or his environment his mania. But there it was, flourishing nicely, ready at any moment to be unleashed with destructive effect; indeed, if I were right, already once destructive!"

There was a chuckle from Hubbard. "Megalomania – the old cry of the herd hurled at the superman. Alexander, Caesar, Napoleon

– oh yes, we admit their greatness, their colossal achievements – then a knowing shake of the head – but they suffered from megalomania." He looked fiercely round him. "Fools, idiots! If you experienced one moment of the blinding sanity that comes to me at times, your poor remnants of brains would shrivel and melt! I go to eliminate Carpenter. I accomplish my purpose. In that moment, when the average man would be palpitating and terror-stricken, my brain works as calmly and quietly as when I walk down Fleet Street. As I pass I notice some cuttings. I pick them up, and – before taking off my bloodstained coat even – very deliberately put them away. You call that insanity." Hubbard burst into a roar of laughter.

Charles looked at him keenly but said nothing. In a moment he resumed his story. "However, even after I made that discovery – which was later made independently by Lee Kum Tong – I still had to find a motive – but now it had to be a much slimmer motive. You see when the world revolves completely around you, the slightest offence deserves capital punishment. It is high treason; an offence against the Lord of the World. Carpenter's offence had been a bitter one. He had laughed and mocked at Hubbard's systematizing: he had called him an old fool; the day on which he died he had threatened to dismiss him. Quite sufficient motive for a megalomaniac. And had not Carpenter, pointing rhetorically to the wall, indicated the means of his own elimination?"

"Yes, that appealed to me more than anything," said Hubbard with relish. "Carpenter was a crass fool and he deserved elimination. But it seemed so delightfully amusing to adopt his own suggestion. Remember Nietzsche's remarks about war, which we may translate a little freely: 'Ye have said a good reason justifies any murder. But I say, a good murder justifies any reason.'" He chuckled again. "Pardon my incurable facetiousness."

"Once I came to this conclusion," went on Charles, again not noticing Hubbard's interruption, "I realized the danger was not confined to Carpenter. Whoever else took up a hostile attitude to Hubbard was in danger; and when I heard you, Mr. Grovermuller, abusing Hubbard and threatening to dismiss him, I felt concerned enough to warn you. You ignored my warning, and as a result I had considerable difficulty in reviving you after strangulation. When you were convinced of Bysshe Jameson's guilt you ignored my warning again. I am afraid that at that time I was wavering myself in my belief in Hubbard's guilt. Circumstances were so challengingly presumptive of Jameson's guilt. I sought desperately for every means of assuring myself that Hubbard was the man. I therefore rather welcomed your attitude. I felt – with all respect – that you might play for me the part of the tethered goat, and lure the lion within range. You will remember that I joined in the farce myself. With the case against Jameson blackening every moment, I told Hubbard that I suspected you. I must say I made out quite a plausible case against you. I stated my belief that in the cuttings lay the clue to the guilt of the murderer. It was a carrot passed gently under Hubbard's nose. He seized it. With typical ingenuity he invented a hypothetical series of cuttings that pointed to Grovermuller's guilt, and declared they were missing. To my delight he went farther. Enchanted by the idea of getting rid of Grovermuller, the object of his hate, without being directly implicated, he forged a letter to Grovermuller from Carpenter, put it in Grovermuller's desk and suggested I should look for it. With the typical inconstancy of the maniac, he was already tired of the brilliant stroke – in which he imagined he had been aided by luck – by which he had involved Jameson in a fatal mesh. He now concerned himself – under my careful suggestions I admit – with the idea of incriminating you. This may seem foolish now, knowing how terribly Jameson was involved. But Hubbard, naturally, did not know that. He thought Jameson was as innocent as you, and that it would be as easy to shift the guilt to you as it was to fix it on Jameson in the first instance. The unconquerable optimism of megalomania again!

"It was essential for my purposes that Hubbard's subtle and perverted ingenuity should not guess that there was any shadow of suspicion in my innocuous manner. I did not dare to take you into my confidence. I was afraid, to be frank, you might not then be able to sustain the part of the innocent man wrongly accused. So I arranged to be found rummaging in your desk, accused you of the murder of Carpenter, and produced the letter. Your indignation at this accusation was natural. I drew Hubbard into a share of the wrath."

Grovermuller smiled. "My final conclusion was that, so determined were you to get Jameson off, that you had decided to fake enough evidence to hang me instead. That belief alternated with a suspicion that some secret enmity was actuating you. In the end I even came to believe that you had strangled me yourself."

"Anyway, you played the part I wanted of you to perfection. It removed all suspicion from Hubbard's mind. My casual statement to Hubbard that you knew of his assistance to me in seeking to prove your guilt was, however, electric in its effect. You had, I said, actually threatened to sack him. Crash came Hubbard's world! Turned out of the *Mercury* what could he do? No time now to enmesh you in a web of suspicion. He must act quickly. His former desire was right. You must be extirpated. And by chance a golden opportunity presented itself. Every month you went on a visit to the East End; you did not wish to be seen; surely in some part of your walk, anxious as you would be to avoid being seen, he could stage a struggle with you, and in the struggle stab you to the heart? Self-defence, of course, with myself as a witness of his innocuous intention to follow you and your sinister record. Preparation, which included scratching your initials on the knife, took only a moment."

Charles paused for a moment. Hubbard's face was turned from the window, his features indistinguishable in the shadow. Manciple, his eyes the only live thing in his face, watched Charles intently. Grovermuller, his cigar smoke spiralling vertically to the ceiling, smiled grimly at a passing recollection.

"I followed, to see that you ran into no danger and to catch him in the act. I regret nothing so much as the fact that I let you two out of my sight. It was either that or coming into the light of a street lamp myself. Of course with his diabolical cunning he had been thinking of that; while without suspicion of me in particular. You passed out of my sight, and a moment later you were struggling. My chance of open accusation, was for the moment gone. Very well, I continued to play the farce."

"As a matter of curiosity," interrupted Manciple, "what was this mysterious East End assignment which you will not reveal? May we ask?"

Grovermuller blushed. "You may – but must I answer? Perhaps I should, but never let it out of this room! I'm an incurable sentimentalist, and there are about fifty crippled East End children to whom I play father and guardian in a little hostel. I go down there once a month to," – he paused shamefacedly – "well, frankly, to *romp* with them, and put on my oldest clothes."

Charles smiled. It elicited from Hubbard a sudden squeak of laughter.

"Next day, you will remember, Mr. Grovermuller, I saw you. It might be described as a stormy interview. But I convinced you at last of my *bona fides* and we went over the evidence against Hubbard together. I explained how I had found his fingerprints in Jameson's room, how Szerky attributed to him the forgery of the diary and the letter to you from Carpenter. I told the secret history of his homicidal attacks on you. But you put your finger on the vital spot. Jameson was guilty. He could not be. You agreed to the final move I suggested to get fresh information about him – the dismissal of Jerningham. But I left you still, in effect, hopeless of incriminating Hubbard.

"Illumination came to me suddenly, while I was discussing it with Lee Kum Tong. Had I – greatest peril of criminal investigators – neglected the obvious? What was the obvious deduction from the fact that both Jameson and Hubbard appeared to be guilty? That both *were* guilty. In collusion? No! And then instantly the whole magnificent hypothesis flicked into shape. Wait though, surely the autopsy would have revealed it? Perhaps it did! Sir Colin had concealed one thing, why not another? The last tessera in the mosaic dropped in the vacant space without a gap and the hypothesis was complete. Startlingly obvious! Chaotically fantastic! From then on it was easy."

"Speaking merely as the tethered goat, I am filled with admiration," said Grovermuller.

"Magnificent," commented Manciple, "but it is not police work. What's the use of a solution without a criminal? Mosaic law, you know – an eye for an eye, and a tooth for a tooth!"

He spoke lightly, even as Grovermuller had spoken, but there was a tension in the silence that could be felt. With a dreadful fascination their eyes turned to Hubbard, with his features indistinguishable in shadow, motionless and silent.

Suddenly he jumped to his feet. "Go on, say it!" he roared. "Say that you hate me, that I oughtn't to be alive. Tell it to me, and get it off your sick puling stomachs." He looked round him with an indescribably hunted air. "You know the story of Gulliver and the Lilliputians. That's what you all are – Lilliputians with your baby moralities, and your petty – infinitely petty – laws and prohibitions. For years and years I've struggled with you." His eyes dilated, gleamed behind his glasses. He made abrupt sweeping gestures with his hands. "It has been my intellectual strength against the millions of you, and it's beaten and broken me." He relapsed into his chair, and his face, quite suddenly, seemed to grow grey and collapsed. "Always the same – a fool of a wife, a harlot of a daughter, and work, work, work!" He looked round cunningly. "Work that no one else could do, mind – no one in the wide world! Oh-ho, they had to admit that. Hubbard was indispensable – fine fellow – complimenting me as if it were a sneer. I've murdered a man, and I've stood up in front of the whole world and told them, boasted of it, bragged of it, flung it in their faces, and they daren't say a word! But I know what they're thinking in their hearts. We'll wait. He'll try and get Grovermuller. He'll go for his wife. He'll stamp on the Lilliputians. Then we've got him – fling in our little darts, boys; wind him up in our threads, we've got him. Stab him, stab him, kill! kill! kill!"

Hubbard stopped short with a squeal. Fascinated, the three watched his face. He seemed to be listening, and when he spoke again his voice was changed too. "I saw a doctor this morning. One of those old, grey, understanding men. Such a nice man." Still as if to catch some ghostly echo, his head turned from side to side. "He asked me the oddest questions. It was just as if he knew all my troubles better than I knew it myself. Even about my enemies."

Hubbard looked at Charles interrogatively. "Have I told you about them? Several people have hired houses in my road, just to sit there and wish me ill. Horrible thoughts they are – I can only escape them when I walk very rapidly with my arms crossed behind my back. People tease me about the funny way I walk. I laugh and tease them back. I nearly told them why I did it once. Suddenly I realized. They were sent by my enemies to try and stop me – spies, you see! Now I never walk any other way. The joke is I know the names of these enemies, and I even know the numbers of the houses they live in. You'd be surprised at their names if I told you. Bishops, well-known novelists, princes of the blood even." He paused for a moment, and drew his hands over his forehead. His eyes seemed to have gone quite dull.

"The doctor man knew their names very well. Apparently he'd known of it for some time. Then he warned me. What was it?" Hubbard's face screwed up in an access of concentration. "I remember he told me I was very ill. I had been over-exerted lately. He told me very soon I might get worse. A weakness might come on me."

He looked round cunningly. "I knew what he meant, although he didn't say it straight out. He meant to warn me that when this weakness came on me, my enemies would try and make out that I'm mad – ha-ha, mad. Me, so clear-headed that I can sit here and analyse my thoughts as if they were moving about under a blinding light."

Charles felt physically sick. He murmured something soothing and looked at the wall, out of the windows, away from those horribly knowing eyes. The climax, when it arrived, was abrupt.

Hubbard's mind had moved on, or rather back. "How did you get on to my wife?" he asked suddenly. "Who told you she knew?"

"Your daughter," answered Charles without reflecting.

The result was dreadful. Hubbard sprang to his feet with a scream. His brow ridged suddenly like that of a gorilla, and a torrent of foul abuse poured from his throat. "God strike her dead," he ended. "Curse–" He choked and ended his sentence with a gurgle. Horror-struck, Charles saw him struggle to finish the sentence. His lips parted abruptly over his teeth with a ghastly rictus, half snarl and half smile. His eyes contorted in a violent squint. Foam gustily flocked from his lips. His arms seemed to be drawn into him with the convulsions of tetany. And then at last articulation came to him. With a horrible wailing cry, a cry that seemed to come not from him, but from something inside him, the epileptic's immemorial hallmark, Hubbard sank to the floor.

Charles knelt beside him. "Pass me that ruler," he said. He prized open the jaws of the unconscious man, and rolled his tongue forward, then rapidly loosened collar and coat. The unconsciousness passed into a sleep, and in his sleep Hubbard's face shed, as deep sleepers do, the torments and hate that seared his waking face with lines. It became almost as peaceful as a child's.

When he woke, his face was still as peaceful as a child's. He lolled his head backwards and forwards and grasped the coverlet. The nurse leaned over him to hear what he was trying to say. He was humming a nursery song.

Hubbard suffered no more from megalomania. He moved vaguely through a drowsy world, in which he recognized and remembered nothing and no one. He developed a simple aptitude for knitting in bright colours at tremendous speed.

— II —

"When do we leave?" Miranda asked, looking up from her work with an absent gaze.

"Monday as ever is." Charles looked at her anxiously. "Are you really sure you want to go to the Fiji Isles?"

She laughed. "I don't want to go to Fiji. I don't want to go anywhere. But one must have some excuse for going to sea, and Fiji seems the best. It's not a place one ever hears of anybody going to. And I've reached a stage where the only thing I want to see is water, everywhere, in every direction, as far as eye can see. Think of the dictionary definition – 'In a state of purity (important that!) at ordinary temperatures (you can never catch them out) a clear transparent liquid, perfectly neutral in its reaction, and devoid of taste and smell.' How soothing – so accurate, and yet so untrue. What could be more exquisitely simple than the chemical formula – H_2O – the name is like a caress. We shall be entirely surrounded by this perfectly neutral liquid for three months at least. Will it cure us? Will it drive us crazy with boredom?"

"My dear old thing," protested Charles. "Bored – with you on board?"

"My God, if that's meant as a joke, I'll never marry you!" protested Miranda. "If it isn't, what a terribly ordinary thing to say! I suppose eventually you'll learn to say things like that, with a coffee-cup poised in mid-air, munching a mouthful of toast, and without taking your eyes off the paper. Everyone will then say, how well I've trained you. However, I'll hurl the coffee pot at you and scream till you look up. A quiet household ours; do you think you will be able to bear it?"

Charles fixed his monocle into position and looked at her gravely. "You do this prattling business remarkably well. It doesn't, however, disguise from your observant lover the fact that you're worried about something. Out with it, or we shall most certainly go crazy before we reach Fiji."

She smiled wanly. "Your insight is appalling. The disadvantage, I suppose, of being a detective. Yes, I am worried. Bysshe again. You know his latest idea – he's qualifying as a doctor, then when he's got his degree he's going to join a medical mission in Central Africa and never return to civilization again. 'Expiating his error,' he calls it. Well, that's not what's worrying me. Knowing his temperament I think probably it will save him – real hard work, danger, and a mission in life and consciousness of doing good unselfishly. But doubt is driving him mad."

"Doubt?"

"Yes. Over and over again, it seems, he asks himself, 'Am I a murderer, or was he dead?' It runs through his thoughts day and night. It is part of his dreams. He can't settle down. He can't think. He's getting to look awful – like he was at the trial. They're threatening to close down on him at King's – he's getting so woolly-minded and distrait."

Charles shook his head. "I'm sorry. Terribly sorry. But what can I do? –

> 'Therein the patient
> Must minister to himself.'"

Miranda looked wearily out of the window. "Isn't there any way you could decide – who did it? It's the uncertainty that's getting on his nerves. I honestly believe he'd rather know the worst – for certain – than have this endless tormenting doubt."

Charles looked grave. "That's a hard saying. It's a big risk, you know, for me to ferret out the truth. Once we know – it's irrevocable."

He turned away. "I'll see him tomorrow and decide."

— III —

Mrs. Jerningham dabbed her eyes delicately with a lace handkerchief. "I've just come away from seeing father," she said. "It's terrible. He didn't recognize me."

Jerningham murmured sympathetically, concern on his handsome face.

"I'm afraid it was my leaving him that broke him up," she said. "If you knew how he depended on me! Inseparable we were! Oh, if only I could have saved him."

"There, there," he said, clumsily patting her. "Shall we postpone the bridge party tonight?"

"No. I must be brave," she answered in a still, small voice. "Mustn't let it get me down!" She smiled wanly.

"God, you're great!" said Jerningham enthusiastically. "Poor little girl – what you must have suffered, with your sensitive, innocent feelings, in that dreadful house!"

— IV —

"Do you realize what you're asking, Bysshe?" said Charles for the third time.

The other, his red hair straggling wildly, thumped the table. "I do. Of course I do. I *must* know, whichever it is! Try and conceive the situation I am in! I tell you I feel everything that matters in my whole life depends on the answer to that question. Perhaps it doesn't matter morally, you'll say! But you're wrong. You're wrong."

He stood up abruptly. His pale face flushed. "Do you believe in guilt? Do you believe in predestination? Unfashionable beliefs perhaps. It's not his fault – a disharmony of the endocrines. Causality is a myth, Eddington tells us. We're a fortuitous concourse of atoms. But I tell you there's a pattern, a pattern of good and evil running through this Universe, and it matters, it matters to me more than anything on earth, whether I'm the black thread or the white. This is the test, I tell myself. Did I murder him? Or was he dead? If I murdered him – well, I accept it. But if he were already dead," – Bysshe's blue eyes flamed with fire – "then indeed, I know that I have been saved, against my will, from the burning – not a material burning, but the consuming fire of conscience. Then shall I know that my expiation is accepted, that the gift of my life and my knowledge, such as it is, has been flung in the balance and been found of true weight."

Charles looked at the pale face, alight with intellect and soul, so strangely, so heart-rendingly reflecting in its gaunt lineaments the features of Miranda. What a strange mixture – Tinker, tailor, soldier, sailor, murderer, madman, hero, saint? He might be any – or each alternately.

"This is the test then," Charles repeated slowly. "But will you abide by it?"

Bysshe's chin went up. "I will," he answered firmly.

Charles was silent for a moment. He drummed reflectively on the desk with his fingers. When he spoke again his remark seemed irrelevant, and the eager flame in Bysshe's eyes flickered out.

"So you're a medical student! How far have you got?"

"Oh, only a few days into it, you know. Absolute A B C of anatomy. I haven't even learned the parts of the body yet."

Charles nodded. "Of course not. Tell me, will you – I'm afraid I must ask this question – how much blood was there on your coat?"

Bysshe's face went white with disgust. "A fairish amount. You see I steadied the body with my arm when I pulled out the knife, and the sleeve all dribbled in it."

"Only the sleeve?"

"Yes, only the sleeve."

Charles offered no comment. He pulled out his watch. "Mrs. Hubbard will be here by now. I asked her to call." He phoned through to the reception clerk. "Yes, send her up."

Mrs. Hubbard, attired in the involutions of widow's weeds,

had magnificent scope for her sartorial untidiness. She took it to the full. It was some time before she ceased muttering and patting herself and subsided quietly in a chair.

"Well, a lot of water has gone under the bridge since we met," said Charles. "I've brought you here to ask you only one question. But it is a question on which the peace of mind of this young man depends."

She looked at Jameson quickly, but made no comment.

"You washed your husband's coat. Was there much blood on it?"

She gave a grimace. "That there was. Fair turned me up, it did."

"Where about was it?"

"All up the front."

"Was it as if the coat had been dipped or rubbed in it, or was it, say, as if it had been splashed?"

"Splashed! That's it!" she said eagerly. "Just the word that describes it! It was just, as you might say, as if he was standing in front of a basin of blood, and something had dropped in it *plomp* and splashed him. That's why I never believed his nonsense about someone cutting themselves. Why, he'd even had to change his collar for the spare one he keeps in the drawer at the office. It was that splashed and specked."

Charles's hand came down heavily on Bysshe's shoulder. "Run back and finish your anatomy studies, old man, for you'll find this lets you out. That's a live man Hubbard stabbed, from whose severed aorta spurted the blood that splashed him. When the second knife wound pierced the artery and auricle, the blood was coagulated in death. Easier for a stopped heart to beat again, for a severed head to speak, than for Carpenter to have been dead when Hubbard stabbed him to the heart."

290

Make sure you check oleanderpress.com for the
latest in the LONDON BOUND series:

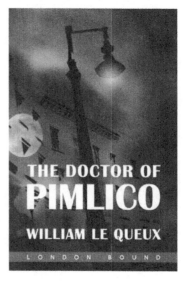

ISBN: 9781909349711   ISBN: 9781909349735